Not Another Happy Ending

David Solomons was born in Glasgow and now lives in Dorset with his wife, Natasha, and son, Luke. He also writes screenplays.

Not Another Happy Ending

David Solomons

Published in Great Britain 2014
by Harlequin MIRA, an imprint of Harlequin (UK) Limited,
Eton House, 18-24 Paradise Road,
Richmond, Surrey, TW9 1SR

© 2013 David Solomons

ISBN 978 1 848 45273 2

59-0114

Harlequin (UK) Limited's policy is to use papers that are natural, renewable and recyclable products and made from wood grown in sustainable forests. The logging and manufacturing processes conform to the legal environmental regulations of the country of origin.

Printed and bound by
CPI Group (UK) Ltd, Croydon, CR0 4YY

For Natasha and Luke, with love.

CHAPTER 1

'Here Comes the Rain Again', Eurythmics, 1984, RCA

Dear Jane,

Thank you for submitting your novel, *The Endless Anguish of My Father*.

Ten years ago it would probably have received a warm reception, but there is quite enough misery to be found on the non-fiction shelves just now, so, in fiction, we're currently very much into happy stories with happy endings.

At the moment we are enjoying wonderful success with a novel entitled *Come to Me*, an exotic and erotic tale of revenge and redemption, with a fabulously feisty female lead and a Hollywood ending. If you *were* willing to make some adjustments to the novel's dénouement you might also be happy to entertain some other minor reshapings: set it in LA or Bangkok rather than Glasgow, say; make your main protagonist a jet-set-y interior designer, for instance, rather than a shelf-stacker; and tweak the key rela-tionship so that, rather than one between father and daughter, it's between our cosmopolitan interior designer—who is actually, despite her success and fabulous wardrobe, just a little girl at heart—and a father *figure*, who happens to be a domineering (but gorgeous!) film producer. If you were to reposition the novel in that kind of way, then I'd be very happy to reread.

You can certainly write, but these days it's so dif-ficult to launch a new writer—however talented—who's writing about the wrong things.

I have recycled your manuscript.

Yours sincerely,

Cressida Galsworthy

Assistant Editor

Well, thought Jane, at least Cressida gets points for sustainability.

She made space on the notice-board—in a moment of dejection she'd referred to it as her Board of Pain, and the name had stuck—and pinned up this latest rejection, then sat back to admire the varied collection of publishers' and agents' rebuffs.

Until she began submitting her novel she hadn't appre-ciated that there were so many polite ways to say no. Forty-seven examples, to date. The rejection didn't hurt so much; the opinion of some woman in W1 she'd never met was of no consequence to Jane. She had survived far worse in her twenty-five years than anything Cressida—or Olivia or Sophie (so *many* Sophies)—could throw at her. But early on in the process she realised that the letters could be useful. There were writers who stuck inspirational messages over their desks to spur them on: you can do it…believe in yourself…open that window of opportunity! But encouraging slogans didn't work for Jane; she shrank from their brimming optimism. She was far more likely to want to jump head first out of that window of opportunity. Instead, she bought the board at her favourite vintage store off Great Western Road, nailed it to the wall by the large bay window of her airy, white flat and artfully arranged the naysaying letters. She could hear their honking dismissals as she penned each new query letter and packaged up the latest hopeful submission. *I didn't love it. I didn't love it enough. I hated it.* Their lack of enthusiasm was grist to her dark Satanic mill.

The printer spewed out another copy of the manuscript, and as she waited for the four hundred pages of her thus far ill-starred debut to stack up she hoisted the sash window, leaned on the sill and took a deep breath.

The air smelled of trees after the rain. Half a dozen slender poplars lined the quiet West End street, in full leaf now that what passed for the Scottish summer had arrived. Beyond them stood a blond sandstone terrace, a mirror to the building Jane's flat occupied. From the top floor someone practised the cello. The doleful strings drifted over the treetops, and suddenly the flats were miserable dolls' houses with naked windows through which Jane glimpsed desperate lives: a raging argument between husband and wife, the tired old lady with no visitors, the self-harming teenage girl crying in her bedroom. On the street below a wan-faced young mother slouched behind a squeaking pushchair, cigarette jammed between chapped lips, flicking ash over a wailing infant.

The cellist took a break from his practice and reality was instantly restored. The windows revealed no more heartache than a tired executive mourning a slice of burnt toast, and in a patch of sunlight beneath the trimmed poplars it was a smart young mother wheeling a silver-framed pram, talking to her child in a voice as groomed as her suit.

Jane roused herself from her melancholy flight of fancy. This was the West End of Glasgow, a dear green place of well-kempt gardens, specialist delicatessens, and more convertibles per square mile than anywhere else in Europe.

She still couldn't quite believe she lived here. She had grown up in the East End of the city. It was four and a half miles away, but may as well have been a million, her life until the age of sixteen spent in one of the brutalist tower blocks more readily associated with the mean city of legend.

Residents never referred to them as tower blocks; they were always the 'high flats'. Plain language hid a litany of flaws as deep as their rotten foundations: walls thin as cigarette paper, alien mould choking every corner, a stagnant pool of water in the basement referred to with typical humour as 'the spa', and stairwells daubed with crude graffiti that always bothered Jane less for its vulgarity than for its incorrect use of the apostrophe (in retrospect, a clear sign of bookish leanings to come). She laughed when she heard people reminisce about growing up on the schemes: 'Aye, we might have been poor, but we were happy.' What a load of crap. It was a miserable place to exist.

She'd only got out thanks to her mum. She remembered the letter arriving on her twenty-first birthday. It was from her mum, which came as something of a surprise since she'd died fourteen years earlier. They'd had so little time together that now when Jane tried to picture her face it was like reaching through water. Turned out mum had squirrelled away most of the wages she made at the Co-op in some kind of get rich quick scheme invested in Jane's name soon after she was born. The letter duly arrived with a valuation and a note on how to claim her inheritance—god, it sounded like something out of Dickens.

She remembered sitting on the floor by the front door reading the contents with growing disbelief. The money was enough for a healthy deposit on her new flat; her new life. It was surprising enough that the dodgy investment had reaped a profit, but the bigger surprise was that her mum had contrived to keep the money out of her dad's thieving hands.

A breeze at the open window ruffled the rejection letters on the board. Set amongst them was a faded Polaroid of an older man, face scored with deep lines, eyes surprisingly soft, one pile driver arm wrapped around a ten year-old girl. In the photograph the late afternoon sun has caught her hair, turning the hated 'ginger' a deep, sunset red. Father and daughter are both smiling. But then, that was the summer before it happened.

Mum had taken the snap on a day out to the beach at Prestwick. Unusually, the sun had shone all day, just like it should in a memory. She remembered on the way home afterwards stopping in Kilmarnock at Varani's for ice cream. Best in the world, her dad used to say. Not that to her knowledge her father had ever been outside Scotland. Of course she couldn't be sure of his travel itinerary since then, not after he walked out on them later that year. He left a few months after the photograph was taken, on her birthday. She laughed. How much more of a cliché could you get? Her hand brushed the faded photograph. That was the last time she'd had ice cream from Varani's.

Her eye fell on a flourishing umbrella plant on her desk, its soft, green leaves trailing across the top of her laptop screen. It had been a present from him a few years ago; the only evidence in a decade that he was still alive. When it arrived she prepared herself for the inevitable follow-up:

the drunken, apologetic phone call in the middle of the night; the knock at the door with a bunch of petrol station flowers. Neither of them came; only more silence.

The leaves were dry to her touch. She gave the plant a quick spray from a water bottle she kept close by. They didn't have a garden in the high flats, but her dad had installed a window box and she remembered planting it with him. It was a shady spot, he explained, so they filled it with Busy Lizzies in summer and hardy cyclamen in winter. The water-spray hissed. Thinking about it, she wasn't even sure why she kept his plant.

With a whine the printer finished its work. She packaged up the latest submission into a large buff envelope and wrote out the address of the next publisher on her hit list. Tristesse Books were based in Glasgow. Tristesse was French for something she couldn't quite remember. She'd taken Higher French at school, but only just passed the exam. *Je m'appelle Jane. J'habite à Glasgow*. That was about the extent of her conversation. That and, at a push, she reckoned she could order a *saucisson*.

Outside, the sky darkened, dampening the earlier promise of sunshine. The wind swirled around the trees, sending a flurry of rain against the open window. Hurriedly, she slid it shut and stood for a moment gazing at her reflection in the rain-soaked pane. Her hair was still long and straight and red, its neat fringe framing a pair of bright green eyes held open in what seemed to be a state of permanent surprise at the vagaries of the big, bad world.

When the kids at school had taunted her for being a 'ginger', her dad had pulled her onto his knee and together they'd watched his (pirated) copy of Disney's *The Little Mermaid*. The first few times she didn't understand the message that however tough the journey, even redheads are allowed a happy ever after. Instead, through a terrible misreading, Ariel and her singing friends gave her a horror of losing her voice, and for years the slightest hint of hoarseness convinced her that the end of her little life was imminent.

The superstitions and playground taunts of childhood were long gone, but now she attracted a different kind of unwelcome attention, from the Armani-skinned lizards with large cufflinks who frequented the bars on Byres Road. And these days there was no dad to tell her it would all turn out happily in the end.

He was the one who'd inadvertently introduced her to the world of books, dropping her off in the public library to wait while he took care of a little business at the bookies across the street and then nipping in for a swift pint—or nine—at the pub next door. As he gambled and drank away their benefit money she immersed herself in books.

Even after he walked out of her life she continued to visit the library, just in case he came back. She hated him for leaving, but more than anything else she wanted him to come back. And as she waited for him to swing through the door with his big grin and too-loud voice, she read. The library was her playground, her university. Here she was surrounded by familiar faces. Hello, Cinderella. Cheer up, Tess. Good day, Mr Darcy. As the years passed, *The Brothers Grimm* became *The Brothers Karamazov* until one day she picked up a pen and began to write her own stories.

Raindrops streamed down the cheeks of her reflection in the window. She remembered what 'tristesse' meant.

*

After almost a decade in Scotland, Thomas Duval still dreamt in French. Four years of university in Glasgow, followed by a brief internship with Edinburgh publisher Klinsch & McLeish (ending in a spectacular bust-up with the notoriously spiky Dr Klinsch) and then five years building up Tristesse had left him a fluent English speaker trailing a wisp of a French accent along with the added charm of a stray Scottish vowel. But at night, in his dreams, he was once more the golden boy from the Côte d'Azur, raised under hot blue skies, bestride his old Benelli motorbike racing the rich kids in their Ferraris and Lambos along the twisting coast road between Saint-Tropez and Cannes. And always with a different girl riding pillion. *Mais, bien sûr.*

But somehow despite the sun-soaked childhood, when he'd first arrived in Glasgow something stirred in his soul. He'd always loved Walter Scott, James Hogg, the gloomy heart of the Scottish canon. The first time it rained he walked around the city without an umbrella until he was wet to the skin. He'd never felt so alive, which was ironic, since he came down with a bout of flu and missed the rest of Freshers' Week. But his affair with Scotland had begun. His family thought he was mad. He ignored them and bought an umbrella. Soon, the tanned limbs of Brigittes and Hélènes gave way to the pale, freckled legs of Karens and Morags.

Still asleep, Tom reached an arm around the shape beside him in the wide bed. He began to mutter in French, a low, rhythmical sound, languid and masculine, capable of snapping knicker elastic at twenty paces, then slid one hand beneath the rumpled sheets—and froze. His smile slipped, replaced with a glower of cheated surprise.

He sat up and flung the covers from the bed. Beside him lay a chunky six-hundred pager. He'd just tried to make sweet love to a manuscript, and not even one worthy of his moves. A glance at the title—*The Unbearable Sadness of Daal*—brought back last night's bedtime reading: mediocre writing, derivative plot and two hundred pages too long.

He huffed and turned a bleary eye to the small bedroom. Manuscripts littered every surface. Uneven stacks of them sprang from the floor like heroes turned to stone by a Gorgon's stare. He was behind in his reading, as usual. He had put his romantic life on the back burner in favour of pursuing a different prize—glittering success as a publisher. So far he was frustrated on both fronts, not helped by his strict adherence to one of his few rules: never shag a writer—especially not one of your own. He was still looking for The One. Just one critically acclaimed—and more crucially—best-selling book would take his struggling company to another level.

Once showered and dressed he stood over the espresso machine as it gurgled and hissed in protest before grudgingly offering up a shot of treacle-black coffee. Tom drained the cup and immediately poured another. His broad frame filled the narrow galley kitchen like a Rodin bronze in an elevator. The living quarters were crammed into a mezzanine above Tristesse's offices and consisted of two small bedrooms and a holiday camp for bacteria masquerading as a kitchen, littered with plates growing more life than the average Petri dish. Less *cordon bleu*, more cordoned off.

He juggled a new manuscript and a piece of toast. Concentration fixed on the page he failed to notice that the marmalade he spread thickly over the toast was in fact mayonnaise. He took a bite. Disgusted, he toed open the pedal-bin at the end of the counter—and discarded the manuscript. Swiping a finger across his phone he checked the time.

'Roddy!' He barked towards the second bedroom. 'School!' There was a thud from inside like a cadaver being dropped by a slippery-fingered mortician, the distinctive chink of many empty beer bottles being inexpertly stepped over and then the door swung open. Out shambled a figure in a state of confusion and a brown corduroy suit.

'Have you seen my tie?'

'You mean the brown one,' mocked Tom, 'to match the *chic* suit?'

Roddy stuck out his chin defensively. He was a slightly built man with the sort of boyish face always ID'd when buying a six-pack. He tugged at one of the large lapels. 'It's not brown,' he insisted. It flapped like a Basset hound's ear. 'I'll have you know this is fine Italian tailoring and the young lady who sold it to me called it *marrone*.'

'You do know that's just Italian for "brown", right?'

Roddy ignored him, moving aside manuscripts to continue his search. 'So have you seen my tie or not?'

'Hey, careful with those,' said Tom, waving his toast at the unread scripts. 'I have a system.'

'Ah-ha!' Roddy produced a red bow tie from behind one of the stacks and slipped it around his neck.

'You're seriously going to wear that to school?'

'It's a valid choice.'

'For Yogi Bear, maybe.'

Roddy frowned. 'That makes no sense. Yogi Bear never wore a bow tie. It was a necktie—and it wasn't even red, it was green. Wait, are you thinking of the Cat in the Hat?'

'If I pretend I just arrived from France and don't understand anything you're saying will you stop talking?'

'Just for that I'm having your muesli.'

Roddy swiped a bowl off the draining board, wiped a spoon on his trousers and dived in.

'Hmm?' Tom looked up from his reading. 'We're out of muesli. Haven't bought any in weeks.'

Roddy gagged as he spat out the ancient slurry. 'Aw, you're kiddin'. That's criminal. That's unsanitary, that is. We live in squalor, you know that?' He threw down the bowl. 'I'll get something in the staff room.' He turned to go and paused in the doorway. 'Oh, don't forget, you've got Nicola coming in this afternoon.'

Tom grunted. A couple of years ago he'd discovered Nicola Ball, a writer of novels set in the unpromising world of public transport (one notable sex scene in her debut had brought whole new meaning to the phrase 'double-decker'). Recently, she'd featured on some influential lit. crit. blog, hovering near the middle of a list of 'Scottish novelists to watch under the age of 30', and the annoying girl wouldn't stop reminding him about it at every opportunity. However, her sales didn't match her bumptiousness.

A buzzer sounded from downstairs.

'Get that, will you?' Tom strolled off, head buried in the latest novel plucked from the slush-pile.

'No can do,' spluttered Roddy. 'I've got *Wuthering Heights* with my Third Years…' He checked his watch. 'In fifteen minutes. Bollocks.'

The buzzer went again and Tom padded resentfully downstairs. Roddy's question trailed after him: 'When are you going to hire an actual secretary?' The answer was simple: when he could afford one. Which right now felt a long way off.

The postman might as well have been holding a ticking bomb. He brandished what Tom recognised through long acquaintance as unwelcome correspondence from the bank and credit card company.

'Lovely morning,' the postman said cheerily, 'though there's a bit of rain forecast for later.'

Reluctantly, Tom took the mail, which included half a dozen fat A4 envelopes—more manuscripts—and closed the door. With a dissatisfied grunt, he shuffled the official letters to the bottom of the pile and made his way along the narrow passage to his office, deftly navigating around towers of cardboard boxes filled with expensively produced books fresh from the printer. He shuddered at the financial risk; each title was a long shot of vomit-inducing odds, a fragile paper boat set sail on the roughest publishing market since William Caxton thought 'Hey, what if I put the ink in here?'

Tom threw the mail onto his desk and sat down heavily. Napoleon glowered up at him. It was a bust of the great Emperor, a gift from Roddy on the launch of Tristesse Books, which Tom was in no doubt also conveyed a pointed comment on his high-handed manner. He looked round his tiny office with its clutter of contracts, press releases and inescapable manuscripts; a battered velour sofa with the stuffing knocked out of it (appropriately) and a couple of low, uncomfortable chairs, perfect to intimidate writers. It wasn't exactly the Palace of Fontainebleau.

He turned his frustration to the morning mail, tearing open the top envelope and removing the bulging manuscript from within. He scanned the cover and blew out his cheeks in disbelief. Then held it out in front of him, squinting at the title to make sure he'd read it correctly. Which he had. There it was, in black and white, Cambria twenty-four point. *Quelle horreur*.

'*The Endless Anguish of My Father*,' he read aloud, allowing each word its full weight and bombast. 'By Jane Lockhart.'

Worst title this year? Certainly it was the worst this month. Briefly he pondered summoning the author for a meeting, purely for the satisfaction of telling her just what a brainless title she had concocted and, he felt confident asserting this without condemning himself to the unpleasant task of reading one more word, that she was a hopeless case with no chance of making a career as a novelist. But he was busy. Taking the manuscript in the tips of his fingers, he gave a shudder of disgust.

'Ms. Lockhart…*au revoir*.' And with that he tossed it into the cavernous wastepaper basket by the side of his desk.

CHAPTER 2

'Tinseltown in the Rain', The Blue Nile, 1984, Linn Records

THE BOWLER WAS a great idea. She rocked that hat. It was her lucky hat, always had been. Not that Jane could recall specific examples of its effect on her good fortune at this precise moment, but she was sure there must have been some in the past.

It was an awesome hat. It had been a last-second decision to take it to the meeting and she'd plucked it from its hook above the umbrella stand along with her favourite red umbrella. Not that the umbrella was lucky. Who has a lucky umbrella? In fact, weren't they notoriously unlucky objects? Yes, it was bad luck to walk under them. No, that couldn't be right. That was ladders, of course. *Open* them! You weren't supposed to open them indoors in case…what? Non-specific, umbrella-related doom, she supposed.

Oh god, she was losing it.

It was nerves. The email from Thomas Duval of

Tristesse Books inviting her—correction, *summoning* her—to a Monday morning meeting had arrived last thing on Friday, leaving her all weekend to obsess. It had to be bad news; nothing good ever happened on a Monday morning. But if that were the case then why demand a meeting? If he wasn't interested in publishing her novel, surely he would have rejected her in the customary *pro forma* fashion, and he hadn't *Dear Jane-d* her, not yet.

She felt a spike of anticipation, which was instantly brought down by a hypodermic shot of self-doubt. Perhaps he was some sort of sadist who got his kicks torturing writers in person. But that seemed so unlikely. She'd been propping herself up with this line of thinking through-out most of the weekend, extracting every last drop of hope from it, until halfway through the *longueur* of her Sunday afternoon she decided to Google him and discov-ered that Thomas Duval was indeed just such a sadist. The Hannibal Lecter of publishing, blogged one aspirant author who'd evidently suffered at his hands. Attila the Hun with a red Biro, recorded another.

She dismissed the opinions of a few affronted authors—all right, fourteen—as a case of sour grapes and sought out a more cool-headed assessment of his reputation. There was scant information available on the *Bookseller*'s site, the industry's go-to journal, but she dug up half a dozen snippets of news. The names changed, but on each occasion the substance remained the same: break-ing news—Thomas Duval falls out acrimoniously with another of his writers, who storms out in high dudgeon, swearing never to write one more word for that arrogant, temperamental sonofabitch.

Well, at least he was consistent.

She jumped on the subway at Kelvinbridge and rode the train to Buchanan Street in the centre of town. By the time she reached the surface, the early rain had given way to patchy sunshine and she enjoyed a pleasant stroll through George Square to the Merchant City. European-style café culture had come late to Glasgow—until 1988 if you said *barista* to a Glaswegian you risked a punch on the nose. But when it did arrive it came in a tsunami of foaming milk. An area of the city once referred to as the 'toun' these days sported sleek cafés on every corner, where, at the first warming ray, outside tables sprouted like sunflowers, and were just as swiftly populated by chattering, sunglasses-wearing crowds who always seemed to be waiting just off screen for their cue.

Jane headed along cobbled Candleriggs past the old Fruit Market, before stopping outside a set of electric gates. One of the residents was leaving and as the gates whirred open she slipped inside, finding herself in a large, sunlit courtyard bordered by a Victorian terrace on one side and a glassy office block on the other.

She made her way over to the far corner and at the door, she inspected the nameplate. This was the place all right. She hadn't really paid attention to the Tristesse Books logo before, but a large version of it was stencilled on the wall: a white letter 'T' suspended in a fat blue drop of rain. As she pushed the buzzer it struck her that it wasn't rain at all, but a teardrop.

*

Jane had been kicking her heels for half an hour, waiting in the hot, cramped Reception room for her meeting with Thomas Duval. She could hear him through the wall, shouting in rapid-fire French. He may not have been ordering a *saucisson*, but it wasn't difficult to catch the gist—someone was getting it in *le neck*.

Though his fury wasn't directed at her, with each fresh salvo Jane shrank deeper into the waiting-room chair. After fifteen minutes of listening to him rant she'd contemplated making her excuses and slinking out, but the possibility that he had read and liked *The Endless Anguish of My Father* was enough to encourage her to stay put and suffer.

Across the room she could see Duval's secretary trying to ignore the furious noises coming from his boss's office. At least, Jane assumed the man sitting at the desk was his secretary. For some reason she'd pictured Thomas Duval's secretary as one of those pencil-skirt wearing, bespectacled ah-Miss-Jones-you're-beautiful types, whereas the figure valiantly shielding the phone receiver from the angry French volcano on the other side of the wall was a twentysomething man in a brown corduroy suit and red bow tie. Now that she studied him carefully, he

looked less like a secretary and more as if he was channelling a fifty-year-old schoolteacher.

'Mm-hmm. Yeah. Oh yeah, he's a wonderful writer. So
unremittingly bleak.' The secretary paused as the caller on
the other end of the phone asked a question. 'No, Tristesse
doesn't publish him any more,' he said haltingly. 'A little
disagreement with…' He glanced towards Duval's office
door, cupping the receiver against the rising din. 'She's
one of my favourites!' he said, responding to a fresh
enquiry. 'Yes, long-listed for the Booker, you know.' His
left eye twitched. 'Right after she was sectioned.' He
listened again, one corner of his mouth sinking mournfully. 'No. She left too.'

This was becoming ridiculous. How long would Duval
make her wait in this tiny, airless cellar of a room? For all
he knew she had taken time off her actual, proper job to
show up at his beck and call. Not that she had a proper job
any more. She'd quit the supermarket at the beginning of
the year, when they offered her a place on the management
trainee programme. She'd started off stacking shelves and
here they were offering her a suit and a key to the executive WC. It was a sign; she knew, that if she took it then her
life would go into the toilet metaphorically as well, taking
her far away from her writing.

In the end it didn't even feel like her decision. She had
to write; it was as simple as that. So she jumped, a great,
giddy, don't-look-down leap of faith. And here she was.
Forty-seven rejection letters later. Savings countable on

the fingers of one hand…Was it stuffy in here, or was it her?

She yawned and stretched her legs, knocking the low table in front of her on which perched a stack of teetering manuscripts. They wobbled alarmingly and she dived to steady them, noticing as she did that the top novel was entitled *A Comedy in Long Shot*. Not a bad title. She immediately compared it with her own, placing each in an imaginary ranking system. Hers scored higher, she felt sure. *The Endless Anguish of My Father* had been tougher to come up with than the rest of the novel. But the day it popped into her head she knew it was the one. It had the ring of authenticity, rooted in truth, in life; six words that spoke to the eternal verities. And it looked good when she typed it across the cover page.

Something glinted behind the paper stack. A single golden page coiled into a scroll and set on a plinth. It was an award. An inscription ran along its base. She picked it up to read: 'Thomas Duval. Young European Publisher of the Year, 2010.' She turned the award another notch. 'Runner-up.'

'Miss Lockhart?'

Duval's secretary had crept up on her. Startled, she dropped the award. It landed against the wooden floor with a resounding clang and rolled under a sofa. Apologising profusely, Jane fell to her knees and scrabbled to retrieve it, a part of her brain belatedly registering that the shouting from the office had ceased.

'What the hell are you doing?

She looked up into the face of Thomas Duval and felt her own flush. He was handsome in a way that would make Greek gods sit around and bitch. It wasn't the rangy stubble, or the thick wave of hair that demanded you run your fingers through its luxuriant tangle, or the intense stare from behind his Clark Kent spectacles. OK, it might have been some of those things. His distracting features were currently arranged to display a mixture of anger and puzzlement, but, she noted with a sinking feeling, they definitely tipped towards anger. She was also vaguely aware of a draught located around her backside and knew then that in her pursuit of the runaway award her skirt had ridden up and currently resided somewhere around her waist. As she covered her modesty (oh, *way* too late for that) she made a show of polishing the golden award with one corner of her sleeve.

'I'm so sorry. I didn't mean to—I was just, y'know, touching it. I mean not *touching*—that sounds like *molesting*, like I'm some kind of pervert...' she drew breath, 'which I'm not.' She ventured a smile. 'Young European Publisher of the Year...Runner-up? That's really impressive.' Don't make a joke. Don't make a joke. 'I have a swimming certificate.'

Across the room the secretary chuckled, for which she was immensely grateful. Duval silenced him with a scowl. Certain that her submissive kneeling position wasn't help-ing her case, Jane picked herself up off the floor, laying a hand on the vertiginous stack of manuscripts for leverage. She leaned on the unsteady pile and the scripts toppled over, crashing to the floor. Random pages flew up around her ears.

Duval narrowed his eyes. 'Who are you?'

She stuck out a hand in greeting. 'Jane Lockhart…?' Duval ignored the proffered hand. She withdrew it awkwardly, turning the action into a waving gesture she hoped came across as insouciant. 'I wrote *The Endless Anguish of My Father*?'

'Ah,' he grunted. 'Yes.' He turned his back on her and began to walk away.

So that was it, she thought—another rejection. And I've shown him my pants.

'What are you waiting for?' he snapped over his shoulder.

She threw a questioning glance at the secretary, who motioned her to follow the disappearing Duval. Hurriedly gathering up her hat and umbrella she stumbled after him.

She was not sure what compelled her to do so—blame it on the confusion of believing she was about to be unceremoniously ejected onto the street—but by the time he had led her into his office she was again wearing the bowler hat. She was confronted with his broad back as he gestured her curtly into a low seat, then slid behind his desk and looked up. He leaned in with a quizzical expression, mouth half open.

'It's my lucky hat,' she pre-empted his question.

'No one has a lucky hat.'

Something about this man made her want to argue. 'What about leprechauns?'

He screwed up his face. 'What?'

'They're lucky. They wear hats.' Oh god, she was doing it again. Stop talking. Stop talking right now. 'Y'know, with the green and the buckle and…Ah…Ah!' She sat up, raising one finger triumphantly. 'You can have a thinking-cap.'

He sneered. 'It's not the same thing at all.'

'No. No it isn't.' Sheepishly, she removed the offending bowler. 'I only wore it to offset the umbrella,' she confessed, then asked brightly, 'Have you ever wondered why it's bad luck to open an umbrella indoors?'

Duval gazed at her steadily. 'The superstition arose during the late 18th century when umbrellas were larger, with heavy, spring-loaded mechanisms and hard metal spokes. Open one in the confines of a drawing room and the consequences could be destructive.'

'Oh.'

He drew a tired breath and fished a manuscript from under a pile. She recognised it immediately as her own, although the pages appeared crumpled at the corners and was that the brown crescent of a coffee stain on the cover? This must be a good sign. Clearly, the turned-down corners were evidence of the hours Duval had spent reading and then rereading; the stain conjured a long,

espresso-fuelled night, his head bent over her novel mes-
merised by the spare, elegant prose, those sharp, intelli-
gent eyes tearing up at the emotive tale.

'I'll be honest with you,' he said, tossing the well-worn
manuscript down on the desk, 'I put this in the bin without
reading a single word.'

Or, there was that.

She looked down and played nervously with her ring.
It was made from an old typewriter key, the word 'back-
space' in black letters on a silver background. She'd
bought it with her last pay packet, a fitting gift to launch
her on her new career as a novelist. She felt a lump in her
throat and swallowed hard. She swore she wouldn't cry in
front of him.

'That title…' He made a long, sucking sound through
his teeth.

She had a feeling it wasn't the only thing that sucked.
She glimpsed a straw and clutched at it. 'But you took it
out again.'

'Hmm?'

'Of the bin. Something must have made you take it back
out.'

'Yes.' He fiddled with the small bust of Napoleon. 'A
fly.'

Had he just admitted to using the novel she'd slaved
over for the last year and a half as a fly swatter?

'It was a highly persistent fly,' he added in a conciliatory tone. He pushed a bored hand through his hair. 'I'm

busy, so I'll keep this brief. I read your novel. I'm afraid it needs work. A lot of work.'

Hot tears pricked her eyes. She blinked furiously, trying to hold back the waterworks. She hadn't cried in years, not since her dad left, and now here was this man making her feel like that little girl again. It wasn't the rejection—she'd shrugged off dozens without resorting to tears. It must be him. The bastard. To actually reject her face to face.

'But it has potential, so I'm going to publish it.'

What a complete and utter shit. Making her come all the way here just to wait in his stupid little office, only to be told—

Wait. What?

'Ms. Lockhart?' He peered into her stunned face. 'Are you all right?'

'Publish? Me?' She just had to check. 'In a book?'

He gave an exasperated sigh. 'I'm offering you a two-book deal. It will mean a lot of rewriting—definitely a new title—and neither of us will get rich. But I think you have it in you to be a writer and, unfashionable as it may seem, that is what I came here to find.'

She waited for the punchline, searching his face for the appearance of a grin that would say, 'only joking', but it didn't come. He was serious. This man wanted to publish her novel. This kind, wonderful man. There was only one rational response to the news.

She dissolved into tears.

She'd always wondered how she'd feel if—she corrected herself—*when* the moment finally came and the flood of 'no's' was stemmed by one small, clear 'yes'. In the end it wasn't even a 'yes' so much as a '*oui*'. *Vive la France*! *Vive le Candleriggs*! But this was more than an air-punching victory, it was…happiness. That's what it felt like. Through great hiccupping sobs she could see him watching her, confused. 'I'm sorry. I didn't mean to…' she blubbed. 'It's been so…so long…so many rejections…I have a board.'

'You have a board?'

'Of rejection letters. I call it my Board of Pain.'

'Well,' he said with a straight face, 'that's completely normal.'

'It is?' Oh good, that was a relief.

'So, how many publishers turned you down exactly?'

'All of them,' she said, palming away tears. 'Well, obviously not all of them. All of the big ones, I mean.' She caught his eye. 'Not that I'm saying you're not big. I'm sure you're very…important. I mean, really, I should have sent you my novel ages ago, given that it's set in Glasgow and so are you.'

'So why didn't you?'

'Umm.' This was awkward. 'Because I'd never heard of you?'

He grunted.

'But then I read *The Final Stop* by Nicola Ball and I loved it and she is really talented and *really* young and I saw your logo on the spine and, well, here I am.'

She lapsed into a renewed bout of weeping.

The office door swung open and the secretary in the brown suit entered, flourishing a paper tissue from a man-sized box. He'd come prepared. 'I'm sorry about him. He was like this at uni. Everywhere he went—crying women.'

She took the tissue and blew her nose loudly.

'Roddy—' said Duval, trying to explain that, as unlikely as it appeared, this time he was not the cause of the great lamentation.

Roddy wagged a finger. 'Uh-uh. You lot are supposed to be charming. *Charmant, n'est-ce pas*?'

Jane shook her head, struggling to form words through the wracking sobs.

'I've told you,' snapped Duval, 'never try to talk French to me, you—'

'Happy!' Jane's outburst silenced both men. 'No, really.' She bounced out of the low seat. 'I've…I've never been so happy in all my life.'

She hugged a surprised Roddy and then circled round his desk to embrace Duval. Gosh, up close he was *very* tall. In her exuberance she knocked over her umbrella. It sprang open, an inauspicious red blot in the centre of the room.

But it was probably nothing to worry about.

CHAPTER 3

'Nine Million Rainy Days', The Jesus and Mary Chain, 1987, Blanco y Negro

'THIS IS THE marketing department...And this is sales...And this is publicity.'

'Hi, I'm Sophie,' said a shiny young woman with a sleek bob and perfectly applied make-up.

'Sophie Hamilton Findlay,' said Tom, 'three names, three departments. You blame Sophie if no one reviews your book, or if you can't find it in all good bookshops. Don't blame her for not marketing it...I don't give her any money for that.'

They turned a hundred and eighty on the spot.

'And this is George. He's production.'

A pinched face looked up from a wizened baked potato overflowing with egg mayonnaise.

'I'm on lunch.'

'You blame George if the print falls off the page, or if the pages themselves fall out. So, you've met the rest of the team. Any questions?'

'Well…' Jane began.

'Good.' Duval clapped his hands. 'Time to get to work.'

*

When he suggested heading out of the office for their first editorial meeting Jane pictured them moving to a quiet corner of Café Gandolfi sipping espressos and arguing about *leitmotifs*. He had different ideas. One thinks at walking pace, he pronounced, and took off along Candleriggs at a clip, brandishing her manuscript and a red pen. *Andante!*

She scurried after him, his loping stride forcing her to trot to keep up. The man thought fast. He did not approve of the modern fashion of editing at a distance, he explained, with notes issued coldly via email; adding with a grin that he preferred to see the whites of his writers' eyes.

'Readers are only impressed by two things,' he said. 'Either that a novel took just three weeks to write, or that the author laboured three decades.' He sucked his teeth in disgust. 'And then dropped dead, preferably before it was published. No one cares about the ordinary writer. The grafter. Like you.'

Ouch. A grafter? Really? She'd been harbouring hopes that she was an undiscovered genius.

'And publishers are no better.' He turned onto Trongate, carving a swathe through commuters and desul-

tory schoolchildren, warming to his theme. 'Do you recall
that book about penguins?'

'Which one?' The previous year the book charts
seemed to be awash with talking penguins, magically real-
istic penguins, melancholy penguins, there had even been
an erotic penguin.

He slapped a hand against her manuscript. 'My point
exactly! One book about penguins sells half a million
copies and suddenly you can't move for the waddling little bastards.' He stopped, slumping against a doorway.
His shoulders heaved like a longbow drawing and loosing.
'The giants are gone,' he said sadly.

Giants? Penguins? Was every day going to be like this?
He set off again at a lick.

'So many modern editors neglect the great legacy
they have inherited. They are uninterested in language
or, god forbid, art; and would prefer a mediocre novel
they can compare to a hundred others than a great one
that fits no easy category. They care only about publicity and book clubs and film tie-ins.' He spat out the
list as if it curdled his stomach. 'Most editors are little more than cheerleaders, standing on the sidelines
waving their pom-poms.' He turned to her. 'I have no
pom-poms,' he growled. Then thumped a palm against
his chest. 'I care. I care about the work. I care about your
novel.'

He stopped again and she felt she ought to fill the
silence that followed. 'Thanks,' she said brightly.

Duval cocked his head and looked thoughtful. 'Of course, it is not a *good* novel.'

Sonofa—

'But it could be.' He pushed a hand through his hair. 'So I say this to you now, without apology. From this moment, Jane, we will spend every waking hour together until I am satisfied. It will be hard. Lengthy. I will make you sweat.'

Uh, could he hear himself?

'I will stretch you. Sometimes I will make you beg me to stop.'

Apparently not.

'I do this not because I am a sadist—whatever you might have heard—I do this to give an ordinary writer a chance to be great.'

That was terrific, she was impressed—moved, even—but could he not give the 'ordinary writer' stuff a rest?

They came to a busy intersection. Pedestrians streamed past them. At the kerb the drivers of a bus and a black cab loudly swapped insults over a rear-ender; the aroma of frying bacon fat drifted from a van selling fast food. He ignored them all, shutting out the traffic and the smells and the noise, for her.

'I promise that no one has ever looked at you the way I shall. Not even your lover.'

Jane swallowed. 'I don't have a lover,' she heard herself admit. 'Right now I mean. I've had lovers, obviously. Not loads. I'm not, y'know, "sex" mad. I don't know why I brought up sex. Or why I put air quotes round it. I'm totally relaxed about…y'know…*sex*. And yet I just whispered it. Very relaxed. I think it's because you're French. You're all so lalala let's have a bonk and a Gauloise. Oh god. I'm so sorry about…well, me, Mr Duval. Should I call you Mr Duval? It sounds so formal. Maybe I could call you Robert.'

'You could,' he said, 'but my name is Thomas.'

'Thomas! Yes. I knew that. I was thinking of the other one. From *The Godfather*? Played the accountant.'

'Tom.'

'No, it was definitely Rob—oh, I see. Tom. Short for Thomas. I had a friend called Thomas. Well, when I say "friend" I—'

'Stop talking.'

'Yes. Yes, I think that would be a good idea.' She dropped her head, stuck out a foot and screwed a toe into the pavement.

'OK,' he declared. 'Now our work begins.'

And with those words the months spent at her desk writing for no one but herself were at an end. Now they would embark on a journey of discovery, together, to prepare her novel for…Publication. Suddenly, the sacrifices seemed worth it: losing touch with friends, turning on the central heating only when the ice was *inside* the windows, baked beans almost every day for three months straight, all to reach this pinnacle of a moment.

'Do you want a roll and sausage?' asked Duval.

'Do I want a—?'

He marched off in the direction of the fast-food van.

'Morning, Tommy,' the owner greeted him. 'The usual?'

'Aye, Calum, give me some of that good stuff.' Duval took the sandwich, then showed it excitedly to Jane as if he were a botanist and it a new species of orchid. 'And not just any sausage, oh no. A *square* sausage. See how it fits so perfectly inside the thickly buttered soft white bap? Genius! But then, what else would one expect from the nation who gave the world the steam engine, the telephone and the television? This is why I love the Scots. Now, a *soupçon* of brown sauce.' He squeezed a drop from the encrusted spout of a plastic bottle, patted down the top of the roll and sank his teeth into it. Paroxysms of delight ensued. 'And to think that France calls itself the centre of world cuisine.'

She wasn't entirely sure he was joking. And then she realised. He'd gone native.

'You must try one. I insist.' He clicked his fingers as if he were ordering another bottle of the '61 Lafite.

Moments later she stood peering at the sweating sandwich in her hands, and beyond it, Tom's grinning face.

'OK,' he said. '*Now* we begin.'

*

Ten minutes later they sat beside one another in the window of a café next door to his office. Between them lay the ziggurat of her manuscript.

'Jane,' he said softly, 'there is no need to be nervous.'

'Nervous? Me? No-o-o. Not nervous.' A coffee machine gurgled and hissed, only partially masking the spin cycle taking place in her stomach. 'OK, a little bit nervous.'

He smiled. 'It's OK.'

It was then she realised what was making her nervous. He was being nice to her. The heat had gone out of his fire and brimstone, his voice, typically tense with anger, now soothed like warm ocean waves.

'Usually I need a run-up before I start editing,' she said. 'Y'know: tea, a walk, regrouting the shower.'

'Or we could just begin?'

'What, no foreplay?' Even as she spoke them she was chasing after the words to stop them coming out of her mouth. But it was too late. He gave a small laugh, the sort of laugh your older brother's handsome friend might give his mate's little sister. Jane's embarrassment turned to disappointment. 'So, where d'you want to start?'

'Call me crazy, but we could start at the beginning.'

'OK.' She nodded rapidly, appearing to give his suggestion serious consideration, hiding her mortification at asking such a dumb question. 'OK yes.' She clouted him matily on the arm. 'You crazy Frenchman.'

He turned the top page of the manuscript. And they began.

*

He gave great notes. They were acute, considered, wise. Intimate.

As he had promised, the process of editing her novel forced them into a curious form of co-habitation. She would arrive at his office each morning and, following his customary breakfast of roll and sausage and black coffee, they would commence work. At first on opposite sides of his desk, then on the third day he came out and sat on the edge, balancing there comfortably, at ease in his body; a move, Jane did not fail to notice, which put her at eye level with his crotch.

Often she felt like the submissive in a highly specific S&M relationship, one with no physical contact but plenty of verbal discipline. I edit you. I. Edit. You. Ordinarily, she wouldn't have put up with any man who bossed her about as much as Tom did, but theirs was a professional relationship, she reminded herself. So she gave herself permission to be spanked. On the page.

Mostly they worked in his office, or the café next door, and whenever they reached a sticky point they would take to the streets and walk it out like a pulled muscle. Occasionally they decamped to her place. The first time he asked her—no, informed her—of the change of venue came early one morning while she was still half asleep, drowsy with last night's notes. He was on his way over, said the familiar accented voice on the other end of the phone.

When the doorbell rang she was in the shower. She stepped out, dripping, to shout down the corridor that there was a key on the lintel above the door and he should let himself in. It felt natural to give this man the run of her flat. After all, he was going to publish her. When she entered the sitting room she found him sprawled on the floor, propped on one elbow, pages scattered about him, red pen zipping through the manuscript. He looked right at home. And, watching him work steadily, intensely, she realised that he was the first man she'd properly trusted since her dad walked out.

They settled into their routine. Every day it was just the two of them, happily suspended in a bubble of literary discourse and fried egg sandwiches. One Wednesday morning, ten chapters into the edit, Jane breezed through the front door of Tristesse Books.

'Morning, Roddy.' She plunked a bulging paper bag on his desk. 'I made brownies.'

There was an urgent rustle as Roddy tore open the bag. With an appreciative smile, she turned towards Tom's office. She liked Roddy; he was a good influence on Tom. If Tom had a fault—and he did—it was an impulsiveness that shaded into arrogance, and Roddy was the one who called him on it, every time. Although it was dubious how he balanced his job as a replacement English teacher with secretarial duties for Tristesse Books, he exuded an air of moral rectitude along with an insatiable appetite for her home baking. He was Jiminy Cricket to Tom's Pinocchio, she'd informed both men one cool summer night, as they sat outside at Bar 91 amidst the buzz of revellers welcoming the weekend. Tom had almost choked on his pint. Roddy just looked disappointed: couldn't he at least be Yoda to a hot-headed young Skywalker, he'd asked.

'Uh, Jane. You can't go in there.'

She stopped at the door, one hand poised over the handle.

'He's got someone with him. They've been in there all night.'

She could hear Tom on the other side, his voice in its by now familiar trajectory, the point and counterpoint of argument, the steady inflection and unwavering logic of his contention. And it hit her. He was giving notes.

To someone else.

She experienced a sudden light-headedness, like an aeroplane cabin depressurising at altitude, and was still reeling when the door opened and a winsomely pretty blonde girl stepped out of the office and collided with her.

'Ooh, sorry.'

'Sorry.'

'No, I should be the one who…sorry.'

They disentangled themselves and the girl introduced herself.

'Nicola Ball.'

She was wearing a severe black pinafore dress on top of a white shirt buttoned to the neck. Pellucid blue eyes gazed unblinkingly from a perfectly oval face. There was a hint of redness around her eyelids, as if she'd been crying.

'*The Last Stop*,' said Jane delightedly. 'I loved that book.'

'Thank you,' said Nicola, a tremulous smile appearing on pale lips. Then her expression hardened and she cast a dark look back through the doorway to Tom's office. 'At least someone appreciates me,' she snarled.

'Why are you still here?' Tom's voice boomed out. 'Stop socialising and start rewriting. Go. Now!'

'I hate that man,' Nicola hissed.

As she said it Jane felt an unexpected sense of relief. Nicola hated Tom. Good.

'Please tell me you're not one of his,' said Nicola.

'Uh, one of—? Oh, I see. Well yes, I am—as you say—one of his,' said Jane, adding an apologetic shrug since Nicola's sombre expression seemed to demand one. 'Tom's going to publish me.'

Nicola took her hand and patted it consolingly. 'I'm so sorry.' She pursed her lips in an expression of graveside condolence, bowed her head and departed.

Jane watched her slip out, the triangle of her pinafore

dress swinging like a tolling church bell, and felt herself smile inwardly; whatever Nicola's experience of working with Tom had been, it bore little resemblance to her own.

'Jane?' he called from the office. 'Is that you?'

She never tired of hearing him say her name. She floated inside on a cloud of happiness ready to embark on the next leg of their voyage of collaboration and constructive criticism, of intellectual discussion and high-minded debate.

*

'Your notes,' Jane spluttered. 'Your notes are burning cigarettes stubbed out on the bare arm of my creativity.' She stepped away from his desk only to return immediately. 'Oh, and there is no such thing as *constructive* criticism. The phrase reeks of foul-tasting medicine forced down gagging throats "for your own good". Constructive criticism is a fallacy; weasel words designed to lure innocent writers like me into an ambush. *This chapter is too long. There's too much set-up. This plotline doesn't pay off.* Uh, perhaps that's because you cut the set-up? *This character is underwritten. Show, don't tell! This chapter is still too long. I like this scene, this is a great scene—it must be cut.*' She stood before him, her face flushed, her breath shallow and rapid.

'Are you quite finished?' Tom responded with irritating calm.

She brushed her fringe from her eyes and sniffed. 'Yes.'
'Good, then we shall continue.'

*

Two months into the edit and Jane had lost all sense of
perspective. Was he a brilliant editor or, despite his earlier disavowal, simply a sadist who enjoyed torturing novelists? Currently, she was leaning towards the latter. She
half suspected that were she to pull at the antiquarian volume of *Frankenstein* squatting atop his bookcase a secret
door would swing open to reveal a shadowy chamber and
the gaunt, moaning figures of his other novelists, hanging
from bloodstained bulldog clips, notes on their last drafts
carved into their skin with his annoying and ubiquitous
little red pen. It pained her to admit it, but Nicola Ball's
expression of pity had been prophetic.

She occupied her usual spot, squirming in the low chair
opposite his desk. They sat in silence as he went through
her latest revisions, the only sounds the dismissive flick
of manuscript pages and the scratch of that damn pen. She
watched as he adjusted the bust of Napoleon, turning it
precisely one inch clockwise, then two inches anti-clock-
wise. He did this with some regularity, but it was only
latterly she'd realised that the tic inevitably preceded his
delighted unearthing of a particularly egregious flaw in
her manuscript.

'This makes no sense at all,' he muttered on cue, striking out a paragraph with a flurry of red slashes.

'What are you cutting now?' Sometime on Thursday she had given up any attempt to hide her irritation.

He looked up and she was sure that his smug, infuriating face evinced surprise at her presence. *Why are you even here?* it said. *What could you possibly have to contribute to this process? You are merely the writer.* Jane struggled out of her chair—she'd meant to leap up for added effect, but her prone position made it tricky.

'I've changed my mind,' she said, reaching across the desk for her manuscript. 'I don't want to be published. By you. Thank you very much.'

She had no practical reason for retrieving the manuscript; if she'd really meant what she said she could simply have walked out of the door, gone home and printed out another—but she wanted to take something away from him. She had gathered an armful of pages when she felt his hand close gently but firmly around her wrist. She was startled; was it the first time he'd touched her?

Last week she'd been surprised that he hadn't kissed her in the French style—not *that* French style—when she'd finally signed her contract and left with a cheque that would pay for a fabulous trip to Moscow (the one in Ayrshire, natch). It had seemed to her that he started to lean in over the signature page for the customary embrace, but pulled back at the last moment. He'd been close enough for her to feel the leading edge of his well-groomed stubble and smell his skin. She'd half expected his natural scent to be Lorne sausage, but instead he was a heady mixture of sandalwood and new books. Then why his hesitation? She had swilled copious amounts of mouthwash that morning in preparation for the signing. Just on the off chance, you understand. So it wasn't her breath. Perhaps he simply didn't fancy the idea of kissing her. Well, his loss.

He was still holding her wrist. And, for a moment, she wondered what it would be like to do it right here on his desk.

'You can't do that,' he said firmly.

'I know,' she said, shocked at where her mind had taken her. 'Knowing my luck I'd probably end up with Napoleon in my back.'

Jane saw that he was looking at her in utter bafflement. She had seen a similar expression on his face earlier that day over a complicated sandwich and a cappuccino at the café next door. Pushing his coffee to one side he had complained that until meeting her he'd imagined his English not only to be fluent, but idiomatic—and prided himself on being almost certainly the only living Frenchman who knew his *bru* from his *broo*. However, in conversation with her he often felt like a foreigner, he said. No. Correction. Like an alien. She hadn't said so, but secretly she enjoyed the thought that she unsettled him.

She shrugged off his hand, glowered at him to get it out of her system and then with a sigh lowered herself into the knee-height chair once more. She waved at him to continue. 'You were cutting what was no doubt my favourite passage.'

'*Bon*,' he said, gratified, and scored viciously through another paragraph.

As she watched his scurrilous red pen she wondered when it had all gone wrong. A few weeks ago she had even made him her flourless chocolate cake. Though now she thought about it the baking interlude had arisen because one of his notes had sent her into a tailspin and she had been unable to write a single word for days. Yes, she realised, he was turning her into a crazy person.

As he droned on detailing the endless failings in her novel, she decided something had to be done. What was it about Tom that made her heed his every pronouncement? It wasn't just the sculpted stubbly chin, it was the self-confidence acquired from years at an exclusive French boys' school followed by university degrees acquired in two languages. The closest she'd come to university was on the tills at the supermarket selling lager to boozed-up students on a Saturday night.

She found herself scanning the contents of the bookcase that filled the wall behind his desk, running her eye across the well-thumbed classics, vintage and modern, dozens of them seeded with slips of paper marking favourite passages. It was a display designed to impress. But then with a little rush she realised that she'd read most of them in the library in Dennistoun during those long afternoons. She sat a little straighter—she probably knew them as well as he did. Her gaze settled on a volume of Greek myths and an idea struck her.

The problem was territorial. Like the myth of the giant Antaeus, who drew his strength from his connection to the earth, all she had to do was separate him from the square mile of the Merchant City and she was sure their relationship would achieve new levels of equality and harmony. She needed to pluck him from his comfort zone and repot him. She smiled to herself—she knew just the place.

CHAPTER 4

'Laughter in the Rain', Neil Sedaka, 1974, Polydor Records

'YOU SAID IT WAS a Highland cottage.'

'Yes.'

'I heard you distinctly. An old crofthouse nestling at the end of a glen, you said.'

'Yes.'

'But…'

'Yes?'

'You made it sound…' he hunted for the right word '…picturesque.'

Ignoring his accusing tone, she motioned towards the small stone dwelling with a gesture of 'ta-da!'

His eye roved suspiciously across the outside. A chimney stack balanced like a drunken man on the roof; weeds sprouted from slate tiles that had been discarded rather than laid; of the two windows cut roughly into the facing wall, one was bricked up and the other colonised by a family of squabbling, drab-feathered birds. The whole structure tilted at a twenty-degree angle, leaning into a relentless, biting wind that howled down the most desolate glen he had ever seen.

'Does it leak?'

Her mouth gaped, offended. 'Of course it doesn't leak.' She turned away, fished out a great iron key from her weekend bag, slid it into the stiff lock and shouldered her way inside. 'So long as it doesn't rain,' she mumbled.

There was a sucking squelch from behind her.

'Of course. What else should I expect? Just wonderful.'

He stood up to his ankles in a sloppy brown puddle. Jane wasn't sure which looked more soggy—his trousers or his face. When she had suggested the trip up north to work on the manuscript—to finish it once and for all—she told him to bring suitable outdoor wear. So, when he'd picked her up in his car that morning, she couldn't help but notice with some surprise that he was wearing orange trainers. She declined to comment at the time; he'd obviously picked them as a reminder that he didn't have to listen to her—he was the one who gave the notes in this relationship. Well, look where it got you, she thought smugly. I say potato, you say *pomme de terre*.

The muddied orange trainers steamed gently in front of the fireplace as Jane stoked the sputtering fire. Beside her, Tom shivered in a faded tweed armchair, hugging himself and grumbling.

'What's wrong now? You haven't stopped moaning since we left Glasgow.' She threw on a handful of kindling. 'Don't you like it here? This was my granny's cottage.'

He snorted. 'You're telling me your granny was a crofter?'

She noted that he didn't say 'farmer', but used the Scottish expression. He was amazing. His English. Was amazing. Not him. He was annoying. 'She worked on the line at Templeton's Carpets,' she explained.

'So, she *bought* this place?' He sounded incredulous at the idea anyone would put down hard-earned money for such a dump.

'She won it. Back in the '80s. One of those dodgy timeshare offers came through the door.' He gave her a blank expression. 'Y'know the sort of thing: *You have already won one of these great prizes: a wicker basket of dried flowers, a canoe, or a Highland hideaway*. All you had to do to claim your prize—and it was always the dried flowers—was sit in a conference room in an Aviemore hotel and listen to some guy's sales pitch. But my granny hit the jackpot.' She motioned, quiz-hostess style. 'The Highland hideaway.'

'And to think she could have walked away with a canoe.' He cast a disgruntled eye around the dim room. 'If you'd wanted a change of scene there are perfectly good cafés on Byres Road,' he grumbled. 'With Wi-Fi.' He flicked the switch on a standard lamp sporting a fetching floral shade. The room remained dim. 'And electricity!' he barked. 'This is not natural.'

'What are you talking about? Outside that door is *actual* nature.'

'Nature is for German hikers in yellow cagoules.' He scraped the chair across the floor, closer to the fire. 'Can't you turn this thing up?'

Jane tossed on another log and retreated to the kitchen to make coffee. It was a while since she'd been up to the cottage. When she'd begun the novel she imagined retreating to its splendid isolation. In her head it would go like this: during the day she would alternate writing by the window (that would be the one window with glass in the frame) with long walks in the countryside where she would be inspired by clouds and daffodils. At night she would curl up by the fire and continue scratching out her masterpiece. She had decamped to the cottage to live the dream, only to find the power out, as usual. Four hours later her laptop battery died and she lost half of the chapter she'd been working on. That was the end of the romance. She returned to Glasgow the following morning and hadn't been back since.

The cupboard contained a single jar of Nescafé, a tin of powdered milk and a suspicious trail of what she hoped were only mouse droppings. She warmed the drink on an old Primus stove. It pained her to admit it, but Tom was right; the place was little more than a ruin. But it was her ruin. Her gran had left it to her, not her mum. Gran hadn't approved of mum's choice of husband—she was an astute judge of character—and though there was no grand title or country estate to disinherit her from, there was the cottage.

Tom called from the other room, imploring her through chattering teeth to hurry up with the coffee. She put up with his hectoring, thankful he wasn't asking where to find the toilet. She was delaying the inevitable moment when she had to explain the purpose of the spade by the front door.

He had moved from the armchair onto the hearth, and as she approached she saw he was holding her manuscript. She sighed. It was straight to business then.

'Sit down.'

'You're incredibly bossy, anyone ever told you that?' she complained, sitting nonetheless.

'Yes. Now be quiet and listen. This is the chapter where Janet goes to her favourite sweetshop—'

'Glickman's,' she interrupted. It was on the London Road. A Glasgow institution, the oldest amongst dozens in that sweet tooth of a city. Her dad used to take her on a Saturday morning to spend her pocket money: a bag of Snowies for her—moreish drops of sweet white chocolate covered in rainbow-coloured sprinkles; and a quarter of tangy Soor Plooms for him that made her mouth tingle. He always let her pay for his—a warning sign of things to come.

Jane folded her arms, bracing herself for his critique.

'OK, so what's wrong with it? Wait, don't tell me. It's the Soor Plooms—too specific—they won't understand the reference in Croydon.'

He said nothing and instead reached into his bag for a small, white paper bag. It rustled with unbearable familiarity.

'Are those from Glickman's?' she asked, already knowing the answer.

He chuted the contents into his hand. Out tumbled white chocolate Snowies.

She felt sick.

He held out a single sweet with the quiet unblinking confidence of a man who knows that when he wants to kiss a girl it is inevitable; at some point she will kiss him back. He offered the sweet to her, both of them understanding that she would succumb.

'Your dad—' He shrugged. 'Forgive me, *Janet's* dad—was an *alky* and a total *bamstick*, but you took that pain and turned it into a novel which, for the most part, isn't awful.'

'I'm not Janet.'

He made a face as if to say, oh really? 'A less scrupulous publisher would insist on calling this a memoir,' he said with a nod towards the manuscript. 'He would conveniently skip over the few sections that *are* fiction and sell a hundred thousand more copies. Readers love pain, particularly if they know someone really suffered.'

'I'm not Janet.'

'Now, for the sake of editorial distance, you need to let her go.'

'Editorial distance?' She felt the sag of disappointment. So this *was* just about the edit.

'Yes. What else?' Tom leant forward. 'Janet is about to have a new life on the page. Soon, your character will belong to thousands of readers—' he grimaced '—well, hundreds. You two need to go your separate ways.' He paused. 'So we are going to make a new memory. One that belongs to you, not her. Here, in this picturesque shit-hole.'

He pushed the Snowie towards her. 'You are not Janet.'

'I can't. I haven't had once since Dad…'

'I know.'

Slowly, she parted her lips. He popped the sweetie on her tongue and her mouth filled with warm chocolate and the crunch of hundreds and thousands.

*

In the morning she found him asleep in the armchair, arms wrapped around her manuscript. Was it possible to feel jealous of your own novel? Nothing had happened after Snowie-gate; he had behaved like a gentleman, keeping the conversation professional, the mood workmanlike. Which was absolutely fine with her. A-OK. Hunky-flipping-dory. After all, it was perfectly natural for a modern young woman to invite an attractive man she barely knew to a cottage in the middle of nowhere. A cottage with one bedroom. There was no pretext; this week-end was all about the sex. *Text*. The fire had burned itself out overnight. No, that wasn't a metaphor. She gathered a handful of kindling from the basket next to the grate and built a new one.

At his suggestion after breakfast they spent the day walking the length of the glen. Around lunchtime it opened out to a dark, glassy loch. The sun was breaking through the thick layer of cloud when they came to a large flat rock by the edge of the water and Tom insisted on stopping. He reached into a chic leather messenger bag, and Jane was sure it was to retrieve the manuscript, but to her surprise he produced a couple of gourmet sandwiches from Berits & Brown and a portable espresso maker, from which he proceeded to make the most delicious cup of coffee she'd ever tasted.

'What are you doing here?' she asked as they ate. The clouds had cleared and now the sun hung awkwardly over-head, lost in an empty sky like a walker who's realised he's been holding his Ordnance Survey map upside down for the last four and a half hours.

'It's a nice day, I thought we should get out.'

'No, I don't mean here. I mean *here* here. In Scotland. At the risk of sounding small-town, can I ask what a Frenchman from the Côte d'Azur is doing running a pub-lishing company in Glasgow?'

He lowered his espresso cup. 'You know, Saint-Tropez is a lot like Glasgow.'

'It is?'

'No. Not one little bit.'

'So, you fancied a change of scene?'

'I had to get out. I was living in a pop song. A *French* pop song. Do you know how many hours of sunshine the Côte d'Azur receives annually?'

'How many?'

'A fucking lot.'

'Wait, you're saying you came to Scotland…for the rain?'

He shrugged and rooted around the ground before picking up a smooth, circular stone.

'Why Glasgow?' Jane continued. 'You do know it's Edinburgh that has the book festival, right? And if you want to be a publisher isn't Paris a more obvious choice? Or London, or New York?'

Gripping the stone in the curve of his index finger and thumb he sent it skimming across the flat loch. It sank on the second bounce. '*Merde!*' He turned to Jane. 'The world has been overrun by *ersatz* writers, musicians and artists. All we have are writers who write about writing, singers who purposely break up with their lovers so that they may sing about heartache. I came because Glasgow is still somewhere real. And I came to find someone real.'

His eyes definitely did not bore into her soul. Real eyes didn't do that. So why did she feel so utterly naked?

'Jane, I think I came to find y—'

'*Guten Tag!*'

Above them on the edge of the loch stood a party of walkers with bare knees, ruddy cheeks—and yellow cagoules. Their round smiles deepened into Teutonic puzzlement when Jane and Tom's laughter shattered the stillness.

*

They returned to the cottage. The weather closed in shortly before they reached shelter and they were both soaked through. When she entered the room, towelling her hair dry, she found him occupying his usual place in the armchair by the fire.

'We need to talk about the sex,' he announced.

The sex. *Le* Sex. *Finally*, she thought.

There were, however, cultural proprieties to be observed. A nice girl simply didn't acquiesce to such an indecent proposal. 'I don't think we do,' she said, folding her arms across her chest. 'I am not talking about "the sex" with you. You've got some cheek, you know that? Just because I asked you up here doesn't mean I'm ready to jump into bed.'

'The sex,' he said evenly, 'in chapter seventeen.' He opened her novel to the relevant page.

'Oh,' she said, unfolding her arms. 'Yes. *That* sex.'

Tom stabbed a finger at a section halfway down the page. 'I'm confused. What is going on here?'

'What are you talking about? It's…' She circled behind

him, craning her neck for a sight of the offending paragraph. 'Perfectly clear.'

'Are they having sex? Because if they are, you should know that it's improbable.'

'Ah, well,' she wagged a finger, 'that's because I'm writing it from the woman's perspective—something you clearly don't understand.'

'Right.' He held the page at arm's length, rotating it first one way and then the other, as if looking at it from another angle would make the scene clearer. 'So where exactly is her leg meant to be?'

Oh, the man was maddening! Jane swatted him with her towel and made a grab for the manuscript. 'Give that back!'

He was too fast for her. He led her around the room, dangling the novel at arm's length, just out of her grasp. At first she requested him curtly but politely to desist in his childish behaviour, but when he ignored her she resorted to a tirade of foul language. He doubled up with laughter at hearing her swear. Which meant that he failed to notice the trailing cord of the standard lamp as he swept around the room once more.

'Ow!' He slammed into the floor, his knee taking the brunt. 'I hate this place!'

She stood over him to gloat. 'Serves you right. It's a good scene. It's full-blooded, lusty—'

Tom rubbed his knee mournfully. '—physically impossible.'

With one final cry of irritation she lunged for the manuscript. He teased it out of reach and with his other hand swept her legs from under her. She crumpled, sinking down beside him. So near to him now she saw that he had kept his promise—no lover had ever looked at her this way.

'It's not impossible,' she said, swallowing. 'You just have to be…bendy.'

That raised an eyebrow. 'This is drawn from personal experience?'

They were close enough to breathe each other's air.

'Well, that's not something you're ever going to find out.' She let the words hang there. Just the two of them in the overwhelming silence of the cottage. Not a milk frother to disturb the stillness.

A small part of her couldn't help but observe the situation from a distance: an unfairly attractive Frenchman, a hearthrug in front of a crackling log fire, a Highland cottage. If she'd written it, he would have struck it out. Infuriating, exasperating man.

She waited. In all the romances she'd read people kissed adverbially. Hungrily, madly, passionately. She wondered what it would be like to kiss him. Wondered about the hardness of his bristles and the softness of his lips. Wondered if she should make the first move.

And then she didn't have to wonder any longer.

CHAPTER 5

'Why Does It Always Rain on Me?', Travis, 1999,
Independiente

'YOU STILL UP?' Bleary-eyed, Roddy surveyed the wreck-
age of the evening: a card table strewn with the last hand, a
drained bottle of something in equal parts cheap and nox-
ious, and Tom. He sat in the quiet darkness of his office
with a supermarket brand cognac, swirling the dregs
around the fat-bottomed glass. The pale liquid caught the
light of a streetlamp.

'I'm off to bed. Got Jane Austen with my Fifth Years
first thing tomorrow,' Roddy said wearily. 'Or, as I prefer
to call it, Pride and Extreme Prejudice. Are you crying?'

'No.' There was a snuffle from the darkness.

'You are. You're crying like a little girl.' He took a step
into the room. 'What are you reading?'

'Nothing.' Tom attempted to hide the manuscript
propped open on his lap, but it was too late. 'It's a non-
fiction proposal,' he said, 'about the endangered Chinese
Crested Tern.' He wiped his cheek. 'Very moving.'

'Bollocks. It's Jane's novel, isn't it?'

Tom shot him a look. 'You can never tell her. Never. Promise me, Roddy.'

'OK, OK. But I don't know what you're so worried about—if you hadn't noticed, Glasgow city centre on a non-football Saturday is *chock-a* with reconstructed males in floods when they discover Boots has run out of their Hydra Energetic Anti-Fatigue Moisturiser.' He yawned. 'How many times have you read that book anyway?'

'A few.'

'Uh-huh. I'll leave you two alone then. There's a box of man-sized tissues by the sofa.'

'Roddy!'

'For the crying, sicko.'

'Ah, right. Thanks.'

Roddy shook his head and, smiling at his friend's mood, set off upstairs.

'She's more real than any writer I've ever known,' Tom whispered. 'She stands there, a red flame in a downpour. I think she's the one.'

Roddy froze, then quickly trotted back to the doorway. 'Oh my god. So it's finally happened. The lothario— what's French for lothario?—doesn't matter—anyway, the great lover from Saint-Tropez meets the girl of his dreams and—*twist ending*—turns out she's a redhead from the Gallowgate. It's love across the borders. *Jeux Sans Frontières*. Or is that *It's a Knockout*?'

Tom scowled. 'She's the one *Tristesse* has been waiting for.'

'Oh,' said Roddy. 'No bridesmaid dress for me then.'

'I don't care if her novel sells a single copy, it is a great piece of work.' He reflected on that with a tilt of his head. 'Naturally, I wouldn't object if it does sell a few copies.'

'Naturally.'

'Shitloads would be good, actually.'

Tom drained his glass and thumped it down on the table. 'But she can write, Roddy. The darkness, the terrible beauty of her prose. She does not mistake sentiment for emotion, she plays with language, sometimes it almost destroys her. She leaves a piece of herself on every page. She is unafraid to use her life, her self—whatever the cost. It's very brave.' He took a deep breath. 'In her soul she is a poet.'

'That's nice.' Roddy studied his friend in the gloom. 'Have you told her?'

'Don't be ridiculous.'

'Why not? People like to be told they're doing a good job.'

'Such petty considerations do not concern an artist such as Jane.'

'An *artist*…?' Roddy's face lit up. 'Oh wait a minute, you *do* fancy her, don't you?'

Tom pursed his lips and blew out dismissively.

Roddy pointed excitedly. 'Did you just *pah*? You did. You just *pah'd*.'

'I did not. And that is such a cliché. I thought you were going to bed.'

Roddy narrowed his eyes. 'Have you two…done it yet?'

Tom threw up his hands. 'Typical Anglo-Saxon prurience. Next you'll be asking me if I first requested her father's permission.'

'You did! You two did it.' Roddy's voice dropped to an appalled whisper. 'But what about the golden rule—don't shag your own novelists?'

'I never said it was a *golden* rule.' Tom shrugged. 'It's just a rule.'

'It's the bloody Prime Directive, mate!'

'This is not the time to be quoting *Star Wars*.'

'*Trek*, you philistine.'

'Well then, say it why don't you?' Tom invited the expected disapproval with a brusque wave. 'No good will come of this. You cannot work together and sleep together. Come on, where is your petty bourgeois censure?'

'*Au contraire*—as we Anglo-Saxons like to say— I think it's a great idea. You two make a lovely couple.'

Tom shook a finger at Roddy. 'Hey, hey, hey—who's talking about a *couple*?'

'Well, I just thought—'

'Do I fancy her? Yes. Did sleeping with her make the edit more enjoyable? Naturally. But for fuck's sake,

Roddy, why does every hook-up have to be Happy Ever After?'

*

Sunday morning tiptoed into Jane's bedroom on a gentle breeze and the muffled blare of a radio from the flat upstairs. Through a gap in the curtains a bar of daylight striped the wooden floors and the bed where the two of them had spent most of the night. The rest of it they'd spent in the bath. And on the kitchen counter. And then on her desk in the bay window.

She lay there watching him sleep. They hadn't really discussed what this was, what *they* were: was this just part of his editing process, along with square sausage rolls and coffee from Café Gandolfi? Was he her boyfriend? Somehow she couldn't bring herself to ask, didn't want to seem needy. She was trying very hard to be cool and aloof—for a change. And anyway she saw him every day and it didn't seem to matter. The edit was intense and intimate, but in all this time he hadn't said those four magic little words she so wanted to hear: I love your novel.

She was wearing one of his shirts, though couldn't remember putting it on. She did remember being naked and the ensuing tussle that had visited every room in the flat and lasted half the night. In their passionate frenzy they'd broken a vase filled with fresh flowers and now the memory of last night's lovemaking was suffused with the scent of peonies. Beside her, he stirred. He rubbed his eyes, kissed her good morning and then reached past her for the manuscript on the bedside table. Slipping on his spectacles he began to read.

They had started the final chapter of the edit last week and now all that remained to review was the ending. She studied him, absorbed in her novel, aware of nothing but her words. He must have read the ending countless times—perhaps more than she had, certainly more than any other section of the novel. Finish strongly, he'd said to her often. It was a rule of writing, like 'cut adverbs', 'show, don't tell', and 'never sleep with your editor'.

'So, the ending,' he said at last.

She propped herself up on her elbows. 'You think it's too sad.'

'I love sad. I'm French.' He propped his spectacles on his forehead. 'The way you describe her mum's death…'

Perhaps it *was* more memoir than fiction, she thought. Certainly it was only the most delicate skein that separated the events in the novel and her real life. But she hadn't acknowledged it—not to him—until now.

'I was seven when she died.'

'You must miss her very much.'

'There were aunties. A *lot* of aunties.'

'And your dad?'

'My dad left us. Me.'

'Do you hate him?'

'It'd be easier if I did, right? What kind of man walks out on his family like that?' She shook her head. 'Maybe I do hate him, but the fact is I don't know him. Is it wrong, but I wish I knew where he was?'

She flung off the covers and swung her legs onto the floor. 'I'm going to jump in the shower.' She stood up. The shirt hung down over her hips, brushing the tops of her bare legs. 'Coming?' She waggled her eyebrows.

'Wait. I have something I need to say.' He sat up and laid the manuscript on his lap. 'Jane, I believe we're finished.'

The room went quiet and she took a breath. In her head she started to give herself a talking-to. *Get it together. We were never really a couple.*

Then he patted the manuscript and said, 'We're finished the edit. I want to publish.'

She exhaled. It took her a moment to register what he'd actually said and then all she could muster was a disbelieving, 'Really, are you sure?'

He shrugged. 'We could go through it one more time if you prefer—?'

'No!' She squealed. 'Oh, Tom.' She leapt onto the bed and flung her arms around him. Finally, it was done. Finished. Over! But even as she thrilled to the prospect of being published she was aware of a small voice in her head ringing like an alarm. 'Oh-oh. Oh-oh.' Done. Finished. Over. The edit, not the two of them. So what *did* it mean for them?

She tried to dismiss the nagging voice. What they had was much more than an edit. Wasn't it? He had shared his deepest feelings. *About her novel.* He'd demonstrated an acute sensitivity to her emotions. *On the page.* She realised with a jolt that everything they'd done together to this point was on the page. Apart from the stuff they'd done under the duvet. Under *this* duvet. Tomorrow there would be no discussion of metaphor, no disagreement over the importance of chapter fourteen. Tomorrow there would be no reason for them to see each other.

'We should celebrate,' she said. 'How about tomorrow I take *you* out for lunch?'

Tom climbed out of bed and started to pull on his clothes, retrieving them from the corners of the room where they had been flung the night before. 'Can't. Off to Frankfurt first thing.'

She was puzzled. 'On holiday?'

'For the Book Fair.' He fastened his jeans. 'I need to find the new Jane Lockhart.'

She knew he was kidding, that this was meant to flatter her. But if that was the case then what was this sick feeling in her stomach?

CHAPTER 6

'A Hard Rain's a-Gonna Fall', Bob Dylan, 1962, Columbia Records

THE DAY AFTER Tom announced that the edit was finished, Jane got all the way to the Underground platform before she remembered. She huffed, irritated at wasting her time until it struck her that she could waste as much time as she wanted now. She had absolutely nothing to do.

She trudged home and proceeded to mooch about her flat, rearranging furniture, desultorily flicking through magazines she had been forbidden from reading during the last few months. When they'd started to revise her manuscript Tom had banned all other reading material. No magazines. No newspapers. Definitely no novels. To avoid the possibility of leakage, he had said. He didn't want her influenced by external factors. What about him, she'd teased, wasn't he external? No, he'd said sternly, from this moment on I am inside you. Yeah, he really didn't hear himself.

When he returned from Frankfurt they met up for

NOT ANOTHER HAPPY ENDING 73

dinner, but without the scattered manuscript pages and the low-level squabbling that invariably accompanied the edit, something was missing. She even missed his red pen. Which, she had to admit, did sound somewhat phallic. And yes, they did sleep together that night, but then around midnight his phone pulsed with a message.

'Who is it?' she asked sleepily.

'Nicola,' he said, the blue glow from the screen illuminating his face. He read her text and smiled. 'Clever. Very clever.'

She felt a stab of jealousy. 'What does she want?

'She's had a thought about how to crack chapter twenty-two and wants to talk it through.' He climbed out of bed.

Stung, Jane sat up. 'You're going?' she said. 'Now?'

Hurriedly he began to dress. 'If I don't go to her now then by morning she will have convinced herself that the idea is worthless. She's not like you. She doesn't have your confidence.'

She tried to accept the compliment and to remind herself that Nicola and Tom really was just business, but as she heard the front door click shut behind him the unease she'd felt through dinner swelled into emotional indigestion.

The next date went better. They'd planned to see a triple bill of Kieslowski's *Trois Couleurs* at the GFT, but over drinks Tom asked her if she had any thoughts about her next novel and as she talked to him she realised that she did. They missed *Blue* as they brainstormed and by the time they made it to the film theatre, they'd lost three and a half hours of Polish miserablism to their conversation and decided to skip the rest of the bill in favour of continuing their discussion over a curry at Balbir's.

As they ate, it occurred to her that as soon as she gave him the next novel it would be followed by another close edit and they'd be back in the place where things between them had flowed easily. She decided to start work on the new novel the very next morning.

*

When she awoke he had already left. Instead of feeling upset she took advantage of his absence and the peace of the empty flat, leapt out of bed, showered, grabbed a bowl of cereal and sat down at her desk. *File. New Document. Save As* Untitled. That would do for now. She was ready to begin. She loved this moment. The anticipation of what happens next. It didn't matter that the ideas which had seemed so sharp the night before now appeared fuzzy. She was fearless before the blank page. She rested her hands on the wrist pad and, taking a deep breath, hurled herself into the white void of the first draft.

*

She quickly lost herself in the new book. Her protagonist, Darsie Baird, began to dominate every waking and most of her sleeping hours. Suddenly, she didn't have time to see Tom and when after a few weeks of writing in her pyjamas she decided it would be nice to shave her legs and drop in on him she discovered that he had gone home to France for a month to see his family. She tried not to be irritated that he hadn't told her, and Roddy mumbled something about him not wanting to interrupt her Muse.

Somehow the weeks had drifted past and now it was the best part of two months since they'd seen each other. A couple of days ago he'd texted her to say he was back in Glasgow and the finished copies of her book were due to arrive that week. She waited as long as she could to call in to the office, unsure which she was more eager to see: her debut novel or Tom.

'Hello?' It was Roddy's voice on the intercom.

She stood outside Tristesse, bouncing with anticipation, mouth tilted up to the speaker, one hand supporting a tray of fairy cakes. 'I was just passing.' Lie.

There was a buzz and a click and she threw herself through the front door. Balancing the tray she skipped down the corridor towards Reception. The fairy cakes were a bluff. She'd been making batches of them all morning, studding alphabet sweets in the icing to spell out highly amusing and piercingly appropriate lines from classic literature.

At least, that had been her plan. Turns out the surface area of your average fairy cake is not nearly expansive enough to accommodate your classic literary quip. And anyway, even had the cakes been bigger, there weren't enough e's in her bag of alphabet sweets to manage more than a couple of zingers from Shakespeare and the opening line of *Moby Dick*. In the end she gave up any attempt at cake intertextuality and settled on dropping random letters onto the icing. She was adamant that if you squinted at the last batch you could see a couple of lines from Emily Brontë.

But the fairy cakes were a decoy. A subterfuge. A Trojan horse in sponge form.

She eyed the stacked boxes that lined the narrow passageway, paying more attention to them than usual. One of them could contain *her book*. She'd been waiting for this moment since Tom announced that the edit was finished. He was happy. Or, as happy as the scowling Frenchman ever got. The manuscript had been scoured for solecisms, corrected for commas; it was ready to go to the printer, he announced. And what about the cover?

'That is up to the publisher,' he'd said. 'Trust me.'

And she had.

Tom had insisted that the delivery date was a rough one, that the books could arrive any day that week. She wasn't taking any chances. But she didn't want to seem too keen. Hence the deceptive fairy cakes.

'Hi, Jane,' Roddy greeted her. 'What are you doing here?'

'Yeah, I was just passing,' she repeated, attempting to sound casual. 'I was baking this morning and made too many of these.' Lie.

'Ooh, fairy cakes. With alphabet letters. Nice touch.' He took a bite out of one, then snapped his fingers and said through a mouthful of sponge, 'You know what would be brilliant—if you used the letters to spell out, y'know, famous lines from novels!'

'Genius!' she exclaimed with rather too much surprise. 'I should do that.' She waited impatiently while he polished off the cake.

'Umm…' she began.

'He's in,' Roddy nodded towards Tom's office door, 'if that's what you're asking.'

'Oh good. Good to know. That he's in.' She scanned the small Reception room, trying to identify any new boxes. 'Umm…'

'Was there anything else, Jane?'

Her gaze fell on a stack propped in front of a life-sized cardboard cut-out of Nicola Ball. They were unopened boxes, shrink-wrapped and pristine, lacking the telltale scuffmarks that indicated stock which had been left lying about the office for weeks. Jane snatched a pair of scissors from Roddy's desk and set about prising open the topmost box. The flaps sprang open and there before her lay four snugly fitting hardbacks.

Her heart sank: it wasn't her novel. The hot pink cover was dominated by a photograph of a grinning little girl under an umbrella, beneath the title, *Happy Ending*. Relief immediately replaced disappointment; it was an awful cover, and the title stank. What kind of a writer would come up with…? Jane's eye slipped down to the author's name.

Her name.

No. That made no sense. She hadn't written a novel called *Happy Ending*. She read it again and felt a sudden sensation of falling, as in a dream, and was aware of eyes watching her. She glanced up at the cut-out of Nicola Ball. The young novelist's knowing, cardboard expression said, 'I told you so.'

'Hey,' said Roddy, studying the top row of fairy cakes with a quizzical expression. 'I'm pretty sure that's the last line of *Wuthering Heights*. Jane?'

But she had gone.

*

'I'll call you back.' Tom replaced the receiver as Jane barrelled through the door, brandishing a copy of her novel, her face red with fury. With a grunt she launched the hardback in his direction. He ducked and it hurtled past his ear, slamming against the wall.

'Now, Jane…' He held up his hands defensively.

'*Happy Ending*? *Happy* fucking *Ending*!? What happened to *The Endless Anguish of My Father*? You bastard, you changed my title! To that?!'

'I told you. The first time we met, I said it must go.'

'But we never discussed it.'

He shrugged. 'I knew how you'd react.'

The supercilious, condescending…she quickly scanned

the room for something else with which to assault him and immediately found just what she was looking for.

'Careful,' he cried, 'that's my Young Publisher of the Year award.'

Jane weighed the gold-coloured trophy and drew back her hand. 'Runner-up,' she said, heaving it at his head.

It flashed past him.

'Sonofa—' cursed Jane, disgusted at her aim—two throws, two misses. What the hell was she doing?

She slumped and the fight went out of her. She studied the man before her, searching his face for a sign, for whatever it was she'd missed that revealed his true nature. Like some spotty teenage girl she'd been distracted by his outward charms. God, she felt such a fool. 'Who are you?'

'What?'

'All that time we spent together working on the manuscript. No one's ever got me the way…You told me to trust you. I did.' She shook her head slowly. 'It was a lie. That man would never have done this.' The words caught in her throat. 'I don't know you.'

'Look, it was a terrible title and I changed it,' he said gently. 'There's no point being upset about it. What's done is done. Let's move on.'

'How can this be so easy for you?' Her voice was low, restrained. 'You bastard.'

He flinched and colour rose into his cheeks. Now he was angry. 'Perhaps because I am not a talented writer whose dad left her with a pathological inability to stop worshipping her own pain.'

'Worshipping my…'

He closed his eyes, trying to regain control of himself. 'Please, sit down. Let's talk about the launch.'

'You know what,' she said quietly, 'our deal is one more book and then what's done is done.'

She wanted to turn smartly on her heel, head held high and march from his office. From his life. She needed a good exit, something to show him what she was made of—a full stop at the end of their stupid little relationship, or whatever this was. But her legs felt like they belonged to someone else. And with each step she told herself don't look back. Don't look back at him. Finally, she was outside and she let the tears fall. She made her way quickly across the empty courtyard and back onto the street. With a whir and a click the gates swung closed behind her.

Au revoir, Tristesse.

CHAPTER 7

'Only Happy When It Rains', Garbage, 1995, Mushroom

IF IT HAD BEEN up to Jane she would have cut all ties with Tom and Tristesse, but there was the small matter of her debut novel to promote. As a result the next six weeks were punctuated with a stream of perky communications from Sophie Hamilton Findlay in her capacity as Tristesse Books' publicity department.

'I'm pitching you to *Vogue/Harpers/Stylist*,' she would announce one day, and follow up two days later with news of a rejection delivered in the same upbeat fashion.

Sophie remained stalwart in the face of endless dismissal, but Jane couldn't help noticing that the scale of her ambition lowered with each round. The glossies gave way to the free sheets. 'I'm pitching you to the *Glasgow West Gazette/The Big Issue*.'

As the weeks wore on, Jane began to worry. Now even worse than the prospect of bad reviews was the distinct possibility of no reviews. It was not so much the sinking of her expectations as their torpedoing.

'We'll start with some events.' Sophie's jaunty voice whizzed out of the phone. 'Nothing glam, I'm afraid. Little bookstores. But we'll grow it.'

'Does that usually work?' Jane asked cautiously.

'It can.'

'Have you ever known it to work?'

Jane listened as Sophie circled the question like a bear trap. 'Really, it's all about word of mouth. Nothing beats word of mouth.'

'But people need to read the book in the first place before they can talk about it, right? You need…mouths.'

'Yes.'

'And how do you get to those mouths?'

'Oh, lots of ways. We have our tricks of the trade. The key is to go where the conversation is happening.'

'But it isn't happening.'

'Not yet.'

'So how do we make it happen?'

There was a pause and then Sophie announced breezily, 'Word of mouth.'

*

Jane perched on a wobbly chair tucked away at the rear of the tiny bookshop in a space in the children's section that when she'd arrived earlier that evening was occupied by a playmat and assorted squeaky toys.

She'd pictured her first book signing a thousand times in her mind: a queue of eager readers snaking round the block, her sitting behind a desk bowing under the weight of books, happily accepting endless, unconditional praise, signing each fresh copy to the accompanying melody of the cash register. Reality was a letdown. Most of her makeshift audience had been lured in by the promise of a free glass of wine, some cheap plonk Tom had ordered for the occasion. She'd sunk two glasses in an attempt to bolster her courage before taking to the stage. Well, playmat.

No one applauded when she finished reading. She'd chosen the chapter in *Happy Ending* in which her protagonist is locked in her bedroom on the twelfth floor of the high flat and can only gaze down at the other children playing outside on the first day of sunshine after a month of rain.

She squinted into the audience. The bookshop owner had helpfully set up a reading lamp. It dazzled her as she looked out and she couldn't see their faces. 'Audience' was a bit grand; she wasn't sure there were enough people out there to fill a lift. Beyond the glare she could hear a cough and what sounded like the rustle of a crisp bag. This was her first public reading and judging from the silence she'd gone down like a slug in a salad.

Nervously she tucked a strand of hair behind an ear and closed the book. The awful title assaulted her from the cover and she flipped it face down on her lap so that she didn't have to look at it one second longer. Her cheeks burned. Tom had foisted the title on her, betrayed her trust and then insisted that she go out and pretend she was happy about what he'd done.

She hated her book. The thing—the object—made her feel sick. Such a shame. All she'd ever wished for was to be a published author, but when it happened it came in a pink cover with a title she loathed almost as much as the man standing at the back of the coughing crowd. She couldn't see him either, but had no doubt he'd be leaning handsomely up against the wall, arms folded, watching her make a fool of herself in front of five women and a dog.

This was humiliating. She had to get out of here. Another cough rattled out of the darkness. And another. Was there something going round? The bookshop owner, a severely thin woman with an orb of white hair, stood next to the lamp. They could have been twins.

'Ms. Lockhart, that was lovely.' There was a catch in her throat. God, there really was some epidemic sweeping the city. 'So, so…' her voice squeaked, 'lovely.'

Jane thanked her quietly and got up to leave, knocking the lamp. It swung out over the audience, illuminating them with a sickly light. They weren't coughing.

They were crying.

At the next book signing the same thing happened. Sniffles became sobs, five people became ten. Then the first newspaper review came out. *Inconsolably, wretchedly wonderful—Jane Lockhart knows desolation.*

At the reading the following evening they had to borrow chairs from the café next door. Jane read, people wept. And a new sound joined the weeping, the ring of cash registers. *Happy Ending is the new black*, ran one style magazine. Young women jostled the middle-aged stalwarts in the queue.

And at the next event more than a few men lined up with a copy—or two—clutched in their hands. *Just buying it for my wife, my girlfriend, my dear old ma*, they stressed in loud voices, then sheepishly would ask for it to be signed 'to Gary'. What was happening here? Sophie Hamilton Findlay had a ready answer.

Tears everywhere. Tears on the bus. Tears on the underground. Tears falling from the eyes of miserable office workers. Wracking sobs in the suburbs. Tom thought about approaching Kleenex to sponsor the rest of the book tour.

First was the Scottish leg and home advantage. Her people; the kind who didn't need a glossary for the slang. Then south, following in the wake of the book's sales success, until finally to London, the great nose-in-the-air of a city. Go on, impress me, said Chelsea and Islington and Shoreditch. A spot on Radio Four—Jane Lockhart unlocked—and a half page in the *TLS*. The literati swooned. Film producers sniffed.

The tour continued with a triumphal return home. The big Waterstones on Buchanan Street opened up specially; tickets had to be purchased in advance now, the wine drinkable.

Jane smiled as she signed each new hardback, her hand aching, her signature no more than a scribble after weeks of constant repetition. She'd sent out so many 'best wishes' into the universe that if there really was such a thing as karma she could expect something wonderful to rebound. She shook herself. What was she talking about? It had already happened. Her book was a hit. After three months on sale so wet with tears was the island of Great Britain it could have been rolled up and squeezed out like a rag.

Tom had wanted to tour with her but she'd roundly rejected the suggestion, informing him flatly that she didn't want him anywhere near her. Grumbling, he had insisted on sending Sophie to play chaperone. 'To look after *me*?' she'd snapped back. 'Or your investment?'

He was here today, in Glasgow, watching the cash registers ring. Typical.

A reader, delighted to be face to tear-stained face with the author of her misery, offered up a copy for signature. She'd read it three times; this one was for her aunty Avril.

The book fell open at the dedication. 'To my dad, wherever he is.'

It had been a suggestion of Tom's which he'd made one Sunday morning in bed, during the last stages of the edit, when things were still good between them. Who knows, he'd said with a boyish shrug, perhaps he'll read it and come looking for you. She'd smiled despite herself—she suspected that Tom was a romantic, even though he kept it extremely well hidden. He caught her eye across the room. Oh, and a complete bastard. Don't forget that part.

She swirled her signature across the page. 'Thanks. Thanks so much,' she said, handing over the book.

The funny thing was that no matter how often she said it, she meant it every time. People were connecting with her novel. It was amazing. There was so much noise out there, so many other books to choose from, it was nothing short of a miracle they'd found hers. Here she sat in a bookshop surrounded by thousands of titles. She could feel them bristling at being left dustily on the shelf; their characters resentful at hers being singled out for attention. She liked to think of her own characters out there in the world, making new acquaintances. Readers were complicit, referring to them by name, as if they were neighbours or friends of the family. Sometimes the sensation was so intense she forgot that they were just that: characters. The only downside to all this gratitude was the dry throat.

The water jug and glass laid out on the signing table were both empty. She turned to the bookseller at her side and asked for a refill, just as the next eager reader placed his copy down in front of her.

'Who shall I make it out to?' she asked on auto-pilot, turning to look up at the man who stood awkwardly before her.

His face was as heavily lined as she remembered, but the skin had lost its sallow complexion and his eyes were no longer dull and milky, but gazed down at her with surprising clarity. In the ageing Polaroid on her Board of Pain he had more hair and perhaps the jaw-line was set firmer, but other than that he appeared younger, more vital than the last time she'd seen him. And he smelt different—cleaner. She knew at once he'd given up the drink.

'Dad,' she whispered.

Benny Lockhart twisted his hands and looked away, unsure what to say. He offered a self-conscious smile.

'Hullo, Jane.'

In the signing line the book group ladies, thirty-something mums and sprinkling of literate males, all highly attuned to drama, sensed a new scene developing before their eyes; a bonus DVD extra playing out right in front of them. Conversations ceased and a hush fell over the room.

Benny shuffled his feet. 'So, how have you been?' He rolled his eyes. 'Christ, what an *eejit*. *How have you been*? Like I just got back from a fortnight's holiday.'

Jane pushed back her chair, walked to the other side of the table and, with another low, whispered 'Dad', flung her arms about him. The embrace was as much of a surprise to her as it was to him.

She could see that he was uncomfortable with the public display of affection. Who was she kidding—he'd always been uncomfortable with any kind of affection.

But then she felt him clasp her tightly, and knew that this time he would never let her go.

*

Two weeks later Jane was taking advantage of some late summer sun with a walk in Kelvingrove Park, ducking Frisbees hurled by pasty bare-chested Glaswegian boys, listening to happy chatter ripened by the sunshine. She imagined that somewhere in the park someone was reading her book. Her idle afternoon threatened to be ruined when Tom's name flashed up on her phone. She ignored him, but he kept calling, and after the sixth hang-up she answered.

'What do you want?'

'You've been shortlisted for the Austen Book Awards. Best New Writer.'

'Oh my god!'

'We did it.'

And for the briefest, blissful moment she forgot about their falling out. Hostilities were suspended in the late afternoon glow. There was a pause and in the silence she could hear the rush of the River Kelvin. She waited for him to say something else, perhaps invite her to lunch for a celebratory glass of champagne. Or maybe she should ask him.

'The ceremony's in London. I'll have Sophie send you the details,' he said, interrupting her pleasant reverie. 'And, uh, there's not much left in the budget, so I'm not sure we can afford the train fare.' He paused. 'How would you feel about taking the bus?'

*

The auditorium was full. Five hundred publishers, authors and agents dolled up in cocktail dresses and dinner suits embraced their rivals with hearty greetings whilst silently wishing upon them ignominious failure.

Someone had described the Austen Book Awards as the Oscars of the book industry. Someone in marketing, of course. The comparison was spurious, but what the book award lacked in star-power it made up for in charm. The trophy—inevitably referred to as 'The Jane'—was a golden statuette of a woman in an Empire line shift, inscribed with one of the eponymous author's less tolerant ideas: 'The person, be it gentleman or lady, who has not pleasure in a good novel, must be intolerably stupid.'

To win a 'Jane' was worth bragging rights for a year, but more importantly a bump in sales of anything from a hundred to two hundred thousand copies; a career-defining number.

'Did you try the fishy one?' Roddy sat awkwardly between a taciturn Jane and Tom. 'Very tasty. I don't normally go for the fishy ones.'

He had been invited to the ceremony less as a plus one and more as a referee, and had so far spent the evening overcompensating for their sullen silence with interminable chat about the venue—'That's some lovely cornicing'—the traffic in the West End of London—'Surprisingly not as bad as I expected'—and now the canapés served at the reception prior to the ceremony—'Wonder what kind of fish it was. Do you—?'

'Eel,' snapped Tom.

'Eel?' Roddy's lip curled in distaste.

'*Raw* eel,' added Tom.

'You're kiddin' me?'

'Not at all. It is only in Glasgow that sushi comes deep fried.'

'Don't you pick on Glasgow,' hissed Jane. 'You're only visiting.'

'Ah, the famous Scottish hospitality,' said Tom. 'Feel its friendly embrace. Come in and warm yourself by this roaring candle.'

'Fuck off.'

'And so speaks the nominee in the category for Best New Writer. Such eloquence.'

Jane wriggled in her seat, incensed. Roddy stuck out a hand between her and Tom.

'Keep the *heid*, Jane—he's not worth it.'

'I wasn't going to hit him,' whispered Jane, mortified that Roddy's restraining arm was meant for her. 'You really think I'd *lamp* him?'

Roddy looked thoughtful. 'You do have a tendency to…throw stuff.'

She heard Tom chuckle, and bit her lip. 'Oh for god's

sake,' she huffed, folding her arms and looking straight ahead, hoping neither man could see her cheeks flush in the dim auditorium.

The event's shimmering host introduced a new presenter. 'Ladies and gentlemen, it's my pleasure to welcome award-winning screenwriter Willie Scott, all the way from LA, to present the award for Best New Writer.'

Willie Scott strutted to the podium, a 'Jane' in one hand and an envelope in the other. He wore a sleek, black suit, his hair surfed across his head in a perfectly coiffed wave, and his skin displayed a taut southern Californian glow, so it came as something of a surprise when he opened his mouth and out came a Scottish accent.

'Good evening, ladies and gentlemen, it's great to be here.' His inflection carried a hint of transatlantic twang. 'Even if it's impossible to get a movie off the ground in this country unless your screenplay's full of kids with head lice and outside toilets and some bastard dying of emphysema.' He flashed a thousand-watt smile. There was some awkward laughter from the audience. 'And it's a particular thrill for an old dog like me to be asked to present the award for Best New Writer.' He fished in his top pocket for a pair of standard-issue hipster black spectacles and when they were in place focused on the envelope containing the winner's name.

'The nominations are: Christian Stromain for *The Sons of Memory*; Sharron Lumb for *The Man Who Bought a*

Bridge and Learned to Love the Starling's Song; Jane Lockhart for *Happy Ending*; and Jaswinder Yamanaka for *Rug*.'

Willie opened the envelope. 'And the winner is…'

Jane didn't hear her name being called out. She was otherwise engaged. 'And another thing, Duval. For the next book I want the final decision over the cover design.'

Roddy pressed himself back into his seat as they conducted their latest disagreement across him.

'Jane,' he said. In an attempt to alert her to the news of her win, he gave her a cautious tap on the shoulder, which she ignored.

'Not a chance,' spat Tom. 'I'm not letting you near the cover. If your design skills are anything like your fashion sense…'

'What's wrong with my fashion se—?!'

'Two words. Bowler. Hat.'

'Jane,' Roddy repeated, louder this time.

'What?' barked Jane and Tom together.

'Uh…' He waved in the general direction of the stage, where Willie Scott peered into the audience with a puzzled expression, wondering if Jane Lockhart was a no-show. 'You won.'

'Omigod. I *won*?'

'She won?' Tom couldn't hide his astonishment.

Jane got to her feet and half in a daze made her way along the row to collect her prize.

Willie finally spotted her as she tripped up the steps to the stage and bounced towards him. 'Ladies and gentlemen, Jane Lockhart.'

A thin microphone poked up from the glass podium. She hesitated, unsure what to say. She hadn't prepared a speech. Never in a million years could she have imagined being lucky enough to—

OK, that was a big fat lie.

She'd been preparing this speech from the moment she wrote the opening line of her very first short story when she was six years old. She thought back. It was possible that the first thing she wrote was in fact the acceptance speech for the award she expected to win for the short story she hadn't yet written. However, for the six-year-old Jane thoughts of an award didn't revolve around commercial success or literary validation, for her it was an escape. To clutch the golden statuette of her fantasies was to transport her to another world, one far away from the concrete tower blocks and endless cold rain.

She leant forward to say a few considered words into the microphone.

'Now what we have here, ladies and gentlemen, is a real writer.' Willie cut across her, nudging her aside so that he occupied the centre of the podium. 'Jane Lockhart has penned an extraordinary debut. At once moving and bleakly inspiring, she writes with an authentic voice, rooted in the reality of misery. And not just Scottish misery, this is universal misery. Now if you've read her novel with as much care as I have you'll know that she goes to some pretty dark places. I get that.' He shot her a look of understanding. 'Writers, eh, Jane? We know what it is to face *el toro blanco*—the terror of the white bull—the blank page. And our curse—or perhaps it's our blessing—is to face it every day of our lives.' Apparently finished, he pursed his lips and nodded in deep contemplation.

'Thanks ver—'

'The bleakness, the terrible beauty of your prose...' Willie hadn't finished. 'You are a writer who does not mistake sentiment for emotion. You play with language, sometimes I could feel it almost destroy you.'

In the audience, Tom looked up from beneath the hand he'd clamped over his face when Willie had begun talking. All that crap about the blank page and the reality of misery, he'd thought, seriously, what the hell? But the stuff he was saying now, that was different.

Tom tugged Roddy's sleeve. 'That's what I said.'

'Hmm?'

'About Jane. That night after the poker game? Remember I told you?'

'Oh yeah.' Roddy vaguely recalled the conversation. 'Shame you never told her.' He nodded to the stage where Jane gazed wide-eyed at Willie Scott.

Willie took her hands in his and said softly, though still loudly enough for the microphone to pick it up, 'In your soul, Jane, you are a poet.'

'*Putain*,' Tom cursed, slamming the arms of the seat. From the row behind, someone shushed him.

Applause rolled out across the hall. The authors in the audience applauded in appreciation of Willie's praise, the rest applauded to encourage him and Jane to vacate the stage.

Jane reeled. Sure, Willie's Hollywood *shtick* was excruciating, but that last part had somersaulted her opinion of him. No one, *no one*, had ever talked about her writing like that before. Willie planted a kiss on her cheek.

'Congratulations. And here, I believe this belongs to you.' With another electric smile he handed her the 'Jane'.

'Hey,' he feigned surprise, 'it's already got your name on it.'

*

The party after the ceremony carried on late into the night. Music! Dancing! Socially awkward writers! It was a rare affair.

Sitting alone at a table on the edge of the dance floor, Jane accepted the congratulations and best wishes of at least, oh, three people. Two of whom were waiters. Tom sent over a bottle of champagne, but he didn't count. She had banished him to the other side of the table. He didn't appear to be suffering, surrounded as he was in a bubble of publicity girls, his greatest hardship the threat of being struck by an errant hair-flick. At his shoulder Roddy flapped hopefully.

Jane knocked back a glass of Tom's champagne and

wondered whether she was being too hard on him. Briefly she considered dragging him away from Sophie, Sophie and Sophie, inviting him over to share their mutual moment of triumph. After all, he was her editor and she almost certainly wouldn't be here tonight if he hadn't spent so long working with her on the novel.

'Y'know, I won an award once.'

Jane looked up to see Willie Scott standing over her, a copy of *Happy Ending* in one hand, a golden signet ring like a sword pommel flashing from the little finger of the other as he drew down a memory from the air.

'Best Moon Landing in a Stricken Rocket-Ship in a TV Movie,' he said, proudly.

'That was you?' Jane said with a gasp of mock amazement.

'I know. Impressive, huh?' He grinned and gestured to an empty chair. 'May I?'

'Sure. Why not.'

He slid in beside her. Somewhere between presenting her on stage with the award and joining the party he had discarded his tie and popped the top two buttons on his shirt, revealing a portion of improbably groomed chest.

Willie was in his forties, though at what end Jane couldn't judge. His age seemed to depend on the angle you looked at him, his face like one of those collector's cards you used to get in cereal packets with a cartoon image of a duck or a monkey which, when you tilted it, would appear to smile or throw a banana. From one angle he displayed enough frown lines to suggest a life well lived, but turning him a few degrees revealed suspiciously dark hair for a man of his age.

Her first impression of him had not been a good one. On stage he had hogged the microphone and was clearly revelling in the spotlight; she'd had visions of having to wrestle the 'Jane' from his grip. Not so much lounge lizard as lounge T-Rex, she'd decided. But then he had said those things about her writing and she had glimpsed someone else behind the smile and the hair: a man not afraid to look her in the eye and say what he felt. And a Scottish man too, which was the biggest surprise. She knew other men of his generation, barely able to speak, only ever dredging up passion on the football terraces or at the dog track. But Willie had left all of that behind to go and seek his fortune in Hollywood. Whether he had hit gold, she had no idea, but she sensed that he had found something infinitely more enriching.

'I know this isn't cool, but, what the hell.' He opened the novel in front of her at the title page and fished a pen from his jacket. 'Could you make it to Willie?'

She laughed. 'I'd be delighted.'

He hunched closer so that they couldn't be overheard. 'If you don't mind talking shop for a minute, who has the film rights?'

'Um, no one.'

'You're kidding me. Well, they'll be snapped up now. Who you with?'

'Who am I *with*?'

'Representation. Who's your agent?'

'Um…'

Willie sat back. 'You don't have an agent?'

'I never needed one. Tom…my publisher drew up the contract and I—'

His face twisted in horror. 'Stop! Please, you're killing me. Here.' He dug out a small silver box of business cards and pressed one into her hand. 'My card. My agent's Priscilla Hess at Clarion Creative Management.' He ran a finger along a name and number printed at the foot of the card. 'That's her direct line. Call her.'

'OK.'

'I'm serious. Actually, forget it, I'll get her to call you.' He motioned to the room and beyond. 'Jane, what you've got to realise is that out there it's just sharks and leeches.' He laid a hand on her shoulder. 'You need looking after.' Then with a world-weary sigh and a shake of the head that suggested he knew what was down the road for her—that he had perhaps been down a similar road himself—Willie gathered his signed book and got up to leave.

'Thanks for this. By the way, I really meant it—what I said on stage—you've got a rare talent. Be careful they don't take too much advantage of you.' He smiled ruefully and began to walk away.

Suddenly, Jane knew she wanted him to stay.

'D'you want some champagne?'

He froze in his tracks, then turned round with a pained expression. 'I can't.'

'Oh, I understand,' she said, trying to make light of the rejection. 'You've probably got some Hollywood starlet waiting at the Ritz…'

'It's not that,' he gestured to the bottle. 'I'm off the booze. Seven years sober.'

A layer of Willie's brash exterior rubbed off with his admission. He looked like a man far from home. And Jane couldn't help reflect that before her dad had shown up in the bookshop three months ago she had often imagined him returning to her with just those words.

'We could just talk,' Jane offered.

He extended a hand. 'Or we could just dance.'

The dance floor was full of middle-aged revellers shimmying and bobbing to the song thumping out of two speakers the size of coffins. She knew this one. She let him steer her into the throng. He was a smooth mover and full of what they called in her town, great patter. But there was more to him than that. She had already glimpsed some part of it; she resolved to unearth the rest. He was damaged and she would heal him.

The song blasted across the dance floor as Willie whirled her around. She threw back her head, and for a moment she noticed a figure at the edge of her vision. It was Tom, a statue on the periphery of the frenetic party. The only cloud on her horizon.

CHAPTER 8

'Dry the Rain', The Beta Band, 1998, Regal

SUCCESS HADN'T GONE to Jane's head. Actually, on second thoughts, that's exactly where it had gone. After winning her 'Jane' she'd gone out the following day and bought herself a hat from the venerable Lock & Co in St. James's, hatters to the gentry since 1676. After contemplating a range of fabulous Panamas (originally made in Ecuador, it transpired) and almost plumping for a cool red Fez with a black tassel, she'd settled on a riding hat— a dressage model in deep blue with a polished fur felt. When she'd studied her reflection in the mirror, red hair tucked out of sight, a few wisps artfully poking out, she decided it made her look like the Mad Hatter. She paid cash.

Back home her spending spree continued. She replaced the threadbare rug in the living-room with a handmade Persian, and the old paper lantern that for years had cast a dusty light from the ceiling-rose gave way to a multi-coloured Venetian glass chandelier, which hung over her latest addition, a polished Steinway upright. Her dad had wanted her to learn the piano—all the posh kids at private school took lessons, he said—and after a lucky streak on the horses he'd paid for her to visit a prim tutor on the Southside, but then, as usual with him, the winnings dried up and the lessons stopped.

The dressage hat wasn't the only thing she'd brought back from London. Willie Scott had called her the following week. He was in town, visiting his old ma in Newton Mearns. He had some news he thought she'd be interested to hear. How about lunch? His treat. They met in town, at Rogano, an upscale Glasgow classic with a dining room like a golden-age ocean liner; the kind of restaurant where the fish was never fried, only ever *tempura*. Jane had mixed feelings about the venue: she'd been only once before, when she signed with Tom. Perhaps this time would take away the sting.

Lunch had gone well. Very well. Willie had no sooner sat down than he informed her that he had passed her novel to a couple of buddies in the business. She hadn't understood. The film business, he'd explained; was there any other kind? Oh, yes. Of course. So, you ready for this? One of them wants to option the book. Did he mean they want to make it into a film? No, he grinned. They want to make it into a *movie*.

Their starters arrived and they ate and talked about growing up in Glasgow and what it was like being an in-demand screenwriter in LA until the waiter cleared their plates. There was one other thing about the movie deal.

Willie dabbed his mouth with a white napkin. 'I want to write the adaptation.'

'You do? But what about all your Hollywood projects?'

She was puzzled—he'd spent the last hour regaling her with tales of his numerous movie deals.

'Oh, them. Aye.' He smoothed the napkin across his lap. 'They can wait. This is what I want to do now. Your novel touched me in a way I've never felt before. I'm from that world. I know those characters.' He reached across the table and took her hand. 'Trust me, Jane. I'm your man.'

They'd started seeing each other the following week. Jane wasn't daft, she knew what people on the outside would say: he wasn't Mr Right, he was Mr Rebound. She didn't care; he was fun, full of great stories and she felt better about herself being around him.

A few things about him surprised her. For a writer he wasn't widely read; adamant that *The Godfather* was an original movie and wouldn't believe her increasingly shrill protests until she marched him to a bookstore and shoved a copy of Puzo's novel into his hands. Even his film knowledge displayed some startling gaps, though he had a ready response for each omission. *Sense and Sensibility*? Frock Movie. *West Side Story*? Musical. *The Seventh Seal*? Swedish. *And* Black and White. *Some Like*

It Hot? He shrugged and then displayed a scoundrel's grin. Nobody's perfect.

Since returning to Glasgow Willie had been staying *gratis* in a suite at an achingly hip boutique hotel, having called in a favour from the manager, a friend from the good old, bad old days. The hotel had been converted from a church, and was perched at the summit of one of the city's many hill streets. Willie had the top floor belfry suite. Jane had slept with him for the first time there, afterwards lying naked on the bed, staring over the city through the long picture window, listening to Willie in the shower belting out a passable rendition of 'O Sole Mio'. Closing one eye, she traced the skyline with a finger. The sex had been good. She revised her assessment. Really good.

Willie moved into her flat the following month. His old friend's largesse having run out, it was either Jane's place or his old room in his mum's bungalow in the wasteland of the suburban Southside. Jane insisted he move in with her. It was only temporary, he said, while he waited for a cheque from LA. Aye, as soon as that big boy landed he'd be out of her hair. Her long, red, sweet-smelling hair. He fancied renting one of those penthouse apartments on the river; sure it wasn't Malibu, but it'd do him nicely. In the meantime the living arrangements would help both of them since she'd be right there when he needed to ask her a question about the adaptation.

Jane sat at her desk in the wide bay window, absorbed

in the latest chapter of her new novel. Her fingers flew over the keys, propelling her protagonist, the spirited and resourceful Darsie Baird, to another dramatic climax in her conflict with the brutal Tony Douglas, mean-spirited owner of the umbrella factory. Darsie and Tony had been going at it like cat and dog for thirty-six chapters. Just one more to go, though even now Jane wasn't sure if finally they'd end up together, or killing each other.

A flurry of keystrokes and the penultimate chapter was done. She reread the last page. She could never trust her judgement when the ink was wet; somehow the words always shone when freshly summoned. They had to stand the morning after test before she knew if they were truly working. There was nothing more to do now but to push on. After a cup of tea. She closed the laptop lid and went to boil the kettle.

Willie's desk shared the space in the bay, arranged to face hers, their ends touching. It was a hulking Victorian thing in mahogany that he'd put in storage when he left for LA, and which she'd helped lug up two flights of stairs. She could still feel the twinge in her back. Its inlaid leather surface was crowned with an ancient typewriter— a Royal portable, like Hemingway's, he'd informed her as he stroked the burnished keys. Flanking the typewriter were two neat towers of paper about equal height; one of them pristine and blank, the other filled with his growing adaptation of *Happy Ending*.

Over the last couple of months Jane had observed

Willie at work, seated upright in his button-backed Captain's chair, methodically feeding fresh pages into the mouth of his typewriter, filling them up to the accompaniment of its machine-gun clatter. When he made a mistake, instead of whiting out the error he would rip out the entire page and begin anew. If it doesn't come out right, he'd explained, then it was a clue to a deeper malaise. He was an automaton, as mechanically relentless as his choice of writing tool. Jane enjoyed the steady rattle and clank. It made her feel as if she was one of those feisty girl reporters in a 1940s New York newsroom, or in Paris, an Alice B. Toklas to his Old Man of the Sea.

For now the room was quiet. Willie had taken himself off for a run in Kelvingrove Park, which he did, regularly, every afternoon at three o'clock. Turned out he was something of a worshipper of the body beautiful, and a practitioner of some arcane martial art that sounded to her like Wang Chung, but which she knew couldn't be right since they were an '80s New Wave band. He had set up a punch-bag in the box room and the sound of whacking and grunting had become part of the background. To the neighbours it must have seemed like she'd installed an S&M dungeon, but apart from the occasional curious look on the stairwell no one complained.

On the wall above Willie's empty chair hung two framed film posters from projects he had written. Their design was similar: a montage of exploding cars, a square-jawed hero flanked by half-naked girls, framed by a pair of woman's bare legs in the foreground, akimbo over the scene. Sub-James Bond stuff. Jane had been staring at the posters for a week before she realised they were for the same movie; just that one of them was in French. *Fatal Payback* was *Vengeance Fatale*, a Kurt Salazar film. She hadn't heard of Kurt Salazar or seen either version, but that was OK since Willie had loads of DVDs.

She sat down with her cup of tea and flipped open the laptop. Inserting a break to make a fresh page, she typed the final chapter number.

37.

Endings were tricky. Even this late in the novel, with the weight of the preceding narrative pressing like dam-waters, she hesitated. A sip of tea always helped marshal her thoughts.

As she drank she reflected on the significance of the moment, for here she was on the threshold of finishing the novel. A spike of mischievous pleasure surged through her and she swiped her phone from where it lay on the desk next to the umbrella plant. It was a childish impulse, one she'd probably regret later, but right now the urge was irresistible. She scratched the itch and dialled.

'Jane?'

He picked up on the first ring, she noted, taking undue pleasure in his surprised tone. He sounded uncertain, as well he should; they hadn't spoken for almost nine months. As part of a set of stipulations, she'd insisted that there be no contact between them while she wrote the new novel, though she had been surprised—and perhaps a little chagrined—when he'd caved in without so much as a '*merde!*'

'I'm starting the final chapter,' she said. 'You'll have the manuscript by the end of next week.'

'It's about bloody time.'

'Ah, Tom, as ever my little ray of sunshine.' She began to spin round in her swivel chair, free as a kid on a roundabout, delighted at the rise she was eliciting from him. 'Well, moan all you like, I've never been this—'

'—Annoying?' he interrupted.

She brought her carefree circling to a sudden stop. He could still get to her. 'Happy. You bastard. Happy.'

The line went quiet and for a moment she wondered if the call had dropped. She was about to ask if he was still there when his voice drawled from the phone again.

'So, one more chapter…' he began.

'Yup.'

'…And we never have to see each other again.'

Did she detect a note of regret? Not after all this time, surely. Most likely it was atmospheric conditions on the line. But he was right—there would be no reason for them to stay in touch.

'Uh-huh.'

'Better get writing then. *A bientôt*, Jane.'

See you soon? Didn't he understand that this was far more final than his expression allowed. At some point next week she'd hit 'Send' and deposit the manuscript in his in-box and that would be that. *Finis*.

'*Au revoir*, Tom.'

She stabbed a finger at the touch screen and ended the call. He was right about one thing—better get writing. She couldn't agree more.

She had begun writing the follow-up to *Happy Ending* with indecent haste, in the full knowledge that when she completed it she would have fulfilled her contract to Tristesse Books and be rid of Tom and his smug, bristly face. Forever. And this time she'd laid down conditions. She refused to have any communication with him during the writing period to discuss her progress. Moreover, she refused to let him give notes on the new novel once submitted. She had expected him to rebuff that one with particular venom, but instead he'd acquiesced at the first time of asking, conceding with a brusque, 'Fine, whatever makes you happy.'

All she had to do was finish the damn thing.

As they'd talked on the phone an idea about how to launch into the final chapter had entered her head, but now as her fingers hovered over the keyboard the words wouldn't fall into place. She screwed up her face, chasing the feeling like she was swatting at butterflies. After a minute or two of increasingly frustrated attempts to remember, she tapped down the lid and went to make another cup of tea.

The conversation with Tom had unsettled her. In retrospect it had been a mistake. There had been no need for them to talk at all, and she certainly wouldn't be calling him again. A second hot cup of tea joined the first, which was still gently steaming.

She wiggled her fingers, trying to transform irritation with Tom into creative calm. She was a virtuoso preparing to perform. An Olympian in the blocks. She could do this. She had done this—for thirty-six chapters straight, without a hitch. She didn't buy into all that crap about waiting for the Muse to strike. You showed up at your desk every day and trusted that she'd be there. For Jane writing was as simple as that old nugget of advice: apply posterior to chair.

The cursor winked on the blank page.

There was a force-field over the keyboard, that was it. What else could be preventing her from touching it? It wasn't as if she didn't know what to write. Right? So what happens next?

The cursor was a large, dark oblong. Like a freshly dug grave.

OK, this was ridiculous. Write your way into the chapter. Just write anything. First thing that comes into your head. Doesn't even have to make sense. As soon as you put something down you'll break this hoodoo. Don't talk about a hoodoo, you'll jinx yourself. Oh great, now she'd invoked a hoodoo *and* a jinx.

The cursor convulsed like a twitching eye.

Jane slammed down the laptop lid. The leaves on her

umbrella plant trembled. She drummed her fingers on the desk. A walk. That's what she needed. What happens next? After a walk it would all be perfectly clear. Now who was it said 'we think at walking-pace'? Someone very wise, she suspected, then remembered with a pang who had given her the sage advice. Dammit.

*

An hour later Jane found herself flicking idly through a rack of vintage clothes. *Mini, midi, maxi*. She was pretty sure that was the Latin phrase for 'I came, I saw, I bought an inappropriate skirt.' Despite what it looked like, she absolutely, definitely wasn't in her favourite store, avoiding work on her novel by embarking on a wholly unnecessary pursuit of a frivolous item of clothing. Ooh, nice jacket. Kind of a Nehru thing going on round the collar and the colour was amazing; it reminded her of a livid sunset over a wasteland of discarded shopping trolleys.

The jacket was the kind of thing Darsie Baird, the main character in her new novel, would wear, and she made a mental note to go back and find a place to insert it. But not now. She'd go back later. Right now there was some serious browsing to accomplish.

And it *was* an accomplishment. Hell, some people did this for a living: stylists, fashion writers, personal shoppers. This was work, dammit. OK, not for her, but someone in the store must be working and she was standing quite close to them.

Research! That's what this was. Writing was a lot like playing dolls' houses. You got to design the rooms, populate them and dress everyone down to the last detail. Clothes could say a lot about your character and her world. There was the obvious stuff: a seamed stocking for a vamp or tweed for a country lady. But there was more to it than that. An undone button in anything written before 1920 spoke of seething passion. A woman putting something in her pocket in an Austen novel was a big deal—it being her only truly private place outside of her head.

There was a rustle of clothing from the back of the store. Jane looked round to see a young woman emerge from the changing room. For a moment she wondered if the velvet curtains concealed a time machine, since the woman appeared to have walked straight out of 1950. She wore a full-skirted berry-red dress nipped in at the waist, a scarf tied movie-star style around her head and a pair of classic big-frame Dior sunglasses. She sashayed past, high heels clicking on the wooden floor.

'Hi, Jane.'

'Hi,' replied Jane automatically. Very occasionally—OK, twice—readers would recognise her in the street and stop to tell her how much they liked her book, but this didn't feel like a fan encounter. For one thing, Red didn't stop to chat, but instead her heels carried her past the clothes racks and out of the shop. The bell sounded a merry ding as the door closed behind her. Jane frowned.

Red looked so familiar, like a distant cousin she hadn't seen in years, but she couldn't place her. Great outfit, though. Maybe she'd put Darsie in that instead.

*

Tom punched his PIN into the cash machine. Internal mechanisms grumbled like a reluctant parent and the screen flashed its decision.

INSUFFICIENT FUNDS.

Letting rip with a sibilant French oath and thumping the keypad, he retrieved his useless card and, with as much dignity as he could muster, struck off past the line of people waiting to use the cash machine. Roddy tripped at his heels.

'So, does this mean I'm buying the donuts again?'

Tom cast him a dark look and watched in puzzled silence as Roddy flipped up the furry hood on his coat so that it completely covered his head. It wasn't raining, for a change, and the city was experiencing that most unusual of phenomena, an actual season. Instead of the indistinguishable mush of weather that passed for a climate, the last week had been discernibly summery.

'I don't get it,' said Roddy's muffled voice from deep within the hood. 'Jane Lockhart made you a small fortune. I don't know anyone who's blown as much money as you have in such a short time. And I know people at the Royal Bank of Scotland.'

Tom refused to engage with Roddy's leading remark,

especially since he had a point. It had been more than a year since *Happy Ending* hit the bestseller charts. The sales numbers were strong, but not astronomical. After all, Jane Lockhart was 'literary fiction', not 'vampire romance'. The book had been profitable, but to sell those big numbers the retailers had demanded huge discounts and marketing bungs, which had eaten into his share.

Then he'd taken the remainder of the money and gone on a spending spree, acquiring three debuts within the space of a month, one of them in a competitive auction against three multinational publishers with deep pockets. As soon as he submitted the winning bid he knew he'd paid too much. Ah well, there was always a chance that *Earnest Shards* would find an audience. Hey, who wouldn't love a star-crossed gay love story set in the world of stained-glassmaking in Renaissance Florence?

Tom could hold off no longer. He had to know. 'Why do you have your hood up?'

'I don't want to be recognised.'

That was not a reasonable answer. 'You're an English supply teacher at a state-assisted secondary school in suburban Glasgow.'

Roddy grasped the cords that adjusted the hood and tugged them sharply, sealing himself inside. 'Exactly.'

Tom's battered green Peugeot limped into a space on the crowded street outside Tristesse Books. The gearbox gave one last tortured whine and the engine shuddered into silence. He climbed out and slammed the door. The catch was broken and there was a knack to closing it properly. Which was to slam it. Repeatedly.

'I can give you an hour of secretarial services,' said Roddy emerging from the passenger side clutching a warm bag of Krispy Kremes, 'then I've got *Great Expectations* in Maryhill.'

Even as the barbed quip formed on Tom's lips Roddy was raising a finger.

'Don't,' he wagged. 'Just don't.'

There was a rumble of tyres against cobbles and the two men swivelled their heads to see the driverless Peugeot roll gently into the car in front. Bumper lay against bumper like a tired drunk resting his head on a friend.

'You should probably get that fixed,' said Roddy.

'Yeah,' said Tom with epic disinterest, already turning his back to punch the code into the door entry system.

*

'I don't care what you think. I'm telling you, that's not an opening chapter, it's an ice age. *C'est une époque!*'

Tom's voice shook the thin office walls as he harangued Nicola Ball, flaying the latest draft of her novel while simultaneously sorting through the mail, making one pile for bills and another for final demands. If he was honest his foul mood was largely down to the parlous state of the company's finances rather than Nicola's inappropriate semicolon on page eight.

Her eyes brimmed with tears. 'You can't talk to me like

that,' she said, her voice quivering. 'I was voted one of Scotland's foremost novelists under the age of thirty…'

He brandished the manuscript. 'And that's why I won't allow this piece of crap to be published with your name on it.'

She pursed her lips and placed her hands on her hips. 'You know what, Tom, you're even more of a bastard since you broke up with Jane Lockhart.'

Roddy stuck his head round the door and chimed in. 'That's exactly what I said.'

'Hey,' Tom snapped. 'We didn't split up. Because we were never together. It was a falling out. Got it? And, do we need to have another chat about your eavesdropping, Roddy?'

Roddy banged the wall. 'Flimsy partition. Loud Frenchman.' He sighed. 'Now I am bound by the man-code to take your side in this, but what the hell, Tom? Seriously, what were you thinking? You changed the title of a book without consulting its author.'

'You changed her title?!' said Nicola, shaking her head in horrified disbelief.

'I know,' said Roddy. 'Right?'

'No wonder she dumped him.'

'Uh. I am in the room. And she didn't dump me. Again, we were never *together*.' He glowered at Roddy. 'What about the man-code?'

'Yes, yes, I know. I suppose we could put your behaviour down to an aberration—a temporary loss of faculties as a result of having sex on a regular basis with the luscious Jane.'

'You think she's luscious?' inquired Nicola.

'Luscious, foxy, a little bit naughty.'

'Oh.'

Tom watched Roddy slowly comprehend.

'Not that I fancy her,' said Roddy quickly. 'Not my type. My type's much more like…um…really looking forward to your book launch, Nicola. Have you seen the venue? It's a bus garage in Bridgeton. It's going to be a swanky affair.' He paused. 'I'm pretty confident that's the first time "swanky" and "Bridgeton" have been used in the same sentence.'

She giggled. 'You're funny.' Then she sniffed and wiped a hand across her damp cheek. 'Roddy, why do I keep letting him do this to me?' She jabbed a finger in Tom's general direction.

'I don't know,' said Roddy. 'Maybe you're a masochist?'

She appeared to give it some thought. 'No, I tried that a few times. I quite liked the being tied up part, but in the end it turns out I'm more of a sadist.'

Roddy gulped. 'That's nice.'

She threw a dark look at Tom. 'It's just him. He's the only one who can make me feel this…'

'Vulnerable? Fragile? Waif-like?'

'…Fucking furious.'

Tom had had enough. He flung a finger towards the

door. 'The two of you. Leave. Separately.' He glowered at Nicola. 'Why are you still here? Go and write!'

Faced with her boiling French editor, her lip began once more to tremble. She gathered the manuscript to her chest and scrambled out.

'Get thee to a Costa Coffee!' Tom half-chased her into the passageway. 'And don't come back until every word sings from the page.'

'Bye then, Nicola,' said Roddy trailing after her rapidly disappearing figure. 'See you at the launch.'

She banged open the front door and hurried out, almost colliding with a woman in a dark blue business suit marching across the courtyard. The square-shouldered suit gave her a purposeful air and she observed the crying girl depart, never once breaking stride in her far from sensible heels.

Tom watched her uneasily from the doorway of his office. Without waiting for an invitation the woman clipped along the corridor, pushed past him, placed her briefcase on his desk and made herself comfortable in his chair.

'If you try to make me cry,' she said coolly, 'I'll inform the Inland Revenue about your yacht.'

'Anna,' said Tom, hoping that he was faking enough sincerity. 'Great to see you.' He paused before adding, 'Wasn't *expecting* to see you.' He followed her inside, inquiring with a nervous laugh, 'Good news?'

Anna LeFèvre possessed a French surname and was

distantly related to a family of 17th-century Parisian tapestry weavers, but that's where the *entente cordiale* ended, much to Tom's dismay. She was his banker; a Relationship Manager in modern parlance or, as she referred to it, 'touchy-feely marketing shite'. Spotting her name on the bank's website back when he'd opened his account Tom had sought her out, confident that their French connection would enable him to shave an interest point or two off his overdraft and perhaps bend the lending rules in his favour. His confidence had proved misplaced. Anna was as severe as her dark bobbed hair—and as straight.

She sat behind his desk in his chair while he squatted in the low seat of shame reserved for authors. Her eyes never wavered from the laptop screen as she scrutinised the company's books. Tom could imagine more painful examinations, but they involved disposable gloves and the removal of his trousers. At least Anna stopped at baring his accounts. She scrolled through various ledgers and bank accounts, pausing from time to time in order to raise an eyebrow or cluck disapprovingly. When she had finished she let out a long, low whistle and finally turned to him.

'You and me are going to lunch.'

'Great!'

Released from the enveloping sense of dread that had descended upon him since she walked through his door, Tom leapt up and announced happily, 'We'll go to Rogano. On me.'

She drummed her fingers on his desk.

'Let's go to the wee café next door,' she suggested, then glanced back at the screen. 'And I think I'd better pay.'

*

A waitress with serious glasses and more serious tattoos landed a couple of plates on their table by the window. Tom surveyed the sandwich on Anna's, then looked at his, then back at hers again.

With a motherly sigh of exasperation, she said, 'Do you want to swap?'

Barely had she finished the question when he nodded—'Yeah'—and was already sliding the plates by each other.

'OK? Now can we talk about Tristesse Books' books?'

Tom took a great bite and answered through a mouthful. 'Mmm-hmm. But if we have to talk figures, can you do that thing where you use vegetables?' He plucked a cherry tomato from the weedy salad that accompanied the sandwich and in a business-like voice intoned, 'Imagine this tomato is my cash flow.'

'Perhaps you've forgotten, but a tomato is a fruit, not a vegetable.' She took the tomato from him and plonked it down on the side of her plate. 'Don't play with your food.'

She hoisted her briefcase on to the table and flipped it open. 'How many new writers have you thrown money away on this year?'

'I only throw money away on good writers. Good

Scottish writers.' He waved his sandwich and grinned. 'I'm very patriotic.'

She drew out a glossy black folder and a typewritten list. 'Good, maybe, but commercial?' She read from the top of the list. '*The Thought's Stream.*'

'It's highly experimental,' he explained. 'The main character is a drop of water.'

Unimpressed, her eye fell upon the next entry. '*Death of a Conductor*?'

'Nicola Ball is one of Scotland's most exciting novelists under the age of thirty,' he shot back confidently, before burying his head in his chest to mumble, 'who happens to be obsessed with public transport.'

She went through the list one by one, tutting like a schoolmistress reviewing an errant pupil's exam results until she reached the final entry. '*Earnest Shards*,' she sighed dismally.

'Ah.'

'Tom, what were you thinking?'

'It's a wonderful book. It deserves to be published.'

Anna sat back and folded her arms. 'I admire the sentiment, but you paid too much for it. Don't argue—you know you did. And there's bugger all chance you'll see a penny of it back.'

'I might,' he said quietly.

She banged the table. 'Not unless you get the author to rewrite it with a bunch of vampires and a lot of kinky sex.'

Tom considered the idea for a moment and then dismissed it with a scowl. He took another bite of his sand-wich. 'It doesn't matter anyway. One hit pays for all the rest—that's how this business works. And I have a best-seller in the wings.'

'Jane Lockhart, yes. So how's the new book shaping up?'

He made a face. '*Je ne sais pas*. I have no idea. She won't let me read a word until it's finished.'

'You're kidding me, right? Your entire business rests on that novel.'

He gulped. It was the first time he'd heard it expressed as bluntly as that. 'Relax,' he said, trying to convince him-self as much as Anna. 'It'll be just like the first one: a bunch of beautifully written, utterly miserable characters, three cremations and seven types of rain. But so long as it does half as well as *Happy Ending*, I'll be able to buy a real yacht.' He sighed. 'OK, a big dinghy.'

'I heard on the grapevine that after she finishes this novel for you she's moving publisher. I have a friend at Klinsch & McLeish says they're in advanced negotia-tions.'

'Klinsch & McLeish.' Tom blew out his cheeks dispar-agingly. 'Y'know what they're called in the trade?' He made a tight fist and then opened it abruptly. 'Clench & Release.' He dismissed them with another puff. 'They're brutal. Bourgeois Edinburgh bastards. They're not right for my Jane.' He corrected himself. 'For Jane Lockhart.'

'So talk to her! Persuade her to stay.'

'I don't want her to stay. After she delivers her new novel, I want her to go. Far away.'

'Oh for god's sake, Tom, Tristesse Books is on the verge of compulsory liquidation.'

Tom opened and closed his mouth without speaking. There was no smart answer to that.

'And I've had an offer,' said Anna.

'Well,' he purred, 'you're a very attractive woma—'

'Shut up.' She took the glossy folder she had retrieved from her briefcase at the same time as the list of unprofitable novels and slid it across the table. 'They're called Pandemic Media.'

An over-complicated logo was emblazoned on the front of the folder, the sort of thing that could only have been designed after going through three committees, a test audience and an in-depth consultation with the CEO's cleaner.

'I can only assume they're run by a suicidal madman,' Anna went on, 'since they want to invest in you.'

He pushed away the folder. 'You mean buy me out, move the company to London and let people called Jocasta and Strawberry cut half the authors from my list. Uh-uh. No way!'

'You have to look at this, whether you like it or not.' She tapped the folder sternly. 'Pandemic Media want the edgy frisson a name like Tristesse Books would bring them. And trust me, you could really do with the cash.'

'I don't need Pandemic Media. I have Jane Lockhart.'

He felt his confidence undercut by the yawning hole opening up beneath his feet. Oh god, his whole business, his whole life's work relied on that annoying woman. 'This time she's going all the way!' he declared with a forced smile.

Anna leant forward. 'Are you sure? Because the trade is waiting. Two thousand bookshops have allocated shelf-space, a hundred thousand readers are stocking up on tissues, and if she doesn't deliver soon…' She pronged the tomato with a fork. Juice oozed through the pierced skin. '…your tomato's looking like ketchup.'

Tom surveyed the perforated tomato and swallowed hard. 'She called me on Monday, said she was starting the final chapter and I could expect it by the end of next week.'

Anna rolled her eyes. 'And when in your experience has a writer ever finished a novel when she said she would?'

Tom conceded with a shrug, unhappy about where this conversation was leading.

'Call her,' Anna commanded. 'Find out how close she *really* is to finishing.'

'There's no point—when she sees it's me she won't even answer.'

Anna placed her own phone on the table. 'I believe it's called a "workaround".'

Tom stared at the phone like it was a revolver with one bullet in the chamber. He didn't want to speak to her. The last time they'd spoken Jane had called him just to give him the brush-off. It was too painful to hear her voice. For a time after they'd broken up he'd sat in his office and played old voice-mail messages from her, just to hear what she sounded like when she wasn't angry with him. One day Roddy had caught him in the act and gently but firmly encouraged him to delete the messages. It was over.

Anna gave him a look like a python considering a plump mouse. Grumbling, he picked up her phone.

'This is a waste of breath,' he said, dialling Jane's number. 'She'll deliver the novel. She may be a miserable pain in the arse, but when she's writing she's like a guided missile.'

*

Jane's hand was a blur as she whisked a bowl full of cake mixture to an elastic consistency. This wasn't a displacement activity. This was baking. Baking could hardly be counted a lesser activity than novel writing. Baking produced actual stuff. Stuff you could eat. Almost every time.

When she'd returned from her shopping expedition she had opened her laptop and tried to squeeze out a few words, but to no avail. Rather than squander the whole afternoon, she had cracked out the flour and butter. When the mixture looked just right she dipped in a finger and tasted. Frowning, she consulted an open recipe book.

'*Tea*-spoon?'

She picked up a tablespoon and studied it accusingly. As she figured out if it was possible to rescue the cake, across the room her phone rang, vibrating against the lid of her laptop.

'Willie,' she called to him, 'will you get that?'

Willie sat at his desk, eyes narrowed at the page cranking steadily through his typewriter. She called his name again, but it was obvious he couldn't hear her over the clacking of keys. With a frustrated puff she blew her fringe off her forehead, shoved the brimming cake tin into the hot oven and marched across the room.

The phone throbbed on the laptop like a pneumatic drill. From the lack of a caller ID it wasn't anyone in her contacts list and she didn't recognise the number. She snatched it up, bothered by a faint sensation that she'd missed something important.

'Hello?'

'Thursday or Friday for the manuscript?'

'Grease-proof paper!' She raced back to the kitchen to find the square of parchment that ought to be lining the cake-tin instead laid out on the counter-top. She stared at it mournfully.

'You're certain it will be finished next week?'

She'd recognised his voice immediately, but her cake crisis had taken precedence. Well, she didn't have to tell him anything. He didn't have to know.

'What are you doing?' Tom probed.

'Nothing,' she said guiltily. She winced—why had she said anything? Hang up. Just hang up now!

'Are you…baking?'

She killed the call and cringed. He knew. He knew what the baking meant.

Almost immediately the phone rang again. She jumped at the sound. It was him, of course, persistent as ever. The handset felt like a hot scone burning her palm. There was only one rational course of action. In one swift coordinated move she swung open the fridge, tossed the phone inside and slammed the door. The muffled ringtone continued through the insulated layers.

She looked round to discover Willie peering at her over his spectacles in bemusement. She wasn't sure how exactly to explain her actions without coming across as a complete nutcase. She smiled weakly. No. That didn't help.

*

Halfway across the city, in the café next to Tristesse Books, Tom stared at the phone in horror.

'She's baking.'

Anna waved her hands in mock terror. 'Oh no! It's a cake-tastrophe!' Pleased at her pun, she was irritated when Tom didn't even crack a smile. 'So, she's baking. What, you don't like her Victoria sandwich?'

'You don't understand,' he said solemnly. Catching a glimpse of himself in the window he saw he was sporting an expression he'd only ever seen on newsreaders announcing natural disasters or the death of a much-loved Royal. He sighed and looked back at Anna.

'Jane bakes when she's blocked.'

CHAPTER 9

'Sparkle in the Rain', Simple Minds, 1984, Virgin

THREE DAYS LATER, Jane was still baking. Four loaves of banana bread nestled under a tiered chocolate sponge. A constellation of cupcakes orbited beside a tray of millionaire's shortcake. The kitchen smelt of caramel and obsession.

She cleared a space on her desk, lowered a cake stand crowned with a freshly baked lemon sponge and flicked her eyes to Willie. As usual he was attacking his typewriter as if leading a cavalry charge. She'd discovered that nothing could distract him when he was in this mood. And she'd tried everything.

'Slice of cake?'

Click-clack-click-clack.

'Any laundry need doing?'

Click-clack-click-clack.

'Blowjob?'

Ting!

Without looking up he swiped the carriage return lever

and began a new line. Abandoning her attempt to divert his attention, she admired the cake one last time and grudgingly opened her laptop. The blank page gaped like a wound. No, not a wound. It stood for the emptiness of the universe, she decided; the infinite nothingness which no amount of sponge cake could fill. Slowly she raised her eyes to peer at Willie over the top of the screen.

He continued to pound away, blithely unaware of the existential crisis taking place only a few feet from him. There was something inhuman about his energy. When he had first moved in she'd gawped at his work ethic, then found that her own increased, as if he was pulling her along in his wake, but lately when she eyed him across the valley of their desks she felt herself recoil. She remembered reading that the great Victorian novelist, Anthony Trollope, famously schooled himself to write two hundred and fifty words every quarter of an hour. Willie Scott farted more words. Jane imagined Willie flipping him the finger in his rear-view mirror as he eased past a furiously bicycling Trollope.

Willie added another completed page to his ever-increasing tower. Soon it would need scaffolding. Jane sighed in exasperation and—OK, she'd admit it—with envy. As he stacked up the pages she just stacked, circling forever over Chapter 37, waiting for permission to make her final approach.

She was stuck.

Blocked.

She tortured herself with idle speculation: perhaps she was fated not to finish this novel. She glanced at the 'Jane' trophy on her bookshelf. Perhaps this would be her *Sanditon*, Jane Austen's unfinished novel. She ramped up the anxiety daydream. Perhaps she'd die of consumption before completing it. She *did* feel a cough coming on. How bad would Tom feel about that? No, not Tom. Forget about Tom. She didn't care how he felt about anything.

She reached for her water-spray. Her hand closed around the familiar plastic bottle, index finger finding the trigger. Aiming it blindly she spritzed the umbrella plant.

'You OK, Janey?'

She wasn't sure exactly when Willie had started calling her 'Janey'. She knew he meant it fondly, so even though she disliked the moniker she hadn't corrected him right away. And now it was too late.

'Yes. Fine. Just one more chapter.'

'You not finished that yet?'

She felt her blood boil and imagined jumping out of her seat, reaching across the desk to grab a hank of his stupid wavy hair, pulling down hard and mashing his face repeatedly into his fucking typewriter. Click-clack-click-buggering-clack.

Ting!

In reality she remained fixed in her seat, smiled sweetly and said, 'Nope. Not quite finished.' Her trigger-finger spasmed and she drenched the plant once more.

'Careful, or you're gonna kill that thing,' he warned her before resuming his typing.

'Yes,' she agreed, her eyes suddenly murderous. 'Yes I am.'

What was she doing? It wasn't Willie's fault she was stuck. With a long sigh she rested her head on the desk. The wood felt cool against her cheek. She glanced at the plant.

'It was a birthday present from my dad. He gave it to me in the morning and walked out on us that night. I often wondered why I didn't just kill the thing. Chuck it in the bin. Now I think it's because I always hoped he'd come back.' She stroked the leaves. 'And that hope, like this ugly little plant, didn't die.'

As she struggled back from the memory she was dimly aware that the atmosphere in the room had shifted. Something significant had occurred.

Willie had stopped typing.

She lifted her head to see him staring thoughtfully into the middle distance. Grateful that her story had affected him so deeply she started to get up from her chair. She wanted to hold him. Kiss him. Thank him for understanding.

And then he said, 'How many p's in "deprivation"?'

She laid her head back down on the desk. 'One. One p.'

The novel may have stalled but her renewed relationship with her dad had taken its first faltering steps. It

had begun with an awkward cup of tea in a café on the
Gallowgate, graduated to bowling in Bargeddie and then
he'd suggested they go to the pub. He saw her face fall
and immediately tried to reassure her. 'A quiz,' he'd said.
'That's how well I'm doing. When I think of a pub these
days it's all about the quiz. I'm even in a team. "Benny
and the Jets". I'd love you to come—meet the lads, watch
your old dad answer a few brainteasers. What d'you say,
darlin'?'

She'd said yes and it had quickly become a regular
thing. The last couple of times Willie had come along
too, but she sensed that her dad wasn't a fan. When she'd
pressed him he'd confessed that while he had no right to
judge, fatherly concern had been stirred by the revelation
that Willie was a reformed drinker. He didn't like it. Not
one bit. Didn't matter how long it was since you last took
a drink, he'd said, it leaves its mark. Annoyingly, Benny
displayed a far better rapport with Tom.

The two of them had met during the book tour. After her
dad surprised her by showing up at the Waterstones signing in Glasgow he'd made a point of attending every subsequent event. Jane was touched by his support, but less
thrilled when at the end of a talk in Stirling she'd found
him and Tom at the back of the hall, thick as thieves. After
a signing in Dundee she'd confronted her dad leaving the
library laden with books.

'Tom gave them to me,' he'd said delightedly. 'I love a
freebie.'

She couldn't disguise her irritation. 'So when did you become such a big reader?'

'Oh, I'm no',' he'd said. 'These aren't *stories*. See, I like facts. Stuff that really happened.'

She'd considered telling Tom to lay off her dad, but that would have involved talking to him herself—something she'd strenuously been avoiding since their last phone call. On that occasion she'd intended to wind *him* up, but the call had backfired and she suspected he'd guessed she was blocked.

Officially, the finished manuscript was due in today, but that wasn't going to happen. She'd work on it over the weekend. And maybe the first few days of next week. What the hell, she'd take the whole week. Really, what was another week? She'd start tomorrow. She certainly couldn't do anything more today, and tonight was quiz night.

*

The Sir Walter Scott pub stood in a gap-toothed block that had for the last fifty years stoically resisted all attempts at renovation, modernisation or, latterly, gentrification. As the rest of the city succumbed to the inevitable arrival of chorizo and avocado the Sir Walter Scott stood tall, a beacon of stubborn resistance held together by spit, sawdust, Sky (football on satellite TV being the only concession to the modern world) and the legendary Friday night quiz.

Not wanting to disturb her dad, Jane stood with Willie at the edge of the bar and watched as 'Benny and the Jets' conducted a practice session.

'Largest planet in the solar system?'

'Jupiter.'

Benny Lockhart was a still centre of concentration, deflecting questions with the liquid calm of a Jedi master as his quiz partners fired them at him from alternate flanks.

'Who did Ali beat to become World Heavyweight Champion for the first time?' asked Rory, a man whose moustache could have earned him a place in the Village People.

'Sonny Liston,' answered Benny without hesitation.

A gaunt man with a bobbing Adam's apple, whose every utterance was punctuated with a hacking cough, hurled the next question. 'Which is the only mammal that can't jump—*ACH*!?'

'The elephant,' said Benny with a weary sigh. 'C'mon, the quiz is gonna be harder than that. Get serious.'

Jane glanced round the dark panelled walls of the pub, stained by decades of tobacco smoke, on which hung a series of heavily varnished paintings depicting various Sir Walter Scott heroes. Ivanhoe, Rob Roy and William Wallace gazed proudly from their golden frames. She knew that this quiz was important to her dad. He had left school at fourteen and never thought much of himself. It was the first time he'd ever been good at anything.

'Who was Shakespeare's wife?'

Jane could tell immediately that he didn't know. She caught sight of Rory's grinning mug, jubilant to have stumped the master. Benny hummed and hawed to buy some time.

'Shakespeare's wife.' He scratched his head. 'William. Shakespeare's. Wife?'

Jane saw him look up hopefully at Scott's heroes on the wall, seeking inspiration. The portraits seemed to confer and then turn to him with a shrug. Got nothing. Sorry.

'Hi, Dad.'

'Darlin'!' Benny spun round.

Things were still new between them, so they danced about as they figured out how to greet one another, ending up in a stiff embrace.

'Anne Hathaway,' she whispered.

'What? Oh, right.' Clearing his throat, he turned back to Rory and with a casual wave gave him the correct answer as if he'd known it all along.

As Benny ordered a round of drinks, choosing an orange juice for himself and one for Willie, Jane watched a familiar figure enter the pub, shake the rain from his Macintosh and bound up to her dad.

'Hey, Monsieur L!'

'Tommy! Good to see you, son. It's been ages.'

Jane couldn't help but notice her dad's face light up when he clocked Tom.

'It has. How are you?'

'Not bad, son. So, where've you been hiding yourself?

Tom glanced across the bar at Jane. She scowled.

'From your daughter mostly.'

'Aye, well, she's a tough customer that one, don't need to tell me. Wouldn't talk to me for years—not that I blame her. What'll you have?'

'Nothing,' said Jane. 'He's not staying.'

'Now Jane, c'mon…' Benny began, but tailed off when he saw the expression on his daughter's face.

'What are you doing here?' she snapped at Tom.

'My favourite author is being adapted by Scotland's most talented screenwriter.' He made a big show of bowing to Willie, turning up his palms in a gesture that said 'much kudos'.

Willie was settling himself happily into Tom's oily praise when Benny clicked his fingers. 'Screen*writer*, that was it,' he said as if it had been bothering him for ages. 'No' screen*printer*. Sorry. Go on.'

Willie's self-satisfied expression slipped for a moment.

Tom put an arm round his shoulders. 'Naturally I want to know how the big man is getting on.'

'I wouldn't say I'm the most talented,' Willie said, demurring with a thoughtful shake of his head. He stopped and seemed to consider. 'But, who else you gonna pick? Eh?'

Deciding this charade had gone on long enough Jane laid a hand on Tom's elbow and steered him to a corner of the bar.

'You've got some cheek, showing up here like this,' she rounded on him when they were out of earshot.

'It's Friday. Where's my novel?'

Such an annoying man! 'I'm working on it,' she said tightly.

Tom shot a sideways glance at Willie. 'So, you're not suffering with *el toro blanco*?'

'What are you talking about?'

'You're not b-l-o-c-k-e-d?'

'Why are you spelling it?'

'It's nothing to be ashamed of, and there are plenty of strategies to overcome it.'

'I'm not blocked.'

'For instance, stimulants and narcotics. For a while there, Hunter S Thompson was permanently unblocked.'

She folded her arms. 'I'm not blocked.'

'OK, then change your surroundings. Take yourself off to that Highland hellhole–'

'You mean the cottage?'

'I seem to remember we had some particularly creative sessions up there.' He winked. 'If you know what I'm saying?'

'Yes,' she said through gritted teeth. 'There are single-cell organisms that know what you're saying.'

He angled his head thoughtfully. 'But Willie doesn't know. About us?'

Jane started to answer, but the retort died on her lips.

'Didn't think so,' he said haughtily.

OK, that was it. Enough. She marched to the door and flung it open. A squall of blustery rain swept inside, stinging her face. 'You have a hell of a high opinion of yourself, you know that? Well, let me tell you this, you are the biggest mistake I've ever made. I know that because I'm with someone who loves me now, someone who isn't afraid to say so. And, in case you haven't heard, I'm moving to a new publisher. For the first time in my life I'm truly happy, and it's no thanks to you. So, goodbye, Thomas Duval of Tristesse Books and late of Saint-Tropez. Oh, say hi to Roddy from me. I always liked *him*.'

Annoyingly, he appeared resolutely unaffected by her speech and merely squeezed past her, much closer than necessary, before stopping in the doorway.

'Out of interest, Jane,' he asked lightly, 'what's the title of the new book?'

She hadn't expected that. Damn it. 'The title? Of the new book?'

'Yes. You have a title, right?'

'Of course I have a title.' She clasped and unclasped her hands.

'Then you won't mind telling me. It'd be useful to announce it to the trade, put up a holding page on Amazon, that kind of thing.'

'What if I do mind?'

A smile spread slowly across his face. 'You don't have a title, do you?'

She hated that he could tell; he knew her better than she cared to admit.

In the silence that followed he leant in towards her; they were almost touching. 'Until you deliver that manuscript,' he growled, 'you're still under contract to me. So, what-ever's going on, snap out of it and get writing.'

Before she could stop him he had taken her head in his hands and planted a kiss on her lips.

'Bye, Jane.'

And then the door banged shut and he was gone without a backwards look.

With a cry of disgust she wiped a hand across her face. What a cheek! She mimicked his smug 'Bye, Jane.'

A quick glance at Willie determined, to her great relief, that he hadn't noticed the kiss. She'd seen what Willie could do to a punch-bag and, whatever she felt about Tom, she didn't want him beaten to a kung-fooey pulp. Not that the kiss had meant anything. It wasn't like she'd enjoyed it. She shuddered at the idea.

Willie made his way over, his big hands wrapped round drinks for her and the now departed Tom.

'He's not gone, has he?' He stared forlornly at the door. 'But we never got a chance to talk about my screenplay.'

The door swung open again and the young woman in the red dress from the vintage store breezed in. She glided past Jane, right under Willie's nose.

'Hi, Jane.'

'Hi,' replied Jane, gawping at the figure as she made her

way across the packed floor of the bar without breaking stride.

It seemed impossible that she could pass unnoticed, but no one gave the stunning figure in their midst a second glance. Even Willie, who, Jane had noted on more than one occasion, could out-swivel an owl when it came to tracking a hot young thing, took no interest in her hypnotically swaying hips.

'The French have always appreciated my work,' he reflected. 'Connoisseurs of *film*, oh aye.'

Leaving him to ponder his own genius, Jane followed Red across the bar.

'We should have him round for dinner,' said Willie, finally realising with an awkward start that he was talking to thin air. 'Janey?'

*

Jane tipped open the door to the ladies' toilets. A single energy-saving bulb cast a weak light across the dingy room.

Red stood over the only working washbasin, carefully applying lipstick in front of a spotted mirror. Something about her was compellingly familiar.

'I know you, don't I?' Jane moved closer. 'Where did we meet?'

Red continued to paint her lips, eyes hidden behind her sunglasses.

'Chapter 2,' she said, between puckering up for the next

application. 'I'm in the opening chapter of course, but I'd say you only really get to know me from Chapter 2 on.'

Jane felt her skin prickle. 'Darsie?'

Red turned to Jane, swept the sunglasses from her face and pouted, showing off a glossy red mouth. 'What d'you think?'

Thought, certainly of the logical, coherent kind, was currently cowering on the unwashed toilet floor of Jane's mind with its arms over its head, taking a severe kicking from the thug of mental illness. 'I think I'm talking to my protagonist.'

'I prefer "heroine".' Extending the lipstick a notch, Darsie began to write on the mirror.

I'm sick, thought Jane. I've actually gone over the edge. 'What…what are you doing here?' she stuttered.

'Nothing's happening in your novel, so…' Darsie shrugged. And then added brightly, 'I think they call it a mini-break.'

Mini-breakdown, more like. 'But…you can't do that. Can you?'

'To be honest, Jane, I needed to get away or I was going to go…' she held her hands to either side of her head and widened her big, dark eyes '…totally mental. It's a very intense narrative. I personally have suffered a broken engagement and two bereavements so far.'

'Yes, I know. Sorry.' Jane winced. Why was she apologising to a fictional character?

'Oh no, please don't apologise. I think it's going to make me a stronger person in the end.'

She was experiencing a hallucination, that was all. A temporary aberration brought on by overwork. All right, not overwork. You had to be actually working for that to happen. Maybe it was something in the sponge cake? Get a grip, Jane. She had to regain some semblance of control over this situation before it got any more out of hand. Darsie had said something about 'the end'.

'The end…yes. So you'll go back? Finish it?'

'Oh, I can't do that, not without you.' She finished writing on the mirror and held out the lipstick. It shone in the dim room like a small red flame. Jane took it unthinkingly.

'Why can't you finish it, Jane? What are you afraid of?'

The toilet door opened and two women in bum-skimming dresses swanned in, brassy and loud, cackling over some shared joke.

Distracted by their arrival, when Jane looked again Darsie had vanished. She was conscious that the other women had fallen silent.

They stared suspiciously at the lipstick clutched in Jane's hand and at the mirror. Jane looked in horror at the phrase scrawled over the washbasin where Darsie had been standing.

Where's my happy ending?

CHAPTER 10

'Sugar Mice (in the Rain)', Marillion, 1987, EMI

EARLY THE FOLLOWING MORNING Tom entered the office to find Roddy lying on the sagging sofa in Tristesse Books' Reception area, hiccupping with sobs, staring at the rain running down the window that overlooked the courtyard. The floor immediately surrounding him was scattered with crumpled, tear-filled tissues and stacks of red and blue covered school notebooks. His knees were pulled up to his chest, a copy of *Happy Ending* propped open on them. He turned the last page, closed the cover and bawled.

'Oh for…get a hold of yourself, dammit!' snapped Tom.

'Gets me every time.' Roddy held up the book. 'Three times now.' He gulped back another wracking sob. 'That ending…'

Tom snatched the book angrily from him. 'Don't talk to me about damn endings.' He gestured to the exercise books on the floor. 'Now do your marking.' With that he marched off towards his office. 'Oh, Jane says hi,' he called over his shoulder.

The mention of her name triggered a fresh bout of blubbering. 'That poor lassie,' Roddy wailed, 'She must have led such a shocking life to write like that.'

Tom stopped at the end of the short corridor. There was something in what his friend had just said that struck a chord. He wasn't sure what it meant yet, but he had a feeling it was important.

'What were you saying?' he asked Roddy.

'The lonely page, the endless introspection, the mind plagued with funky thoughts. It's how writers tick, isn't it? No misery, no poetry.' Roddy reached for another tissue and blew his nose loudly.

Tom heeled shut his office door, flopped down in his chair and, muttering a few choice oaths, hurled the offending copy of *Happy Ending* across his desk, knocking Napoleon to the floor. As he bent to retrieve the fallen emperor his phone rang. He swiped at it irritably.

'What?'

'Pandemic Media have upped their offer,' said Anna, ignoring his bad-tempered tone. 'But they want an answer by the end of the month.'

He didn't want to hear that, especially not after today. Jane Lockhart had writer's block; their exchange at the Walter Scott had confirmed it. Her new novel wasn't arriving today or any day soon. 'Anna—'

'Tom, you're going bankrupt.'

He didn't respond.

'Did you speak to Jane?' she asked after a few seconds' silence.

'Yes,' he said eventually. 'She's very happy. Happier than she's ever been, apparently.'

'And her novel?'

Happy. A small thought started to form in Tom's mind. Not like a gentle root sprouting from the rich, loamy earth into the warmth of a clear spring sky. Nothing as bright and hopeful as that. This was a thought born in a much darker place; an evil twin of an idea that latched onto his back with scaly fingers and was now pressing hard. Do it. Do. It. As he considered whether or not to pursue the devilish brainwave, he felt the idea already growing.

'Hello? Tom, you still there?'

He could still hear Anna talking on the other end of the line, but she seemed far, far away. He couldn't do it, could he? It was thoroughly reprehensible, morally repugnant, potentially unforgiveable.

He smiled thinly.

Who was he kidding?

*

He met up with Roddy that evening at the multiplex on Renfrew Street. It wouldn't have been Tom's first choice, but Roddy had insisted. Roddy had a soft spot for the more mainstream Hollywood offering, especially if it hung on some improbable high concept—sharks in space; the president's a time-travelling robot—or it was part of a series whose sequels had reached upper single digits.

'I can't believe you actually pay to watch this crap.'

Tom clutched two twelve-ounce Cokes, one of which he could feel leaking stickily over his hand. He looked on with undisguised disgust as Roddy chuted an assortment of synthetic looking pick 'n' mix sweets from their hatchery tanks into a cavernous bag.

'One,' said Roddy, raising a finger. 'Don't dismiss *Werewolf House 6: This Time It's Were-sonal!* until you've seen it, you snobby git. And two. *You* paid.' He grinned. 'Compensation for the benefit of my about-to-be-imparted sage advice.' Roddy gestured to a shovel laden with yellow and white rubbery sweets. 'D'you like Fried Eggs?'

'I'm not eating your disgusting Pick 'n' Mix.'

'OK. What about white chocolate-y mouse things?'

'Put them back.'

'But they're so sugary and delicious.'

'Roddy…'

'OK, OK. Jeez.' He closed his eyes, weighed the bag in his hand, went back for another scoop of sour fizzy dummies and waited. Tom realised after a minute that he expected him to pay. Grumbling, he put down the drinks and took out his wallet.

'What's French for Pick 'n' Mix?' asked Roddy.

'There is no word in French for this nutritional tragedy.'

Roddy took a long pull on his Coke and smacked his lips. 'So, what was it you wanted to ask me, *Grasshopper*?'

Tom manoeuvred him away from the growing line of people, vaguely aware of the surprising number of them eagerly queuing for such a terrible movie franchise. In a low voice he said, 'I have a problem I believe may be suited to your particular talents.'

'Top Trumps and badminton?'

Tom was in no mood for jokes. Especially not bad jokes. Which didn't bode well for the looming film experience. He took a deep breath and launched into his plan.

'Let's say a miserable writer, through the supreme efforts of her publisher, becomes successful and happy. Are you listening?'

Roddy was watching a couple of pretty teenage girls swing past in cut-off shorts up to their bum cheeks. The first girl flicked her blonde highlights in his general direction.

'Hello, sir.'

'Amber, Roxanne,' said Roddy, acknowledging them with a look of cold terror.

'Out on a school night, sir?' she said teasingly.

'This your boyfriend, sir?' added her friend, thumbing at Tom.

The girls sloped off in giggles through the double doors

that led to one of the auditoriums and some movie that they were, on the basis of their interaction with Roddy, about three years too young to see.

'Say nothing and keep very still—you don't want to antagonise them.'

Tom sighed. 'Can we get back to my dilemma?'

'OK, OK. Miserable writer becomes successful and happy—I get it. And?'

'And being happy she is unable to complete her latest miserable novel. So, in order to help her, the selfless publisher embarks on a course of action to return her to the fragile mental state in which she wrote her highly profitable debut.'

He finished his explanation and looked expectantly at Roddy. His friend mulled over the speech in silence, his thought process evidently aided by chewing a handful of jelly beans.

'Let me get this right. You want to make Jane Lockhart's life a misery so she'll finish writing her book?'

Tom nodded, gratified not only that his friend had cottoned on to the plan with such alacrity, but moreover that he hadn't reacted with deep moral outrage. At least not yet.

'That is seriously messed up,' said Roddy. 'Do they teach you this stuff in France?'

Tom shrugged. 'We study a broad curriculum.'

'You are a deeply warped individual, you do know that?'

'She'll get over it—she got over me fast enough.' This was going even better than expected. 'Now, let's talk about the details. Clearly, it is not practical to have Coldplay on wherever she goes, or force her to sit through an endless loop of Lars von Trier films. So, how do you make someone completely, totally miserable?'

The movie was about to begin. Roddy explained that he couldn't possibly devote mental resources to Tom's question during the imminent werewolf hijinks, but promised to think about it when he was less busy, say when he was teaching the following week.

'Shall we take our seats?' said Roddy primly. 'I believe I hear the bell for the commencement of the first act.'

Reluctantly, Tom followed him inside the auditorium. As they passed through the doors Tom experienced a fleeting pang of guilt at the course of action he was now embarked upon. He reminded himself that Jane wanted to finish her novel as much as he wanted her to finish it; in a way he was lending her a helping hand. Thankfully, any further feelings of compunction were lobotomised by two hours and twenty minutes of werewolf-on-cheerleader action.

*

It was the middle of the week when Tom rocked up to the West End secondary school where Roddy was sub-stituting. His battered car grumbled across the tarmac, wheezing past a square of artificial turf that served as

a games pitch, before collapsing outside the main building in a bay marked Deputy Head. He spent the next
few minutes attracting the attention of half the school by
repeatedly slamming the driver's door in a futile attempt
to lock it. Across the glass-fronted building windows
swung open and curious heads craned out to see who or
what was making such a racket.

'Hey!' A familiar voice hailed him from a second-floor
window. 'Up here,' called Roddy, gesticulating wildly.
'Wait there. I'll be right down.'

When he arrived a few minutes later, Tom was already
in the entrance foyer, having been buzzed inside the
building by a helpful pupil, despite the proliferation of
notice-boards plastered with dire warnings about stranger
danger and online grooming.

'So, what have you got for me?' asked Tom.

'It's nice to see you too,' huffed Roddy.

'Roddy, I don't have time…'

'OK, OK. Walk with me. I've a few minutes before
Wordsworth.'

They headed across the brightly lit entrance and up a
central staircase. Endless corridors thronged with pupils
moving between classes. They parted for the grim-faced
Tom like shoals of fish before a predator.

'I still don't know why you asked *me* to help you
make Jane's life a misery,' whispered Roddy as he led
them through the library. Inquisitive faces peered out
from behind homework books. 'I've dedicated the last

ten years to encouraging young minds, planting hope and aspiration—'

Suddenly, he turned and barked at a small boy with a shifty expression and a permanent marker. 'Benson, put it away! Stand in the corner! Face to the wall!' Then muttered under his breath, 'Little shite.'

When he looked back at Tom, it was with a sheepish air. 'OK, so maybe I have some experience in the field…'

Roddy's classroom was filling up. Students wandered about the fluorescent room, thumbs flying over their phones as they dispatched breathless texts, probably to each other. Some girls sat on desks, swinging their legs and chatting loudly. Several boys occupied windowsills, heads buried in their mobiles, shooting up aliens (which was at least preferable to just shooting up). The only places not being used for seating were the chairs.

Roddy slid behind his desk and rooted through a pile of books. Shooing away a surly schoolgirl perched on one corner, Tom occupied her vacated spot.

'So I've given it some thought and I have an idea,' said Roddy, examining the book spines. 'There's no point just shouting at her. You've done that. She just shouts back.'

It was true. Jane stood up to him in a way few of his authors ever did. It was a quality in her that he admired, even though it undercut his most potent weapon.

'Jane is a writer,' Roddy continued, 'so the trick is not simply to upset her. You have to get her in the right mood. Ah-ha!'

He tapped the cover and raised an eyebrow. 'See?'

Tom scowled as he saw what he was holding. 'Yes, I see. I see Keats. John Keats.'

'Just listen, will you?'

'What's the point?' Tom asked. 'Your plan involves actual poetry. I think by definition that makes it a shit plan.'

'You're not getting it,' said Roddy. 'It's a special kind of misery you want. *Melancholy*. That dull sense of dissociation and alienation that's the source of every artist's creativity. It's like drain unblocker for novelists.'

Tom was on the point of launching into another tirade when he paused. Melancholy. Hmm.

'You know what, that actually makes sense.' He congratulated himself on his foresight at choosing Roddy to help him with his delicate mission. 'Yes, very nice. I see where you're coming from.' A plan was already forming as he made his way to the door and out into the corridor.

Just then the buzzer sounded and Roddy attempted to shepherd his class into their assigned places. 'Settle down, you lot, settle down.' He opened another book of poetry. 'William Wordsworth.'

The class gave a collective groan. Roddy stared them down until they had occupied their seats and some semblance of order had fallen over proceedings.

'Wordsworth was, of course, the first of the Romantics to use a MacBook Pro…'

By the time Tom reached his car he had settled on a

course of action. He knew Jane intimately. Knew what mattered to her. Knew precisely how to get under her skin.

'One melancholy writer,' he announced with unconcealed glee, 'coming up.'

CHAPTER 11

'Ten Days of Rain', Rod Stewart, 1986, WEA Records

RAIN FELL ON the headstones, it bounced off the roofs of the grand Victorian mausoleums and puddled on the path that wound through the cemetery. Jane and her dad sheltered on a bench beneath the outstretched stone wing of an angel.

'Coffee cake?'

She popped the lid on a plastic box containing two fat slices.

'That was your mum's favourite,' said Benny with a sad smile.

'I know,' Jane said quietly, passing him a slice.

'Come to think of it, she was a big supporter of cake in general.' He took a bite. 'That's lovely, that is. I'm just amazed you have time to do all this baking when you're so busy writing.'

Guiltily, she looked away. 'Mum always made a cake for my birthday.'

Benny nodded fondly, tilting his head as a memory

returned to him. 'D'you remember when you were six—you, me and your ma went to Edinburgh Zoo for your treat?'

'I remember.'

'Monkeys threw rotten fruit out the cage and I slipped on it,' he added rather less fondly. 'Fractured my foot in three places. I swear those monkeys were laughing.'

'Yeah, I remember all of it,' she said quietly.

Benny shot her a sideways glance. 'It's in your book, isn't it?'

'Well, yes, the main character does go to the zoo with her dad, but he's not you, and they're not monkeys, they're penguins.'

Benny lowered his coffee cake and frowned. 'How do penguins throw fruit?'

'It's different. It's a story, not real life. They're not the same.'

'Whatever you say, darlin',' he said, unconvinced, then mumbled, 'Damn monkeys.'

It was the first time they'd visited her mum's grave together. Jane had made the cake intending to leave a slice on her grave. She'd seen *Schindler's List* and knew that Jewish people left stones instead of flowers; and, really, was a slice of cake so profane? Her mum always appreciated a good bake. But when it came to it and she'd been standing over the headstone she felt foolish and wished she'd brought flowers like her dad.

'So how's the new book coming along?'

'It's…' She struggled for the right word. Seemed she'd spent the last week failing to find the right word. '…cooking.'

'And Tommy?'

Her dad's familiarity with her soon-to-be-former publisher was a hot button. 'Don't call him that. His name is Thomas Duval. He's from Saint-Tropez. A place they named a fake tan after. You call him Tommy you make him sound like he's from here. Like he's…normal. With his "pah" and his stupid stubbly face. See a lot of Thomas Duvals round here?'

Benny considered the question for a moment. 'There *was* a Jean-Claude Darcheville played for Rangers.'

'Forget about Tom. I'm about to sign with a new publisher. Klinsch & McLeish—y'know? With the red and white covers?'

'I liked Tommy…Tom,' he corrected himself swiftly.

'Da–ad!'

'Well, I did. No one else wanted your wee book, did they? He showed faith in you.'

'No, he showed faith in my book. You know he changed my original title?'

'Was it a good title?'

Oops. How had that happened? She *really* didn't want to tell him her original title. Tom had inadvertently saved her from that conversation and she had no inclination to open it up now. 'That's not the point.'

'So what was it? The original title?'

'Uh…nothing. It doesn't matter.'

He sidled along the bench. 'No, go on. I like hearing the stuff no one else knows. Makes me feel, y'know, closer to you.' He looked at her with imploring eyes.

She swallowed, knowing in that instant that she'd backed herself into a corner. That she would have to tell him now.

'OK, but…OK. I was going to call it…' She took a deep breath. It'd be all right; she'd explain and he'd understand and they'd laugh about it. Hahaha. '*The Endless Anguish of My Father*,' she blurted.

Jane looked down at the ground, then up at the rain running off the end of the stone feathers, anywhere to avoid her dad's face. He was quiet. That was promising. Perhaps it wasn't such a big—

'For fuck's sake!' He strode out onto the wet path. The rain beat down on his balding head. '*Endless Anguish of My Father*…I knew it. I *knew* it was about me.'

'No, that's not how—He's a character I made up.'

'The folk at my work looked at me funny when it came out. God, I'm such an idiot.' He turned his back on her and began to walk away. 'I have to get back to the depot.'

Jane felt a nudge of guilt that was instantly swept away by indignation. 'You never read it,' she said. 'You're not allowed to be hurt until you've actually read the damn thing! D'you not think I'm hurt my own dad hasn't read my novel?'

He stopped walking. She could see his shoulders heave as he tried to breathe some control back into his body, but he was stung by the criticism, trapped in his rage, and for now it had the better of him.

'I will read it,' he snapped. 'Soon as I'm over my *anguish*.' And with that he stalked off along the path, quickly vanishing amongst the statues and the rain.

*

Willie had gone out for his usual afternoon run, leaving Jane alone in her flat with her thoughts.

And her main character.

Darsie sat on the edge of the kitchen counter, dangling her legs, drinking her way steadily through a large glass of red wine. Jane checked on an apple strudel she'd been making. She peered into the oven. The key was the pastry; according to the recipe it had to be brittle yet yielding. It had been in for thirty minutes and was just starting to turn golden brown.

Darsie glugged down a mouthful of wine.

'Is it not a bit early for that?' Jane asked gently.

'It's not my fault I'm an alcoholic,' said Darsie. 'You wrote me like this.' She drained the glass and reached for the bottle.

Jane snatched it away. 'You're not an alcoholic. You're a binge drinker. You only drink when you're unhappy.'

Darsie stared mournfully at the out of reach bottle. 'I'm unhappy a lot.'

'Yeah.' Jane felt bad about that. On the page Darsie Baird was one thing, a character she could put through the grinder without misgiving. But sitting here in her kitchen, drinking her New Zealand Shiraz, large as life, Darsie posed a moral quandary. Every indignity Jane had subjected her to in the novel provoked a pang of conscience.

'Can we talk about your book?' asked Darsie.

Jane perked up. This was progress. She felt sure the mental aberration that manifested itself in the form of her main character was inextricably bound to her new novel. Perhaps she could talk her—*it*—out of existence.

'Yes. Let's talk about the book.'

'I was wondering. The way you write about Glasgow, it comes across as kind of a miserable place. When I'm walking through the streets it's always raining, the people are grey and beaten, but I've been out here two weeks now and I've got to tell you, this is a dead nice town. Most of the people I've seen are well fed, if they're not driving convertibles then they're out walking in parks, which, by the way, are beautiful—and I haven't seen a single deep-fried Mars bar. Not one.'

'I'm depicting the *real* Glasgow.'

'I don't know, that other stuff seemed pretty real to me. Have you seen that new Spanish deli on Byres Road? The Serrano ham looked melt-in-the-mouth. Y'know that bit in your novel where I'm running through the derelict housing estate being chased by a pack of feral kids with their dogs?'

'Yes?'

'Maybe, instead of that, I could go to the Spanish deli and buy some nice ham.'

'I don't think so.'

'Why not?'

'I don't write about delis.'

'No. You don't.'

'I write about the other side,' said Jane sharply. 'The non-Serrano ham eating Glasgow.'

'Why?'

'It's what I know. Where I came from.'

Darsie toyed with a chrome Alessi fruit squeezer. 'But you're not there now.'

Jane folded her arms defensively. 'So you're saying I should forget about my past?'

'No. I just wonder who you're writing this stuff for. Because, I'm telling you, the kind of people you write about in your book aren't the same ones reading it. If I saw your novel in Tesco, I'd never pick it up—and it's *my* story.' She cocked her head. 'Not like you'd ever write me going to Tesco, either.' She slipped off the counter. 'You'd like to think you're exposing the dark underbelly, but in fact all you are is a misery tour guide.' She stepped lightly through the door into the hallway. 'This way, nice ladies and gentlemen, for the awful tale of Darsie the Dipso.'

Irritated, Jane followed her out.

'What you're doing is dishonest,' said Darsie. 'You live in one world and write about another.'

'That's not fair,' Jane objected. 'I'm rooted in that world.'

'Aye, right. Rooted.' Darsie sniffed. 'So how's that filo pastry coming?'

The pastry! Jane scampered back into the kitchen and flung open the oven door. The strudel was beginning to catch around the edges. Quickly slipping on a pair of oven gloves she rescued it and put it to one side to cool. She pressed a finger to the outside. Brittle and yielding. If she were a pastry, she thought, she'd be filo.

'Am I you?'

Jane jumped back, startled. Darsie stood next to her, swirling a now-refilled wine glass.

'Don't be ridiculous,' said Jane.

'That's a relief.'

She wished her protagonist didn't sound quite so pleased. 'What do you mean?'

'I have an arc. My story's going somewhere. I have the capacity for change—you've written me that way. But you.' She shook her head. 'You I'm not so sure about.'

That cut deep. There's nothing like being judged wanting by a figment of your own imagination, Jane decided. But Darsie was wrong. She could change. Just look at her—unrecognisable from the little girl regularly locked up in the twelfth floor flat while her dad went out drinking. Life wasn't neat like a novel, but that didn't mean people were incapable of change. An insistent chime swam up through her thoughts and it was a moment before she realised it was the doorbell.

'Dad,' said Jane on opening the door, surprised to find him on the threshold. Their last encounter had ended with him stalking off in a fury. She was used to him walking out; seeing him again so soon after was novel.

Benny said nothing. He stared at the doormat, clearly wrestling with some internal struggle.

'Come in,' she said, holding up her oven gloves. 'I just made a strudel.'

Benny looked up at last. 'I can't stay. I just wanted to…' He raised his eyes to the heavens and sighed. 'I had it all straight in my head…what I was going to say. You wouldn't understand, being a writer—can't imagine you're ever stuck for words.'

Ha! These days she seemed to spend her life stuck for words.

'Truth is, we don't really know each other and…I'd like to. Get to know you.' He shook his head. 'And I'm messing it up. Like at the cemetery. I was out of order and…I'm sorry, darlin'.'

In that moment she couldn't remember if he'd ever apologised to her. Taken aback, she said nothing. Couldn't find the words, ironically enough. His face crumpled; she saw that he took her silence as a rejection.

'Right. I've said it. I'll be off then. Got to meet the boys for quiz practice.'

He began to trot down the stairs, his polished shoes clipping on the stone steps and echoing off the high Victorian ceiling.

'Dad.'

He paused, standing there like a small child awaiting the next blow.

Rooted in that world. Whatever her alter ego said, she knew how to connect to this man.

'Can I be on your quiz team?'

Benny's face creased into a question and for a moment Jane was sure she'd misjudged the situation.

He shook his head. 'You're too busy to be bothered with a daft wee pub quiz.'

'Please,' she insisted. 'I'd like to. Get to know you.'

He stood in front of a large window that overlooked the communal back court. The residents of the flats shared a square of lawn and a border planted with camellias and rhododendrons. Every year since she moved in she'd planted Busy Lizzies, just like she and her dad had done together in the window box on the twelfth floor. The buzz of a lawnmower rose up from below.

'Be great to have you on the team,' he said, his voice breaking. He cleared his throat, gathered himself. 'We need you. Between you and me, I think Rory might have a touch of dementia.'

*

Tom watched Jane and her dad leave. He and Roddy were parked in a disabled bay opposite the front door. A less noticeable spot would have been preferable but it was the last space available. They slumped down in their seats to avoid being spotted. Roddy followed the departing Lockharts through a pair of high-powered binoculars.

'Are those entirely necessary?' Tom asked doubtfully.

'*Entirely*,' insisted Roddy.

Tom shook his head. Although initially a reluctant participant in the plan, Roddy had quickly become obsessed over every detail of the operation. Or 'op' as he preferred to call it. As well as his ubiquitous parka jacket, he sported what appeared to be a leather helmet and goggles belonging to a World War One flying ace. Apparently, they'd come as a joint lot with the binoculars. This was their first time out in public. Or, as he would have it, 'in the field'.

'OK, she's gone.' Roddy lowered the binoculars and arched his wrist. He wore a watch with a face the size of a dinner plate on which glowed a myriad of tiny luminescent dials.

Tom reached into the back seat for his 'tactical mission equipment', which was contained in a plastic supermarket bag. Once he'd gathered it up, he opened his door. Roddy put out a hand.

'Wait, where are you going?' he said. 'We haven't synchronised watches.' He adjusted the bezel on his enormous wristwatch. 'Aw, bugger it.'

'What?'

'I think I reset Karachi.'

Tom sighed. 'I'll be back in ten minutes. Just warn me if either of them comes back.'

Roddy put aside the binoculars and reached for his mobile phone. He held it up to his mouth. 'Copy that.'

Tom rolled his eyes and slipped out of the car. He made his way inside the tenement building and up the stairs to Jane's front door. After carefully setting down the plastic bag he reached above the door and felt along the lintel. The spare key was where she always left it. With a pang he remembered that the last time he'd used it they'd still been together. He closed his fingers tightly around the key.

'Target acquired. Over.' Roddy's voice whispered from his mobile.

Tom knew Roddy would be in the car, pointing those stupid binoculars at Jane's bay window. He muttered to himself and then responded. 'It's a pot plant, Roddy. Not a North Korean reactor.'

'Roger. That's a solid copy.'

Tom swept up the plastic bag and let himself into the flat. He padded along the empty hallway to the living room.

Willie's presence pervaded the space. He'd spread

through Jane's delicate quirky flat like knotweed. Half-naked women burst from his film posters, on the bookshelves screenwriting manuals pushed out Jane's vintage Penguins, framed photographs of the grinning Big Man with his arm round a succession of Hollywood B-listers colonised the windowsill and coffee table. In the bay window his hulking desk seemed to mount her slender-legged writing table. Tom shook himself. He didn't have much time and this was not about Willie. He was here to create some low-level misery in Jane's life. He crossed to her record player and riffled through her vinyl collection.

'Upbeat…upbeat…upbeat…ah!' The Prophetic Sad. That was more like it. He moved the album to the front. It wasn't going to make her melancholy all by itself, but he figured that every little would help.

He noticed her laptop open on her desk and a thought struck him. Would it be so wrong to take a peek at her novel? There wasn't time for an extensive read, so perhaps he would email himself what she'd written so far. OK, so yes, he'd agreed not to read a word until she finished the manuscript, but she was so nearly done and, after all, he'd paid her a fat advance. He sat down in front of the laptop and prodded the spacebar. The dark screen pulsed into life, presenting him with a password request. What the hell! This wasn't like Jane. When had she become so paranoid? Who was she trying to keep out, for god's sake?

With a stab of regret he realised the answer. She was trying to keep *him* out.

After the sixth failed attempt at cracking her password he gave up. No matter. The mission was still on course. His eye fell on his principal target. Once Roddy had seeded the idea of putting Jane into a state of creative melancholy, it hadn't taken him long to fasten on this object as the means to the success of the plan. He made the exchange and was about to head out of the living room when his pocket grumbled. His phone was tucked in there, the line open to Roddy's so they could maintain contact. He pulled it out and listened. Roddy wasn't trying to warn him of Jane or Willie's return, he was sitting in the car, bored, evidently having forgotten that Tom could hear every word.

'Maverick to Iceman, we are Oscar Mike.'

It was sub-Hollywood action movie gobbledygook. No wonder the British education system was in such a dire state if this was the nonsense spouted by its teachers.

'We are five klicks from extraction point—' A sudden clatter from the other end of the line, suspiciously like a phone being dropped, and a muffled shout of 'Bollocks'.

Tom had had enough of Roddy's *Mission Impossible* routine. His finger slid towards the disconnect button and was a heartbeat away from killing the call when Roddy's voice burst from the handset.

'Tom. Tom! She's back.'

He crossed hurriedly to the window and scanned the street. He could make out Roddy in the car, waving up at him and gesticulating wildly to the tenement entrance. Tom glimpsed a flash of red hair beneath the canopy of trees as Jane disappeared inside.

'She's coming up the stairs! Get out of there!' yelled Roddy. 'Abort! Abort!'

'Shit.' There was no time. If he went out now he'd have to pass her on the stairs. There was only one way in and out of the flat and these old buildings had no fire escape. He looked around for a place to hide.

Jane's key turned in the lock and the front door swung into the hallway. Tom ducked behind a bookcase and held his breath. Moments later Jane dashed into the living room. It seemed to Tom that she was in a hurry, as if she'd forgotten something. That made sense, since she'd left with her dad less than fifteen minutes ago. There was one bonus being trapped in here with her; it provided him with a ringside seat for the scene that was surely about to happen. He ventured a peek over the counter.

Jane dug down the back of the sofa and turned cushions over in search of whatever she had forgotten. Not finding it, she moved to a bookshelf. As she made her way round the room she eventually reached the desk in her bay window. She stopped and let out a little gasp.

She'd seen it.

Her precious umbrella plant lay before her, shrivelled and brown. She stood there staring at the plant, not making a sound, her shoulders shaking. He was pretty sure she was crying. God, he hated it when she cried. But that was the point, wasn't it? He'd coldly calculated what would reduce her to tears and had hit the bullseye. He knew how Roddy would characterise it: Mission Accomplished! So why didn't it feel like a victory?

He crept out to the hallway, picked his way across the stripped wooden floor, conscious of every creak and bow, to the front door.

A minute later he hustled out of the tenement and clambered into the car, relieved to be out of Jane's flat. Roddy was glued to his binoculars, which were trained on the bay window.

'Ooh, that's horrible. She's really upset. I'm not looking at that.'

Tom snatched the binoculars out of his hands and focused on Jane. She sat despondently at her desk, the dead plant before her. From time to time she wiped a palm across her cheeks.

'OK,' he said. 'That should do it.'

Roddy landed a punch on his upper arm. He felt it go numb and rubbed vigorously.

'Ow! What was that for?'

Roddy gave him a reproachful look. 'You're enjoying this too much.'

Was he? It didn't feel like that inside. 'It's for her own good. Remember? And it's not as if I actually killed her plant.'

He rustled in the plastic bag and carefully withdrew Jane's umbrella plant, as healthy and flourishing as ever.

Roddy tapped a finger against the side of his nose. 'Ah yes, the old bait and switch. Works every time.'

'You've done this before?' asked Tom.

'Well no, not as such.' He could see Roddy thinking it over. 'Not at all, actually.'

There was a ping from the handbrake and the car began to roll forward, inching towards a polished Mercedes saloon. Tom yanked the brake back on before they collided.

Roddy checked his giant glowing watch. 'If you put your foot down I might make *Hamlet* with 5c.'

That was code. Tom understood. 'So, we take the scenic route?'

'Yeah,' Roddy nodded. 'I think, all things considered, that would be best.'

*

Jane couldn't understand how it had happened. When she'd left the flat she was sure the plant had been in perfect shape. It was a mystery. Perhaps Willie had been right and she'd overwatered the thing. She could only assume it had been on the brink of dying and something had pushed it over the edge. It was just a plant. But it connected her to her younger self. The last gift her dad had given that Jane. Now it was gone. She started to cry.

She pulled her laptop towards her and keyed in the password. She'd meant to change it ages ago, but hadn't quite got round to doing so. There were too many PIN numbers and passwords to remember, so it was a complete hassle to continually refresh them. That's what she told herself. With a twinge of discomfort she typed 'Tristesse' and the splash screen gave way to her novel and the gaping chasm that was Chapter 37. She glanced at the dead plant, palmed away another tear and rested her fingers on the keyboard. An idea, a beginning, uncurled in the great swirling confusion of her head and she—

'Janey, you OK?'

It was Willie, back from his run. He stood in the doorway, breathing lightly. 'I thought I heard crying. Was it you?'

She shook her head numbly. A couple of long strides took him to her side. He wrapped his arms around her. She couldn't stop herself. Tears fell freely.

'It's OK, Janey. It's OK,' he soothed.

'It's…dead.'

'What's dead?'

Through great gulping sobs she said, 'My…dad's…plant.'

She saw him clock it on the desk, grey leaves clenched with rigor mortis. He grimaced and then his face lightened. 'Aw come on, nothing a splash of Baby Bio won't fix, eh darlin'?'

She let out a snort of laughter.

'That's more like it. That's my Janey.' He kissed her

neck. 'Now, I'm going to jump in the shower, but what do you say afterwards we go to that nice wee Italian place on Ashton Lane you like?'

She nodded again. 'I'd like that.'

He kissed her again. She watched him walk away and smiled, feeling lucky that at last she'd found a man who wanted to make the world right; who wanted to make her happy.

CHAPTER 12

'A Little Fall of Rain', Les Misérables Original London Cast Recording, 1985, Red

FIRST, SHE ORGANISED the pencils in order of colour, ranging them according to the spectrum, but that didn't take long so she tipped them out of the holder and started again, this time cataloguing them in order of height, from tallest to shortest, but when she laid them out on her desk they formed a ragged line that was patently unsatisfactory, so in search of a neater arrangement she fished out a pencil sharpener and spent the next ten minutes whittling them all to the same length.

It wasn't procrastination, it was preparation. Coloured pencils were for making notes on the paper manuscript; a different hue to track each character. It was a system she'd used to great effect when editing her debut. But that novel and that time felt far away.

She remembered the ease with which she used to write, as if she'd been possessed by her characters, channelling their words through her fingers. All she had to do was get out of their way and let them tell their own story. Not like now. Now she sat here day after day, head in her hands hoping to squeeze out a single word. She gathered up the pencils and jammed them back in the holder. She wouldn't be needing them anytime soon. There was no manuscript to edit. Not yet. Perhaps not ever.

Her eyes flicked to the laptop. The stubbornly empty page was like a mute scream. Silence would have been a blessing, but her misery had a soundtrack. The bullying rattle and clank of Willie's typing filled the room. It wasn't his fault; he couldn't know the anguish he caused her, and anyway, what could he do? He was on a deadline, his screenplay due in a matter of weeks. It wouldn't be fair to ask him to change his routine, especially when it was obviously going so well. Disheartened, she turned to the window and began to count the leaves on the trees outside.

Another sound joined Willie's relentless typing: the tapdance of fingers leaping across a modern keyboard. For a moment Jane imagined that she'd been possessed by one of her characters again. She looked down, hoping to see her hands moving unbidden across the laptop the way they used to. But instead they lay folded in her lap. The sound was coming from the other end of the room.

Darsie sat with her legs elegantly crossed, pencil skirt smoothed to mid-thigh, a neat silver laptop balanced on one knee. Long, tapered fingers worked up and down the keyboard with the practised ease of a concert pianist. Her hair was swept back today in a ponytail, which swung in metronomic time to her typing. A pair of black-rimmed spectacles perched schoolmistressly on her nose. She leaned in; her hands became a blur. Jane recognised the signs—whatever Darsie was writing it was reaching its climax. Sure enough, she performed a final flourish and sat back, hands still frozen in the shape of the last word. She let out a long, low breath and her body relaxed.

Jane snatched the laptop from her knee.

'Hey!' Darsie objected. 'What d'you think you're doing?'

'I'm supposed to be the writer. You're the character. Remember?'

'A character without an ending,' she muttered, folding her arms.

Jane ignored her and turned to the screen. Delicate sentences formed succulent paragraphs stacked one on top of the other, baked together into a firm, crisp page. Jealously, she began to read. Absorbed in the text she walked back to her desk and set the laptop down beside her own.

Darsie hovered at her shoulder, looking from the screen to Jane, eager for praise. 'So, what do you think?'

'I think,' began Jane, 'that this is the end of *Les Misérables*.'

Darsie's eager expression didn't alter. 'Yes. You should write something like that.'

'Thanks. Great suggestion. Bit French, perhaps? People dying of consumption and all that? I'm a bit more…urban Scotland, Primal Scream, unhappy '90s childhood…'

Willie looked up, some part of the conversation having pierced the armour of his typing. 'Sorry?'

Darsie raised a finger sharply. 'She wasn't talking to you.'

It took a moment before Jane remembered that Willie couldn't see or hear her. 'I wasn't talking to you,' she said apologetically.

'OK,' said Willie uncertainly, glancing around the room in case he'd missed the arrival of someone else. Then he loosened his shoulders with a shake and returned to work.

Jane studied him. He was a writer, a kindred spirit. She couldn't imagine that he'd ever suffered from writer's block, but perhaps he could offer some wisdom on the subject. 'Willie?'

'Hmm?'

'Do your characters ever…' She hesitated. 'Talk to you?'

Willie broke off and leant towards her, his eyes locking with hers. Oh god, what had she said? She shouldn't have admitted it. She was a madwoman.

'Sure,' he said at last. 'All the time.'

Relief surged through her. She wasn't alone. He under-stood.

Willie patted his typewriter. 'That's why I've got this.'

A half smirk. 'Drowns out the bastards.' He sniffed. 'See, when I'm writing, I only want to hear the one voice.' He angled his hands towards his chest and made a flicking motion. 'Mine.' Without another word he went back to work.

'Charming,' said Darsie, arching one perfectly plucked eyebrow. 'Quite the hero.'

Jane considered the man opposite her. She'd come to the conclusion that there were two Willies: one the supportive, caring man who'd held her when her plant died. The other was a bit of a bastard. Not that there was anything wrong with that. Made things interesting in all sorts of ways; from the bedroom to the bay window. With two writers living under the same roof there was bound to be a bit of creative friction—and some healthy competition. Currently, the score was a whitewash. She was getting creamed.

Moreover, she knew that on some level he thrived on her discomfort. The longer she was stuck on Chapter 37, the better he looked, sailing through his screenplay. And the reason she knew with such certainty was her own dirty little secret. Uncomfortable as it was to admit, if the situation were reversed, she'd feel the same way.

There was the ping of the carriage return and Willie tore another finished page from his typewriter. He caught her eye. A flicker of a smile.

'You still blocked?

She felt her cheeks colour. It was time to face it: no one

else was going to help. It was down to her to do something about her damn writer's block.

*

Mocha Books was that rarest of flowers, a new independent bookshop flourishing in the shade of the national chains and supermarkets. With a gourmet café grafted onto the bookselling side it had quickly established itself as much for its selection of artisan cheeses as its bold selection of literary fiction.

Jane pushed open the door. A bell rang to signal her entrance; more like a temple gong, she thought. She pulled up the collar on her coat, eager not to draw attention to herself.

She hadn't been to Mocha Books before, which was the point of coming here today. Given the delicate nature of the book she planned to purchase she wanted somewhere she was unlikely to be recognised. Not that celebrity was a pressing issue; it was a rare occasion when she was stopped in the street by a fan. And though she'd appeared as a guest on a couple of TV culture shows, they were of the variety broadcast between the hours of midnight and three a.m. on a channel no one had heard of. However, while ardent fans weren't a problem, her local bookstore was. She'd done several signings there and the staff knew her too well. Today she wanted to go incognito. Hence the trip to the north side of town, where the bears lived.

She went inside and made straight for the self-help

section. The plan was to get in and out with as little fuss as possible. She'd even remembered to bring cash in order to avoid having to use a card with her name on it. She browsed the bookshelves, running a finger lightly over the spines as she skimmed the titles. Finally, she landed on a likely candidate and, with a glance over her shoulder to make sure no one was watching, scooped it off the shelf.

'*A Hundred and One Ways to Beat Writer's Block*?' said a loud voice.

Jane winced and turned to see a familiar figure. 'Hello, Darsie.'

Her alter ego had picked up on the undercover vibe and sported a pair of dark glasses and a headscarf. Jane experienced a twinge of envy. Whenever she'd tried to pull off the Grace Kelly headscarf thing she always ended up looking like a nineteenth-century peasant. Darsie wore it with aplomb. Rather unnecessarily she raised the sunglasses to show that it was indeed her beneath.

'Keep your voice down,' whispered Jane. 'Please.'

'Hey,' said Darsie, tucking a stray hair under her scarf. 'I'm not the one drawing attention to myself by muttering into thin air.'

She sashayed along next to the shelf, plucking a series of books, reeling off their titles and loading them into Jane's arms. '*Beat Your Block to a Pulp. Knock that Block! Lost For Words. What would Jesus Write?*' She screwed up her face at this last one. 'Seriously?'

Irritated, Jane set aside the books on a nearby table. One would do—she wasn't *that* blocked. She swiped the top book from the stack. She'd had quite enough of her fictional shadow.

'So, what's the deal, are you going to stalk me until I finish the novel?'

'Yes, I believe that's how it works,' said Darsie matter-of-factly. 'Now, can we talk about the last chapter?'

'What about it?'

'I'm a romantic heroine—I don't want to end up unhappy.'

Jane shrugged. 'Plenty of heroines don't get happy endings. Anna Karenina, Juliet Capulet, Tess of the d'Urbervilles—'

'Tess?' Darsie tutted loudly. 'Oh come on, Jane. Spoiler alert.'

Jane ignored her. 'And anyway, I'm not yet sure what happens to you at the end.'

'But you could make it anything you want,' Darsie pleaded.

'That's not how it works.' There was a rhythm to these things; a rightness that could only be achieved by surrendering utterly to the pull of the story. 'You don't really get to choose your ending. It has to follow from what comes before, or it doesn't feel true.'

Darsie stopped walking. 'But that's not fair!' she wailed. 'What comes before my ending are four hun-

dred pages of unrelenting Celtic misery.' She locked eyes
with Jane. 'Tom's right—you can't stop worshipping your
pain.'

Jane stared back at her creation. Darsie needed to
understand. 'Life is hard.'

'OK, yes,' Darsie nodded, 'but can it be someone else's
life?' She clutched Jane's hand in hers. 'Please, I want it
all to turn out OK. Jane…'

'Jane Lockhart?'

Jane turned to see a formidable lady in a twin set, a bale
of bubble-wrap in one hand, a copy of *Happy Ending* in
the other, open at the author photo. She looked from the
photo to Jane, and beamed.

'I thought it was you.' She marched over, tucking
the bubble-wrap under one arm in order to offer up a
firm handshake. 'Shona Heywood, proprietor of Mocha
Books.' She gestured grandly to the shop, and then laid a
hand lightly on Jane's arm. 'And may I say it's a pleasure
to meet the woman who helped pay for my new kitchen.'
Shona chuckled at her own little joke.

Jane joined in with a polite laugh. Behind her, Darsie
threw back her head and guffawed. Jane sighed inwardly;
so much for going incognito. This was exactly what she'd
hoped to avoid by coming to Mocha Books. She pressed
the cover of *Beat Your Block To A Pulp* against her chest
and hoped Shona hadn't noticed.

'It is. It's her!' Shona pointed excitedly and suddenly
an ambush of excited booksellers and customers material-

ised from the corners of the shop to surround Jane, cooing praise and hurling questions.

Her head snapped back and forth to keep up with each fresh voice.

'I just loved *Happy Ending*…so sad…'

'Can't wait for your new one…'

'Come to our book group…'

'What's it called…?'

'What's it about…?'

And then from the muddle a clear voice rang out. 'When's it out?'

She looked round at the expectant faces. Good question. 'Umm…'

Shona hadn't taken in that Jane was struggling to provide an answer; the bookshop proprietor's mind was on loftier ground. 'It must be difficult,' she pondered aloud, 'having so much to live up to.' She waved a hand as if trying to trap the thought. 'Really, how does one follow such a staggering success as *Happy Ending*?'

By getting stuck on the last chapter of the next book for the rest of your life, thought Jane. She smiled and nodded inanely.

Shona's hand was at it again. This time it performed a graceful swirl like some interpretive dance move. 'But we're interrupting the Muse,' she said huskily. 'I'm sure you're eager to get back to the page.' And then with a twinkle, 'And I have my eye on a gorgeous new bathroom.'

She chuckled again. Jane forced another laugh and Darsie mimicked her. But then Shona motioned to the book Jane was clutching guiltily to her chest. For a moment, Jane was sure the game was up.

'Oh, and you must take the book,' said Shona generously, 'with my compliments.'

'Thank you,' breathed Jane, relief washing over her. It looked like she'd make it out of here without exposing her secret.

'I must just run it through the till.'

Before Jane could react, Shona had wrested the book from her grasp.

'No!' Jane cried out, her outburst startling the crowd.

But it was too late. Shona's smile slipped as her eye scanned the title. 'Blocked?'

She sounded so disappointed that Jane felt even worse. The others could see the offending book now too and a whisper went through the gathering.

'Yes, blocked.'

'She's blocked.'

They surrounded her in a tight circle. 'Sorry,' she heard herself say. 'I'm really sorry.' Abandoning the book she pushed her way through the throng, unable to avoid the disillusionment in every face. Flustered, she stumbled to the exit, yanked open the door and hurried out. Behind her the bell tolled.

CHAPTER 13

'Rain Dance', Big Country, 1984, Mercury Records

A PAIR OF black umbrellas stalked along Wilson Street,
rain bouncing off their taut canopies. Beneath them, Tom
gave Roddy a dark look.

'Your powers are useless, old man,' said Roddy. 'The
Duval Death Stare won't work on me, pal. I'm immune,
see.'

'It's been a week,' Tom complained. 'My inbox is
empty. Nothing. *Rien du tout*. Where's my novel?'

'Unfinished?' Roddy ventured.

'Precisely. She's not as melancholy over her stupid
plant as you said she'd be. So much for your plan.'

'Hey, you said it was a great plan.'

'That was before it failed utterly.'

'Whoa, relax. You need to take a breath. You know
what impatience gets you? Heartburn. So, chill. Leave it
to me. In the words of The Carpenters: We've only just
begun.'

'First Keats, now The Carpenters? I'll give you this, you're nothing if not eclectic.'

'Oh yeah. I've got moves you wouldn't believe.'

They came to the corner of the street just as a car raced through a puddle, sending a spray of dirty water over them.

Tom hurled abuse at the disappearing tail lights and then wiped a hand across his rain-smudged face. 'Does it ever stop raining in this damn country?'

'No. Obviously,' said Roddy, shaking one sodden trouser-leg. 'But I'll tell you where it doesn't rain. Saint-Tropez.' He shivered. 'Here's a thought. Why don't we put a pin in this business with Jane and take a wee holiday…?'

Tom stood like a statue. A wet statue. He grimaced. 'You don't know what it's like. There it is just sports cars and yachts and beautiful women.'

'Uh-huh?' Roddy turned his damp face up hopefully.

'I came here to get away from that.' He stared grimly into the middle distance. 'I grew up in a swimming pool, Roddy. My adolescence was an endless parade of girls in bikinis. By my late teens the summers were a succession of Brigittes, Mariannes and Nathalies, riding around aimlessly on the back of my motorbike. We led hollow lives with nothing to do but drink wine and have meaningless sex beneath an unrelenting sun.'

Roddy sniffed. 'It's a wonder you're not scarred.'

Tom ignored him. 'When the sun is shining nobody can think.'

'Well,' said Roddy with a rueful smile, 'we get to do a lot of thinking round here.'

'And that is why I like it.' They turned into Candleriggs and walked the short distance to Tristesse Books' gated entrance. 'So, what do The Carpenters say we should do about Jane now?'

Roddy nodded, gathering his thoughts. 'OK. Right, get this. Stephen King, John Grisham, JK Rowling—what've they all got in common?'

'If I published any of them, I wouldn't need Jane Lockhart?'

'Well, yes, but apart from that?'

'Just spit it out, Roddy!'

'OK, OK. They were all, at some point, rejected by publishers.' He cocked an eyebrow. 'Yeah? Clever, huh? Smart, with a twist of *bwahahaha*!'

Tom thought for a moment. 'I can't reject her novel—the point is, I want it.'

'But you're not seeing the big picture. This isn't about you. Once she's delivered on her contract with Tristesse, you said she's moving to Klinsch & McLeish, right? Big Edinburgh rainmakers. Publishers to the elite. The red and white covers every writer dreams of being published in. Well, what do needy writers hate above all? I'll tell you. Not being loved.'

He left a pause.

'Are you waiting for applause?'

'Maybe. Yeah.'

'Just get to the point, will you?'

Roddy mimed sucking a pipe. 'So, Watson, if we want Jane to fall into a state of melancholy, then we must engineer her new publisher to dump her. It's…' He raised his chin, inviting Tom to finish the line.

'I'm not saying "elementary",' Tom said flatly. However he couldn't help but agree that despite the shocking Sherlock Holmes impersonation Roddy had hit on something. What he said about authors was true, in his experience. They were all needy. It was understandable. Most spent their formative years opening the morning mail to find a rejection letter tucked in with the bills. But the same thing marked them out: no matter how conditioned they were to failure, they all lived in hope. Extinguishing that was bound to crush Jane. Tom balked at the thought, but consoled himself that he had embarked upon this distasteful project in order to help her. Crushing her hope was necessary only in the short term.

'The hypothesis is sound,' he agreed. 'But how do we get Klinsch & McLeish to drop Jane?'

'Two words,' said Roddy, raising one finger and then another. 'Glen. Buchan.'

*

There was an old adage that crime and horror writers exorcised their demons on the page and as a result were amongst some of the most well–adjusted, easy-going individuals you could ever hope to meet. Glen Buchan proved

the exception. Despite attaining a level of financial success that would choke a banker and critical praise that
had elevated him from genre writer to literary darling, he
remained the same misanthropic bundle of hang-ups that
Tom had known back when he'd almost published his
debut. All of which, Tom reflected with a thin smile, made
him perfect for the next phase of the plan.

The sign in the central foyer of the Thistle Hotel pointed
to the conference suite where the creative writing workshop was due to take place that afternoon. When Tom
swung through the entrance he found the workshop organ-
iser—a crinkly poet in Harris tweed—standing over the
sign locked in a heated discussion with a lanky duty
manager.

'But that's what it says,' said the duty manager
patiently.

'Wind Jar,' said the poet, evidently not for the first time.
He spoke with a singsong cadence, his voice a gentle lilt,
until it rose to an exasperated squeak. 'Not *Whinger*.'

'Yeah,' agreed the puzzled duty manager, shrugging his
epauletted shoulders and pointing to the sign. 'Exactly.'

Tom followed his finger. On the sign was an illustration
of a curving amphora pot encircled with a sentence in a
faux Celtic script. It read: 'Whinger Scotland—*Capturing
the Creative Breath*.'

The duty manager gave one last shrug of incomprehension and politely excused himself, leaving the poet to
grumble his dissatisfaction to the air.

'Donald,' Tom hailed him, 'still pedalling that Hebridean doggerel you call poetry?' He made his way across the tartan-carpeted foyer towards the old poet. 'I could never understand a word of it. Particularly when you read aloud.' He shook his head. 'That ridiculous accent.'

'Duval, you little prick,' chanted Donald MacDonald. His shaggy white beard parted like curtains to reveal a broad smile. 'Fucking marvellous to see you.'

The two men embraced warmly and Tom was hit by an overwhelming scent of pot.

'You're one to talk about my accent, young man,' said Donald. 'You, with your *unfathomable* vowels.' He looked past Tom's shoulder.

A curious assortment of people had just walked into the hotel. A mixture of young men in black sweaters shouldering battered leather messenger bags, old men in tweed jackets like Donald's, a sprinkling of women in floral skirts and sandals, and a few more in standard issue gothic black.

'Wind Jar?' ventured Donald.

The group replied with amorphous nods and muttered yesses.

'Welcome, writers, *makars*!' he boomed. 'Registration is in the Robert Louis Stevenson Suite. Second floor. Please enjoy a complimentary bacon roll. Halal, kosher and vegetarian alternatives are available.'

The aspirants filed past towards the lifts. Donald shook some hands and made throaty noises of recognition. When they were out of earshot, he gazed after them with a sag of disappointment.

'Same old faces. Same old rubbish. Not a real writer amongst them.' He shook his head sadly. 'I hope you didn't come here hoping to find the next Jane Lockhart.'

'No, I came to see Glen,' said Tom.

Donald swung round sharply. 'Is that a good idea, Duval? He's not as fond of you as I am—and I'd happily shaft you for a five-hundred-quid advance and a book tour of the provinces.' He pursed his lips. 'You're sure about this, after what happened last time?' Tom nodded determinedly. With a dubious sigh Donald reached into his jacket. 'That Edinburgh Book Festival ban must be up soon, hmm?'

Tom pretended to ignore the remark. 'Where can I find him?'

The old poet unfolded an itinerary of the day's events.

'He's doing a session on "Generating Conflict" in the James Kelman Conservatory. Ground floor.'

When Tom arrived the workshop had yet to begin. A pretty volunteer in a purple Wind Jar T-shirt was setting out chairs while at the far end of the conservatory the guest speaker paced up and down between two ferns, head buried in what Tom assumed were his notes for the session.

Back when Tom had almost published him Glen Buchan had cut a figure as taut and lean as his prose, but almost a decade on his belt was a couple of notches looser and there was the shadow of an extra chin. His debut had launched him onto the literary scene with the force of one of his famously propulsive sentences. Hailed variously as a stunning new voice, a firebrand, and a disgrace, he had gone on to confirm his reputation with his next two novels, at which point the consensus was that he'd peaked. He had produced three more novels since then, failing with each to rouse the same passions as his earlier work. And he knew it. Crippling neurosis was punctuated by moments of unbearable bumptiousness. It was during one of these moments, in a tent at the Edinburgh Book Festival a few years previously, that Tom and he had come to blows. In his usual fashion Tom had bluntly expressed his opinion of Glen's latest novel, his editor and probably his mother. Things had deteriorated swiftly. Eventually the police had to be called and Tom received a five-year ban from the festival.

By the door was a table piled with copies of Glen's latest novel. Tom picked one up. It was entitled *Paranoia Avenue* and clothed in one of Klinsch & McLeish's ubiquitous red and white covers.

'Are you here for "Generating Conflict"?'

Tom looked up from the book to see the pretty volunteer smiling at him.

'Oh, absolutely.' He beamed back and then banged the book down on the table. The impact echoed round the room like a slapped face. Glen stopped pacing. Irritated, he turned to locate the source of the interruption.

'Hello, Glen,' said Tom smoothly.

'Well, well,' sneered Glen, 'if it isn't Pepe Le Pew.'

'Mr Buchan,' asked the volunteer gingerly, 'should I fetch security?'

He screwed up his face. 'Do we even *have* security at this shit excuse for a writing workshop?'

'I don't—' she began.

'Bugger off, there's a good girl.'

'Yes, Mr Buchan.' She scurried from the room. As she passed Tom, she muttered, 'What a total *shitebag*.'

Tom opened his arms in a gesture of familiar greeting. 'Glen.'

Glen's right eye twitched and he smoothed a lick of sandy hair that had fallen across his shining forehead. 'Bloody writing workshop, can you believe it? What the hell am I doing here?'

'Giving something back?' Tom suggested.

'Bollocks. I fucking hate other writers.'

'Weren't you married to one?'

'I hate her especially. You know she won the Costa?' He paused. 'Bitch.'

An armchair nestled beside a low table on which sat a bowl of nuts and a jug of water. Glen poured himself a glass and drained it in a few noisy gulps.

'So, what brings the great Gallic phallus into my presence?'

'I know we've had our differences over the years,' said Tom.

Glen snorted.

'But we go way back. And after what happened at Edinburgh the other year, I feel I owe you.'

Glen tensed, his hand going to his cheek as if remembering an old wound. 'Go on.'

'So I thought I should tell you. About Jane Lockhart.' He took a couple of slow steps into the room. 'Rumour has it she's about to sign with Klinsch & McLeish.'

Glen's whole body, which had wound itself into a tight ball of expectation, relaxed into indifference. 'Is that all? I knew that. Everyone knows that.'

'She's good.'

'I know. I read *Happy Ending*.'

Tom blew out dismissively. '*Happy Ending* was merely a warm-up. Wait till you read her new one. Reminds me of you…four or five books ago.'

Glen shrank into himself, folding and unfolding his arms.

'I'm a far better writer now. Technically, I was all over the place back then.'

Tom helped himself to a handful of complimentary nuts.

'Sure, Glen, sure. I'm not one of those people who think your best work is behind you.'

'Is that it? Is that all you came to tell me, because—'

'There's something else, Glen.'

His other eye began to twitch.

'It's common knowledge your deal with Klinsch &

McLeish is up after this book.' Tom held up a copy of
Paranoia Avenue. 'Now there's absolutely no truth to the
rumour that Klinsch and McLeish are planning to dump
you.' He let the idea hang for a second. 'Even if your sales
numbers recently have been heading down faster than a
flaming 747.'

He tossed the book to Glen, who fumbled the catch
with nervous hands. It thudded against the floor. Glen
swallowed and stumbled to the chair. He flopped down,
gripping the arms to steady himself. Tom knew he had
him almost where he wanted him—the pantechnicon had
pulled into Paranoia Avenue. Now all he had to do was
move Glen into his new address.

'No, for me,' said Tom, snatching another handful of
mixed nuts, 'there's only one important question.'

'What?'

'Is Klinsch and McLeish big enough for Glen
Buchan…' he paused '…*and* Jane Lockhart?'

Tom studied Glen's face for a reaction. The author
had broken out in a red flush that was spreading rapidly
upwards from his throat. Glen squirmed in the chair, his
breath coming in frantic puffs.

'You're right,' he gasped, his eyes wide with fear. 'It's
either her…or me.'

Tom looked away to hide his smile of triumph. He
would congratulate Roddy later on what had turned out to
be a formidable plan. Klinsch & McLeish would be forced
to ditch Jane and she'd come back to him nicely miser-

able, novel in hand. Perhaps if she was suitably contrite he might just agree to publish novels three and four.

'Tom, I want *you* to publish me.'

That wasn't the plan. That was the *opposite* of the plan. Tom started to choke on a complimentary nut. Glen leapt up and hammered him helpfully on the back.

'You discovered me. I've always felt bad about not going with you at the time.'

Tom gagged. The heel of Glen's hand resounding against his back was only making it worse. He tried to tell him to stop, but the nut had lodged tight in his airway. His vision began to blur.

'As you rightly observed,' Glen went on with self-involved obliviousness, 'my deal with Klinsch & McLeish is up. Yes, my numbers are a little weaker than the good old days, but I'm still a strong seller. So what d'you say? Tom?'

Nothing! He could say nothing. He was choking to death on a nut, couldn't Buchan see?

And then suddenly he could breathe again.

Two things flew out of his mouth. The first was a half-chewed walnut; the second an emphatic '*Non.*'

The answer took them both by surprise.

Tom sucked in a few deep breaths. Had he really just turned down Glen Buchan? Dazed, he headed for the door.

'What d'you mean *non*?' Glen's anxiety was quickly replaced by righteous indignation. 'You can't say *non*.

Word is Tristesse Books is folding. Just one of my novels would turn it round, like that!' He clicked his fingers.

'I…I know,' said Tom quietly, continuing to make his way out.

'Don't you walk away from me, Duval. I swear, you take one more step and I'm moving to Penguin. I mean it.'

Tom exited the conservatory and trudged along the dim tartan corridor, Glen's voice ringing in his ears, at once strident and wounded. 'There's something else going on here, isn't there? Don't try to hide it—I'm a master of subtext, you know.'

CHAPTER 14

'Over the Rainbow', Eva Cassidy, 2001, Blix Street

JANE STARED FIXEDLY from the carriage window at the countryside as it sped past in a blur of green fields and industrial estates on the short hop between Glasgow and Edinburgh. She was on her way to meet Klinsch & McLeish, her new publishers. Well, they would be, as soon as she discharged her obligation to Tristesse and delivered her latest novel to Tom.

She'd left the flat that morning with Willie's objections ringing in her ears. He supported her move to the new publisher, but couldn't understand why she would do so without an agent. It was like taking a carrot to a knife-fight, he said.

Perhaps she would have signed with an agent if he hadn't gone on about it with such feverish enthusiasm. Since they'd met he'd been trying to push her onto his agent, Priscilla. You two would be great together, he said. Two strong, powerful women who know what they want and aren't afraid to get dirty in order to win. It felt less like he was setting her up with an agent and more like he was encouraging her to take part in some girl-on-girl mud wrestling.

Eventually she'd caved and agreed to a meeting. She took the train to London—Priscilla only ever came north for the Edinburgh Festival—and pitched up in Soho outside Clarion Creative Management's offices. Priscilla was out. Of the country. After that Willie stopped bugging her about agents.

Jane intended to sign with Klinsch & McLeish today, despite Willie, Priscilla, and especially Tom.

She stole a look at the middle-aged woman in a mother-of-the-bride dress occupying the seat beside her. She had boarded the train at Falkirk and stowed a giant handbag in the overhead rack, but not before removing a book from it. It was *Happy Ending*.

Last year when her novel had made the *Sunday Times* bestseller list, Jane, not unreasonably in her view, had jumped to a number of conclusions. One of which was that she'd see it everywhere. However, while bookstores displayed it prominently in their windows, she searched in vain for evidence of people reading it in the real world. And while the book climbed the charts it remained steadfastly invisible on buses and trains, and in the West End cafés she frequented. So during the eight weeks when she was a fixture on the chart she found herself using public transport more than usual and drinking a great deal of coffee across the city. Not that she was looking for people who'd bought her book. Obviously. That would have been hugely egotistical. OK. Maybe looking, just a little. But despite her survey, remarkably, there on the ten-thirty to Edinburgh Waverley was the very first time she'd come across someone reading *Happy Ending* in public.

She'd rehearsed the encounter a hundred times. In her imagination it went something like this.

Jane (dead casual): How's the book?

Perfect Reader: Unable to speak owing to overpowering emotion laid bare by novel and damp handkerchief clutched to mouth, utters a single moan that expresses her appreciation of writer's deep humanity, flawless plotting and vibrant characterisation.

Jane (modestly): Oh, I'm glad.

Perfect Reader: Reacts with questioning look that slowly brightens, like the dawning sun, into an epiphany of understanding, since she is Perfect Reader. Turns to cover, points wide-eyed to author's name. Are you…?

Jane (diffident nod): Well, yes.

In reality, Jane couldn't bring herself to make eye contact with the woman. What if she was crying? What if she *wasn't* crying? There was the flick of another page turning. Jane held her breath and strained to hear anything more indicative of the woman's state of mind. There was a whimper. Oh, good. She risked a glance. The woman was strangely quiet. But a Highland Terrier across the aisle whimpered again, begging for a bite of its owner's sausage roll. As Jane looked away disappointed her eye fell on the book. She couldn't help it. And then she found herself face to face with her reader.

'I'm her,' Jane blurted.

The woman gave a quizzical stare.

'Jane Lockhart,' she explained. 'I wrote the book.' Then, for the purpose of avoiding doubt, added, 'The book you're reading,'

'Oh.' The woman looked carefully from the cover photo of the crying girl and then to Jane, as if trying to establish some resemblance.

'Hope you're enjoying it,' Jane said, trying without success to keep the note of pleading from her voice.

'Oh,' repeated the woman. 'I don't know.'

Why not? Is there something wrong with you? Are you incapable of independent thought? Jane wanted to yell. Then noticed the woman's index finger holding her place a few pages into the book.

'Just started it?'

'Yes,' she said. 'I found it on the platform. Someone had left it on a bench.'

*

The train arrived at Waverley on time.

Jane scurried out of the station and, with an eye on the lowering clouds gathered over the castle, jumped into a taxi for the brief journey to Klinsch & McLeish's offices.

She paid the driver, checked the address, which she'd scribbled down on an old receipt, and slowly lifted her eyes to take in the impressive neo-classical façade before her.

Her new publisher occupied two elegant Georgian townhouses situated in the New Town. The main entrance was through an imposing black panelled door, a fan-light arched over it like a supercilious eyebrow. The door entry system was resolutely old school—a heavy brass knocker. She rapped twice, feeling like Macduff knocking at the gate in *Macbeth*, except that her murderous act had yet to be committed. Not long now, and Tom and Tristesse would be consigned to her past. Dead to her.

As she waited, she reflected on how easily Tom had let her go. Not that she'd have stayed, however hard he might have fought for her. But he hadn't. The door swung open and a pretty young woman with a sleek bob and a land-owning accent welcomed her in.

'Ms Lockhart, do please come in. I'm Dr Klinsch's assistant, Sophie.'

Sophie ushered her into a grand parlour overlooking a peaceful sunlit garden overflowing with white roses and deep-pink peonies, shaded by a grove of stately Scotch elms. The walls of the parlour were painted in one of those drowsy heritage greys and lined with bookshelves parading what Jane quickly realised was every edition of every book published by Klinsch & McLeish. Their distinctive red and white livery hadn't changed over the years, and the candy stripes contrasted the chalky walls.

She felt a spike of anticipation; her next novel would be published in one of these covers, and find its place in the continuum of great writing discovered and nurtured by the legendary Dr Klinsch and Mr McLeish.

They didn't make her wait long. True to her name, Klinsch marched up to Jane and flung her arms about her in a tight embrace. The good doctor was a small, boisterous woman with vivid blue eyes and perfect skin. She reputedly owed her complexion to a regime of bathing in the blood of debut authors who had 'disappointed her'.

'Welcome!' said Dr Klinsch, hugging Jane to her. 'Welcome to the family!'

'Thanks,' said Jane, slightly bewildered. 'Thank you so much.'

Just behind Klinsch the saturnine figure of Mr McLeish loped into the room, bony head bowed, hands clasped behind his back.

'Please excuse Dr Klinsch,' he said in a rich, bass rumble, 'she does have a tendency to pee her pants when we sign a new author.'

Dr Klinsch gave an indignant tut.

'That was one time,' she muttered.

They made small talk for a while, the publishers expressing their admiration for Jane's devastating talent and their delight at the imminent prospect of her elevation to the ranks of their authors. Jane responded with suitable modesty, but couldn't help thinking that in all the time they'd been together Tom had never praised her like that.

Not that she craved praise. Although, it would've been nice if he'd shown his appreciation once in a while.

Sophie returned carrying a tray with a bottle of champagne, three glasses and several copies of Jane's new contract. During the last few months she had scoured it from cover to cover, suggested a handful of alterations that Klinsch & McLeish had been only too happy to accommodate. It felt good to be listened to—made a refreshing change from dealing with Tom. Not to mention that the advance they were offering was generous. No less than you deserve, they'd said. Such thoroughly nice people.

Jane noticed the champagne glasses on the tray were old-fashioned saucers rather than flutes. Tom had half a dozen similar *coupes*, as he called them. They'd drunk from them the night before she discovered he'd changed her title. She shook herself and remembered where she was. Tom was her past. Today she would drink to her future.

'Klinsch & McLeish,' she said in an awed tone. 'I can't quite believe it. I'm going to be published in one of those classic red and white covers.' She caught herself. That sounded a bit shallow and she didn't want to be taken for a lightweight, not in this company. 'Obviously it's not just about the covers—but they *are* so pretty.' She really had to stop doing that. 'Your list is amazing too. I mean, you publish Glen Buchan.'

'Ah yes, Glen,' said McLeish. 'Fabulous writer, a prose alchemist, popular without being populist.'

Klinsch chimed in, expressing her high regard for their star author before adding, 'You know you have something in common.'

OK, that was more than she'd ever expected; they were comparing her to Glen Buchan. To Tom she'd been no more than a grafter. Well, ha! Stick that in your Gitanes and smoke it, Duval!

'Really? You think so? I mean, he's up there with McEwan and Byatt.'

An awkward glance passed between Klinsch and McLeish. 'Quite possibly. No, dear, what I mean is that you were both discovered by your former publisher.'

She hadn't been comparing her to Buchan after all. Jane felt her cheeks redden; no doubt they were now the same colour as one of the legendary covers.

'Tom discovered Glen Buchan?'

'It didn't last,' said McLeish with a dismissive wave. 'They had a terrible falling out and went their separate ways long before Glen's debut was published.' A smile slid across his thin face. 'By us.'

'Yeah,' said Jane. 'Sounds like Tom.'

'Anyway, enough of the past,' said Klinsch, producing a fountain pen. 'Here's to the future.'

With a gentlemanly flourish McLeish drew out a seat for Jane and spread the contract on the table before her.

Klinsch eased the pen into Jane's hand. The contract lay

open at the signature page. All she had to do was reach out and make her mark.

That was all.

'Blocked on this too?'

Darsie sat on the other side of the table, wearing a long, green silk gown with a lace neck, her hair hidden under a wimple. Stretching her long neck and angling her head to take advantage of imaginary footlights, she declaimed, 'I am in blood Stepped in so far that should I wade no more, Returning were as tedious as go o'er.' She grinned. 'What d'you think? If the romantic heroine thing doesn't work out, I'm thinking of a sideways move into tragedy.'

Jane was acutely aware that she'd frozen over the contract. She could feel Klinsch & McLeish's expectant gaze.

'Will you excuse us—*me*—for a moment?'

She had to get out of there and collect her thoughts. A splash of water would help. Klinsch pointed her along the corridor to the nearest bathroom. Avoiding their perplexed looks and apologising as she left, she hurried out.

Jane closed and locked the door. The bathroom was little bigger than a converted cupboard and painted a deep red that tricked her focus and made the room swim. She felt like she was standing inside a beating heart. Darsie leaned against the basin, leafing through a Klinsch & McLeish classic edition of *Macbeth*.

'It's funny, at the start I thought I was Lady Macbeth,' she said, 'but now I'm wondering if I'm Banquo's ghost at the feast, haunting you for your unforgiveable crime.'

'What crime?'

'Killing off Tom.'

'I'm not killing him off,' Jane objected. 'He's not a fictional character.'

Darsie planted a hand on her hip.

'Oh, so if he were fictional it'd be all right to snuff him out, yeah, is that what you're saying?'

'Yes,' said Jane. 'No.' She looked at herself in the bathroom mirror. 'I don't know. I'm leaving him. It's not the same thing.'

'He could've tried a bit harder to persuade you to stay.'

'Yes.'

'But he didn't.'

'No.' The red walls pulsed.

'You should ask him to help you. With the ending.'

Jane snorted. 'No way.'

'Why not? He's good at that stuff. Didn't he make *Happy Ending* a better novel?'

It was true. She'd given him a ragged manuscript full of stray commas and potential. He'd shaped her—*it*—into a novel. But she couldn't ask him for help—wouldn't—not after all that had happened. If she crawled back to him now he'd gloat and she couldn't bear the look on his smug, handsome face.

'I have a few ideas,' said Darsie. 'For the ending.'

Jane stiffened. 'You're giving me notes?'

'At least I'm trying to finish it. What are you doing—taking day trips?'

'I'm doing my best. It's just…hard.'

'Yes. Well, I've figured out what's going on.' Darsie adjusted her wimple. 'You can't write the last chapter because once it's done you'll have no reason to see Tom ever again.'

Jane paused and then let out a loud laugh.

'Jane, dear?' From outside the door came Dr Klinsch's concerned voice. 'Everything all right?'

'Yes. Fine,' she called. 'Be out in a minute.'

Jane opened both taps on the basin and rounded on Darsie. The running water muffled their conversation.

'In case you haven't noticed I'm about to go back in there and sign with a new publisher. Oh, and one more minor detail—I'm not writing my ending. I'm writing yours. And I'm not you.'

'No, of course not,' said Darsie. 'And your first novel wasn't a barely fictionalised account of your relationship with your father.' She smiled knowingly. 'Oh, and remind me, what's your middle name again? Jane *Darsie* Lockhart.'

'That means nothing,' she blustered. 'And anyway, I was thinking of changing your name. I…'

Deciding that arguing with her creation was a frustrating exercise that kept leading her back down the same dead end, Jane resorted to a more basic tactic. She shut her eyes and counted to five, then opened them again, hopefully.

'Still here,' said Darsie gleefully.

When she returned to the parlour it was to find Mr McLeish holding out the fountain pen and contract.

'Now then, young lady,' he said. 'All ready to go with a real publisher?'

Jane hesitated, at once unsure and excited. It was time to make up her mind. But really, was there anything to decide? As she reached for the proffered pen Dr Klinsch was already uncorking the champagne.

CHAPTER 15

'Rain, Rain Go Away', Bobby Vinton, 1962, EMI Columbia

THE AROMA OF viciously fried and battered fish filled the tiny kitchen. Tom sat gloomily at a pullout table watching Roddy bustle about in a black and white pinny that looked suspiciously like half of a kinky French maid's outfit, and a pair of oven gloves emblazoned with the line, 'souvenir of Arbroath'.

Tom reflected on the latest plan, not that there was much to reflect upon. It had nose-dived. Like the previous one. And not only had he failed to make her miserable, but he'd also lost her to Klinsch & McLeish.

He didn't want her back—she didn't want to stay—but knowing that there existed a piece of paper with her signature on it next to Klinsch & McLeish's felt like divorce, not separation. Sure, they were never going to reconcile, but until today the door had been open. Now it was shut and padlocked.

Roddy knelt at the oven, peered through a dark glass

door smeared with the burnt-on fat of a lifetime of reheated takeaways and ready meals, and made appreciative noises at two chunky paper-wrapped bundles inside. With the care of a *cordon bleu* chef he adjusted the oven temperature a notch. It was Thursday, and on Thursday dinner consisted of a couple of large fish suppers from Mario's.

The notion of a fish *supper* was peculiarly Scottish, considered Tom. Before he'd arrived in Glasgow the word 'supper' conjured for him a plate of food, flavours and textures distinct and in balance, beautifully seasoned, accompanied by a selection of appropriate side dishes, all perfectly cooked. Here, it meant fish. And chips. The latter dished up with what he could only describe as a shovel. It wasn't food; it was heavy artillery. He loved it.

Roddy shook his head gravely and for a moment Tom was sure that the fish suppers had gone the same way as yesterday's steak pie, which had ended its useful life as a burnt offering to the god of blocked arteries.

'You really turned down Glen Buchan?' Roddy collected cutlery from a grimy drawer, wiped it carefully on his sleeve and laid two place settings.

'I don't want to talk about it,' said Tom.

Roddy studied the wine rack, humming and hawing over his selection to complement tonight's repast, which puzzled Tom since there were only two bottles on the rack, and one of them was vodka.

'Call him,' said Roddy, sliding out a cheeky Chilean

Sauvignon Blanc. 'Tell him you made a mistake, that you'd be honoured to publish him. Then you can stop all this nonsense with Jane.'

Tom toyed with his knife. There was a stain of indeterminate origin on the stainless steel.

'But I don't want him. I can't publish Glen Buchan—I hate his writing.'

Roddy unscrewed the wine cap, making a 'pop' with his mouth as he did so, then filled two glasses.

'So, let me get this straight, you only take on writers you love?'

Tom wasn't falling for that one. '*Writing* I love.'

'How *intéressant*,' mused Roddy, ducking down to open a cupboard under the sink.

'No. No, it isn't. Now can we get back to making Jane miserable? I know, we could force her to read her Amazon page. Or make her go on a "Meet the Bloggers" tour.'

Roddy stood up holding a pair of silver candlesticks, yellow with tarnish. Two stubby ends of candles poked up from their holders. He placed them on the table next to a hulking ghetto blaster that appeared to have fallen through a wormhole from 1985. It wasn't obsolete technology, Roddy maintained, it was vintage.

'I could show her *the* review,' said Tom. Jane's debut had been greeted with overwhelming praise in every quarter, except one. The *London Review of Books* had dedicated a whole page to an excoriating review. Thankfully, the publication was subscription only and he'd destroyed the office copy before cancelling his own subscription. He was sure she'd never seen the offending article.

'You wouldn't,' said Roddy uneasily. 'Remember Keats.'

'Again with Keats!'

'One bad review finished him off. Never wrote again. You want Jane melancholy, not rocking in a corner staring at the wall.'

Roddy shared out the fish suppers from the oven and sat down.

He dimmed the overhead light, struck a match and lit the candles. A soft glow suffused the room. He stabbed the big plastic play button on the ghetto blaster's tape deck and Scottish sadcore drifted across the table.

Tom was suddenly aware that the room had taken on a romantic ambience. He looked slowly from the candle-sticks to his friend. 'You know,' he said. 'One of us really needs to get laid.'

There was a crinkle of paper as Roddy unwrapped his supper. He glanced up with an expression of yearning.

'Oh god, yeah.'

They ate quickly, talking through mouthfuls of orange haddock and salty chips.

Tom paused, a forkful midway to his mouth.

'OK, here's a thought.' He made tiny brooding circles with the fork. 'We could kill her dog.'

Roddy looked confused. 'I didn't know she had a dog.'

Tom waved the fork meaningfully. 'She doesn't. We could buy her one…and then kill it.'

Roddy gave an uneasy glance.

'It wouldn't be a cute dog,' Tom said, not altogether reassuringly.

Roddy swallowed a bite. 'You don't think that's a bit, how can I put this…' He paused. 'Psychotic?'

But Tom wasn't listening; another idea had sprung from the first.

'You're right, she hasn't got a dog.' He grinned darkly. 'But she does have a screenwriter.'

The fork made more lazy circles as he figured out a plan. He'd tried to sabotage Jane's career, but that had failed. It was time to get personal. Her relationship with Willie was a pillar of her life; if he could topple it then she was sure to descend into melancholy.

Roddy looked alarmed. 'I'm not helping you kill Willie Scott.'

His voice was a distant buzz. This would work, Tom decided. Willie would fall. He must.

'It's simple, really. Willie is patently out for all he can get from Jane. He's inveigled his way into her life, moved into her flat, and has persuaded her to let him adapt her novel even though a brief look at his résumé demonstrates how ill-suited he is to the task.' Disappointment kindled into determination. 'All we have to do is open Jane's eyes. She will see that she's with a man who doesn't care for her beyond what he can extract from her talent. She will end it with him and be left miserable and alone. The perfect combination to get her writing again.'

Roddy chewed thoughtfully. 'But if you've proved he was so terrible for her then why would she be miserable about ending it?'

Tom shrugged. 'Everyone is miserable after a break-up.'

'Like when you and Jane broke up?'

'How many times must I say it? We never broke up because we were never *together*. But just for that I'm eating your chips.' He reached over and, ignoring Roddy's protests, grabbed a handful from his plate.

He ground the hot chips between his teeth. He couldn't stop her getting together with Klinsch & McLeish, but he was damn well going to make sure she dumped Willie Scott.

*

A red double-decker bus threaded its way through the city centre, circled George Square half a dozen times and then headed east towards its final destination in Bridgeton. Tom had chartered the bus at great expense for the launch of Nicola Ball's latest, *Death of a Conductor*, and he intended to get his money's worth. The bus side was emblazoned with a suitably moody poster advertising the novel: an image of a lonely, rain-streaked bus shelter, and the terse log-line: *Stop Means Stop*.

On the upper deck Tom guided Nicola through a round

of interviews with print journalists and literary bloggers. The questions were always the same. Is it based on real life? How much are you like the main character? Listening to her answers, he wasn't sure if Nicola was selling herself or her book, and more to the point, whether these days there was a difference.

He didn't organise a public launch for all of his authors—most of them weren't great in public, either too easily flustered or, frankly, staggeringly dull—but Nicola was young and pretty and at ease in front of a microphone.

'I'd like to talk about the character of the conductor's widow,' began the literary editor of *The Scotsman*. 'Now, your own mother was widowed in a tragic bus accident…'

Tom tuned out. Jane Lockhart had also suffered from this line of questioning. Too many readers believed what she did was simply raid her family archives and dump her feelings onto the page. But there was so much more art to her writing than that and in his opinion Jane hadn't received nearly enough credit for the alchemy she performed in transforming reality into fiction. With a twinge of regret he remembered that he was one of those who had never said it to her.

The big depot doors rattled apart and the bus grumbled through into a vast shed lined with commercial vehicles decked out in the bright corporate liveries of half a dozen Scottish operators. Corinthian radiator grilles of Leyland Lions and Albion Valiants shone in serried ranks along each wall. The punchline to the joke that began 'How do you lose a ten-ton bus?' was right here.

They came to a halt with a squeal of air brakes at the edge of a crowd of invited guests. Tom turned his attention from Nicola to look out the long window. In a space set aside for the event, waiters ferried trays of sparkling wine and canapés between small knots of people significantly overdressed for a Friday afternoon in Bridgeton. He had sent Jane an invitation to the launch, signing it from Nicola in order to ensure her presence. He searched the gathering and saw that his ruse had worked. She was here, and she'd brought Willie. In Roddy's suburban commando speak, the plan was 'good to go'.

Tom frowned. As well as her useless boyfriend Jane had also brought cupcakes. She balanced the array of sickly coloured treats on a tray.

He disembarked and addressed the guests, saying a few words about Nicola's prodigious talent, which made the young writer well up (a glance at Jane confirmed that his praise had elicited a pleasing shade of green from her, or perhaps it was just the reflection of the coachwork on the Glasgow Corporation omnibus she was standing beside).

He toasted his young charge and passed her into Sophie Hamilton Findlay's capable hands. When she was safely ensconced behind a tower of hardbacks at the signing table, Tom snagged another glass of wine from a passing waiter and prepared to initiate the plan, which Roddy had bestowed with the name 'Kill Will'.

'Ah, the number 15 to Meiklewood.' Roddy ambled up and cast a wistful look at the destination board on the front of a green and white sixty-seater. He creased his brow. 'Where the fuck's Meiklewood?'

Tom ignored him. He tracked Jane through the crowd as she passed out cakes from her tray. 'She's still baking,' he said sullenly.

Roddy held up his fingers in the sign of the Cross. 'Back, cupcakes of Satan!'

'You don't understand,' said Tom. 'Baking is bad. Baking is the writer's dirty little secret. First, it involves lots of time-consuming measuring and many, many bowls. Then they have to keep checking the oven so they can't possibly write anything in between, and clearing up all those bowls takes ages. Before you know it, the afternoon has disappeared. But, most importantly, people eat their cake and instantly appreciate what they've done. So, although they've written absolutely nothing all day, it makes them feel productive.'

Roddy shook his head. 'Devious bastards.' He took a sip of wine and glanced at Nicola. 'Though she's a nice kid. Bet she doesn't know one end of a slotted spoon from the other.'

Tom frowned. 'Surely it's obvious.'

'Well, yes, but…I was just trying to make a point. About Nicola not being a devious baker.'

'I'm not even sure you use a slotted spoon in baking.'

'All right! God, I really don't care. I was just remarking

upon what I perceive to be the amiability of Nicola Ball. *Nice kid*.'

'Kid? She's not much younger than you.'

'Yeah, but you know. I'm a man of the world, me. I couldn't see myself with a girl like that.' His voice rose to a strangled pitch. 'Could you?

'No,' agreed Tom, barely listening.

Roddy tutted. 'Thanks. Thanks very much.'

'What did I say?'

His eyes widened. 'She's coming over. Don't look!'

'Roddy, what the hell are you on about?'

'Tom?' Nicola stood before him, a hand on one hip, an indignant flash in her eye.

'Yes, Nicola?'

'I was just propositioned by Tiny Tim's Crutch.'

'That's disgusting,' sputtered Roddy.

'It's the name of a literary blog,' Tom explained.

'Oh.' He lowered his head and took another sip of wine.

Nicola was still cross. 'He's a pervert. And not in a good way. He's the one who mailed me his socks. I don't know why you invited him.' She huffed. 'I hate these things.'

'Yes,' said Roddy, clearly unable to stop himself, 'I prefer the old Routemaster Two Seven Six Oh, myself.'

Nicola and Tom turned slowly to face him.

'It's a bus joke,' he shrugged. 'Sorry.'

Tom was about to change the subject when Nicola piped up. 'No, no, I get it,' she said gazing at him. 'It's just, I've never met anyone *else* who made a bus joke before.'

Tom watched in disbelief as the two of them stood in a silence full of potential. Roddy and Nicola? What was happening here?

'Typical,' said Roddy, gawping at Nicola, 'you wait a century for a vintage bus…'

'Then ninety-three of them come along at once,' she finished.

Both of them smiled.

So bewildered was Tom by the romance blooming before his eyes that he almost missed Willie wandering off from Jane's side. She was on her own. Now was the time to strike.

'OK. Here goes.' He drained the glass and thrust it at Roddy, adding with a smirk, 'Don't forget the golden rule.'

'Bollocks to that,' Roddy snapped back. 'I'm not her publisher, remember?'

'What's the golden rule?' Nicola asked innocently.

'Uh, nothing.'

'And if you break it,' she smiled coyly, 'do you get punished?'

Roddy swallowed hard.

With a bemused puff of his cheeks, Tom struck off into the crowd.

'Hello, Jane.' He shot out of the press of people like a shark after a particularly succulent seal.

'What do you want?'

He snatched a cupcake from her tray and took a bite.

'I'll tell you what I don't want,' he mumbled through a mouthful of sponge, screwing up his face and slapping the half-eaten cake back on the tray. 'I don't want a cupcake.'

He flicked a nod towards Willie, holding court amidst a clique of pretty young women in dark, tailored suits. 'I wonder what the collective noun for a group of publicity girls might be? A release? A puff?'

'A buzz,' said Jane.

He snapped his fingers. 'Very good. See, not so stuck for words after all.'

She threw him a reproachful look. Which was good, he thought, since in order for his plan to work he had to aggravate Jane to the point where she would take action. Roddy had informed him, rather unkindly he maintained, that he would have little trouble accomplishing that particular feat.

'So...' he said, commencing his attack, 'two writers living under the same roof, how's that working out? I imagine it's *fantastic*: sharing ideas, the ebb and flow of discussion. Willie must be...a great boon.'

He could see immediately that Jane didn't recognise the description of her boyfriend.

'Yes. Yes he is,' she said.

It was a game attempt to cover her unease. Emboldened, he pressed on. 'And what does the Big Man make of the new novel?'

'Uhh…'

'You're right—it's not fair to ask you.' He started to move off. 'I should ask him.'

A look of panic flashed across Jane's face and she shot out a hand across his path. 'He loves it,' she said quickly. 'Just loves it.'

Tom saw in her expression that she knew she'd over-sold Willie's unconditional ardour. She attempted to shore up the lie. 'Naturally, he has notes.'

'Naturally.'

He signalled to a passing waitress and plucked two more glasses of wine from her tray, offering one to Jane, who declined with a brusque shake of her head.

'A *buzz* of publicity girls,' he repeated in an admiring tone.

There was another phrase on the tip of his tongue; a French one. He had lived here so long that his native tongue sounded odd in his own head, showing up like an unexpected member of the family. The British had adopted this phrase, perhaps, he speculated, because it was a peculiarly French concept.

He was about to deliver the *coup de grâce.*

He touched the glass to his lips, felt the cold wine and then the prick of bubbles on his tongue.

'Willie has not asked to read one single page of your novel, has he?'

A gratifying red flush coloured Jane's throat. 'He's…he's very busy with his screenplay.'

'Ah yes, the adaptation. How's that going?'

'Terrific. It's going terrific…ly.'

He gave a small laugh. 'You don't know, do you? He doesn't discuss it with you.'

She was irritated now. 'What's your point?'

'He's using you.' He was aware that his voice had grown loud. Roddy had cautioned him not to shout and he knew it wouldn't help to get angry. He tried concentrating on his breathing. It sounded like an angry rasp.

'Using me? That's rich, coming from *you*.'

'Oh, come on,' he fumed. 'I checked and the last script of his someone actually made was an episode of *Rain Town*.'

'There's nothing wrong with writing a soap,' she said defensively, though evidently a tad embarrassed. 'And it was the Christmas episode.'

Why was she with this waste of space screenwriter? Tom wondered. Never mind what *he* thought about Willie, why would she do this to herself? She drove him insane. Out of the corner of one eye he was aware of Roddy shaking his head in a warning—don't lose it, don't lose it.

Too late. He lost it.

'Willie Scott's writing career peaked sometime around 1998,' he raged. 'He is a talentless hack without a brain or conscience who doesn't give a damn about you. Even your novel has become about him!'

The last syllable of his tirade sailed down the long line of buses and echoed back from the depot wall at the far end. An appalled silence descended over the party guests. A lone speaker, aware that his voice was the only one in the room, swiftly petered out.

Even the smiles of the publicity girls froze on their shining faces. Willie emerged from their midst, his expression twisted into a grimace, and marched over.

Tom opened his arms in a gesture of conciliation. 'Hey. Big Man. No harm done.'

Willie didn't break stride.

Tom swallowed. 'Yet.'

'Willie, no!' yelled Jane, but it was too late.

Willie dipped his right shoulder and then his fist split the air. There was a crunch of bone as the punch landed against Tom's cheek. As his head snapped round he glimpsed Jane's horrified expression, which gave him a fleeting sensation of pleasure, right before someone turned out all the lights.

*

He dreamt he was aboard the number 15 bus to Meiklewood. In the dream Jane was driving. She looked cute in a peaked cap. Roddy and Nicola were a couple of school kids kissing in the back seats. He was ordering them to stop, quoting reams of what sounded like bus company policy. In the dream he looked down to see he was wearing a jacket with a column of polished brass but-

tons and his hands clutched a ticket machine. He was the
bus conductor. Alarmed, he glanced at Nicola. She smiled
wickedly. He knew how this novel ended.

Jane jerked the steering wheel, the bus swerved and he
lost his balance. The force of the turn flung him through
the open rear door, tumbling out onto the road. As the hard
tarmac filled his vision he felt something cold and solid
against his forehead.

Tom sat up with a start. He was on the open top deck of
one of the buses in the now empty depot. Below, waiters
cleared away the remains of the launch party. In the seat
beside him Jane sat holding a cake to his forehead, lending
weight to his suspicion that he had yet to wake up from the
dream.

'Is that fruitcake?' he ventured.

'Yes,' said Jane.

'I detest fruitcake.'

'Frozen.' She rapped it against the seat in front to dem-
onstrate. 'It's for your head.' She pressed it there again.

He winced.

'I'm sorry about Willie. He shouldn't have hit you, even
though you did deserve it.'

'He caught me off guard. Usually I don't go down after
the first punch.' Tom considered his chequered past; it
wasn't the first time he'd provoked a jealous boyfriend
to violence. 'Usually it's about the third or fourth.' Still
dazed, he looked around, taking in the open deck. 'How
did I get here?'

Jane continued to tend to his injury. 'I made Willie carry you.'

Tom recoiled. 'No you didn't.'

'What's wrong now?' she sighed.

'It's not very manly…' he complained, 'being carried upstairs by another bloke.' Then an unmanly thought occurred to him. 'He's not still here, is he?'

'Relax. I sent him out—to cool off.'

He glanced down, noticing her handbag open on the floor. 'What's the capital of Ethiopia?' Was not what he intended to say, but he'd been distracted by the book poking from the top of her bag. He took it out.

'*1001 Tricky Trivia Questions*? What's this for? Your dad hasn't…?' He liked Benny Lockhart. He hadn't wanted to, knowing how he'd walked out on Jane, but Benny had turned out not to be the monster he'd built up in his head. He was a hard man who'd softened around the edges, and he carried a burden in the sacks beneath his eyes; a taciturn man, animated only when talking about Jane, or his beloved pub quiz. Next to his daughter it was the most important thing in the world to Benny. What *was* the capital of Ethiopia? That was going to niggle him. Tom looked into Jane's face. '*You're* on the team?'

'We're in the finals, actually.'

Tom swayed in his seat still woozy from his battering. Jane reached out to steady him. He felt her hand touch him. It was a good feeling to be here with her like this.

'Jane. There's something I need to tell you. Something I've never said before…'

He was finding it difficult to focus and currently there appeared to be two Janes, both of them annoyed. He knew he had a plan—something devious and clever he was sure—but at that moment he couldn't remember exactly what it involved. He didn't know what he was going to say next, which felt oddly freeing. And a little dangerous.

'Ah, no. No I…what I meant to say was…is…*Happy Ending*…at the end, when things became…y'know… with us and the title and…I never told you…the book. It's good.' This was going really well. He was fascinated to hear what he had to say next. 'No, it's…better than that. It's like *la musique triste*. The saddest music I've ever heard.'

He could sense something in the air between them like a charge before a lightning storm. In that split second he felt connected. To everything. The world spun on a shifting axis, the poles flipped. The moment surged with possibility.

'What the hell was that?' Jane stood up abruptly. Her expression curdled, as if she'd swallowed something nasty. She took a wary step back into the aisle. 'What are you up to, Duval?'

'I'm not up to anything,' he protested, just as it all flooded back to him. Kill Will. Ah, *oui*. So, yes, technically she was quite correct. He was up to something, had invited her here expressly in order to be up to something.

But not just then. What he'd said about her novel, he meant it.

'All this "It's like sad music" crap, and trying to put doubts in my head about Willie.'

He could see she was reaching for something to unlock his odd behaviour.

'Why would you do that…? Unless…' A fog lifted. 'Oh, wait a minute, I know why. I'm onto your little scheme.'

Oh, shit. 'You are?'

Her mouth coiled into a smirk as she delivered her brilliant deduction. 'You want me back.'

He unclenched. She was off target. *Way off* target. But he could tell that she believed she'd scored a direct hit and ploughed on.

'Well, if you can hear me through the obvious concussion, pay attention.' She paused, winding up for a big finish. 'It's. Never. Going. To. Happen.'

He laughed. Couldn't keep the derision out of his voice. The very idea!

Hang on.

'I have a concussion?'

She flung out a finger pointing to the stairs. 'Off. Get off this bus.'

He swayed to his feet and took an exploratory step into the aisle, testing his balance. The deck seemed to rock like a sailing ship in distress. He locked onto Jane's angry face, in part for a fixed point to steer by.

'You really think I'd want you back…?' he said. 'Why? Why would I do that to myself? You're distant at the best of times and when you're writing you're utterly self-absorbed. Sometimes I thought your characters were more real to you than I was.'

Curiously, at that moment he saw Jane jump, then turn and direct a low whisper at an empty seat. The girl clearly needed help. Well, she could find it from someone else.

'So, no, Jane,' he said, walking away. 'I do not want you back.'

CHAPTER 16

'It's Raining Again', Supertramp, 1982, A&M

JANE COULDN'T CONCENTRATE and it was all Tom's fault. Back at her desk early the following morning she kept replaying yesterday's events in her mind. All of those hurtful things he had said about Willie. She ought to be annoyed. She had a right to be angry.

How dare he meddle in her life; she wasn't his girl-friend any more. Soon she wouldn't even be his author. She wasn't his anything. But truthfully it wasn't anger she was feeling it was—what was the word? Melancholy. And not because of Willie. So why did she feel like this? Why was Belle & Sebastian playing inside her head? It couldn't be because Tom said he didn't want her back. No, that was ridiculous. She pushed it from her mind.

Grudgingly, she'd taken a piece of his advice on break-ing her block and had turned to the classics. Who bet-ter to inspire her than the finest author named Jane ever to put pen to paper? Jane Austen. She remembered read-ing somewhere that Austen spent seventeen years drafting and redrafting *Pride and Prejudice*; but then she probably didn't have an angry French publisher breathing down her neck.

The wall clock showed seven o'clock. Willie didn't usually rise before half past. She took a deep breath and relaxed, enjoying the stillness.

'It is a truth universally acknowledged that a young author in the midst of her sophomore novel must be in want of an ending.'

Darsie swept into the living room wearing a white Empire line shift dress, long silk evening gloves, her hair in a soft chignon exposing a flash of nape.

'I see number nineteen has been let,' she said, lowering herself demurely into a seat and folding her hands in her lap.

Jane frowned. 'Number nineteen?'

Darsie inclined her head. 'Opposite the chippy.' She played with her gloves and added in a Heritage Drama accent, 'We ought to pay a call.'

'I'm sure there's a good reason why you're dressed like Elizabeth Bennet–'

'Oh,' interrupted Darsie, disappointed. 'I was going for Kate Winslet as Marianne Dashwood.'

'Of course you were.' Jane leaned back in her chair. 'OK, so what's the big idea?'

Darsie cleared her throat. 'Jane Austen is the greatest writer in English, of all time, right?'

'No argument from me.'

'So, if you could write a book half as brilliant as one of hers, you'd be pleased.'

'Half would be arrogant. I'd take an eighth. A sixteenth.'

A smile flickered across Darsie's lips and quickly vanished; Jane recognised it as the expression of someone who had just pulled off a clever conversational manoeuvre.

'Well, all of the heroines in her novels have one thing in common.'

Jane guessed what was coming next half a second before Darsie said it.

'They all have happy endings,' Darsie declared triumphantly. 'So, if it's good enough for Jane Austen then it should be good enough for Jane Lockhart.'

Jane suppressed a chuckle. On some level she was aware that this conversation existed entirely inside her deranged mind, but Darsie seemed so real. Large as life and twice as persuasive. Perhaps she was right; maybe her story would end up happily ever after. In all honesty, Jane didn't yet know.

She looked down at the open book she'd pulled from the shelf. It was *Persuasion*, her favourite of Austen's six novels. Anne Elliot breaks off her engagement to Captain Wentworth, then years later they meet again and, finally, are married. On the face of it a happy ending, except that it wasn't that simple. But for a terrible mistake the lovers could have been together years earlier, and the shadow of that lost lifetime hangs over the ending. As does another loss. It was Austen's last complete novel before she died, aged forty-one, and for Jane Lockhart, *Persuasion* would always be suffused with unutterably sad endings.

She read a few more chapters and set the book aside. With dismay she realised that if Jane Austen couldn't help her she was screwed.

Willie bounced into the room, black coffee in hand, eyes shining with anticipation as he lowered himself into his chair and strapped himself in for blast-off, his relish for work undimmed by fisticuffs in bus depots. Abruptly, a fresh sheet of paper was led out like the accused, fastened to the platen, blindfolded with a ribbon and summarily dispatched in a fusillade of struck keys.

Jane's eye drifted back to the blinking cursor on her empty page. It was too early to make an excuse and leave the flat and she didn't feel like baking. The conversation with Tom came back to her like a bony finger poking her in the ribs. *The adaptation. He doesn't discuss it with you.* She was annoyed at herself for allowing him inside her head.

'So, how's the screenplay coming along?' she enquired gently.

Willie continued to type. 'Hmm?'

'Your screenplay? I was just thinking we haven't really discussed it much…at all…and since, well, I wrote the novel, maybe I could, y'know…' She plucked one of her

editing pencils from its holder and underlined her suggestion in the air. 'What I mean is, we should have more ebb
and flow.'

Willie paused for what seemed an age, pursing his lips
in contemplation.

'That's not a bad idea,' he said at last, nodding.

Jane felt a weight lift, a sudden sense of vindication
sweeping over her. Ha! Tom Duval. Ha! In your fuzzy
face! Shows what you know. My screenwriter boyfriend
and I are going to sit here and have a far-reaching discussion about his adaptation of my novel. We are together.
We are *as one*.

'You know that scene in the book where her father
goes on a bender and doesn't show up for the mother's
funeral?' Willie shuffled the pages of his screenplay, finding the relevant section.

Of course she did. Jane lost herself in the awful memory
of that day. 'Yes. I remember,' she said quietly.

Willie propped his spectacles on his forehead. 'Would
you miss it?'

Her mouth flapped. It was a key scene, a devastating
moment in her life and her fiction. If he was messing with
that, what the hell else was he doing to her book?

'What? You can't—Willie, I think we need to talk this
through.'

'I know what this is about,' he said in a voice of irritating calm.

'I really don't think that–'

'You haven't written a word in two weeks so you want to talk instead of dealing with your blockage.'

'How many times, I am not blocked.'

He stroked his chin. 'This writer I knew on *Rain Town* got stuck on a Long-Lost Sibling story arc. Thought it would end his career, but he beat it.'

She knew she should have pressed him on what other drastic changes he was making to her novel, but he was offering a potential cure. She cursed herself for asking. 'How?'

He raised an eyebrow. 'Wrote naked.'

'Yeah, right.'

'Seriously.' He leaned in, resting his arms on the desk and fixing her with a meditative gaze. 'Being naked you release yourself from the restrictions of the everyday so that you can express your ideas in an uninhibited fashion.'

She wasn't buying it. 'Uh-huh. You just want to be able to sit there and write while you stare at my tits.'

He grinned. 'They *are* great tits.'

*

The excitement began after lunch. Willie had insisted on taking her out to the Ubiquitous Chip for a quick bite of baked parmesan custard with anchovy toast; his way of apologising for the 'crude remark about her tits'. The quick bite had turned into a lazy lunch. Jane's sclerotic progress with the last chapter ensured she was in no hurry to return to the flat, and Willie was on good form, displaying his usual mix of crude humour and flashes of boyish vulnerability. She laughed a lot around him when he was like this; it reminded her why they were together in the first place. It was sometime after 3 o'clock, over cheese and tequila, that the call came in from his agent.

Willie examined the phone. He was an analogue guy and the touchscreen was his bane. In his eagerness to answer he stabbed at it, inadvertently putting the call on speaker.

'I have Priscilla Hess for you,' chirped an assistant at Clarion Creative Management.

There was the click of a connection being made during which Jane watched Willie straighten in his chair. His expression swung between hope and dread. He was like this every time she called. Priscilla brought tidings from the wide world of showbiz. It could be a request for a meeting from some hot director or a new screenplay commission. However, in the time she'd known him he hadn't received one of those calls. It was always the other side of the coin: a producer passing on one of his pitches, the heart-sickening thud of rejection.

'Willie,' said a clipped female voice from the phone. It sounded as if she was in traffic.

'Priscilla,' said Willie with forced bonhomie. Jane knew he just wanted her to deliver the news fast, and if it was bad that it not spoil his lunch. She felt stirrings of sympathy. 'How ya doing?'

'I'm in LA. Thought you were in town.'

Willie cleared his throat with an awkward cough. 'Not for a while, Priscilla. I'm on the *Happy Ending* script, remember?'

There was a pause that might have been a transatlantic time delay, but which Jane had a feeling was Priscilla deciding whether or not to bother lying that she did recollect what her low-level client was working on.

'You'll be getting a call today about a new project.'

'Oh yeah?' He adjusted his grip on the phone.

'From Fox.'

He fumbled the handset, which fell into the dregs of an espresso granita. 'Shit.'

'Willie?'

He bellowed into the speaker as he retrieved the phone. 'I'm here. Right here. Did you say Fox?' He shook off the coffee drips. '*Twentieth Century* Fox?'

There was a sigh from the other end of the line. 'One piece of advice,' offered Priscilla.

'Yes?'

'Don't fuck it up.'

The line went dead. Willie lowered the phone and looked at Jane, his anxiety melting away like warm granita, replaced by a youthful grin.

They headed back to the flat immediately. He wanted to prepare for the call: throw a few punches at the speedbag, centre himself with a spot of yogic breathing. Jane was curious why Priscilla hadn't imparted more details. What was the new project about, for instance? She hadn't forgotten their earlier conversation in which he'd all but confessed to perpetrating a wholesale rewrite of her novel and despite the nice lunch there was a part of her that hoped the answer to her question, 'will you have to go to LA?' would be a big, fat 'yes'.

'Don't worry about that, Janey,' said Willie, putting an arm round her. '*Happy Ending* is my number one priority. Until I write Fade Out, The End, it's all about your novel. Well, my adaptation.'

'Oh. Good,' she said, trusting that in his excitement he wouldn't notice her lack of enthusiasm.

The call came just before four-thirty. Willie would usually have been returning from his daily run in the park about then, so he was fizzing with pent-up energy when the withheld number flashed up. He put the phone on speaker and began to pace back and forth in front of his desk.

'Mr Scott?' an American voice blared out.

'Mr Fox!' said Willie and then grimaced. 'I mean, you're the guy from Fox, right? Not Mr Fox. He'll be the boss I'm guessing.'

He glanced over at Jane who was holding her head in her hands.

'Yeah. So, Mr Scott—Willie—let me get right to it. Our senior development executive has been looking for a screenwriter with a distinctive voice for a very special project we have slated for next year.'

Willie shot an excited glance at Jane.

She motioned him to keep cool.

'Oh aye?' he swaggered.

She motioned again: OK, not that cool.

'Aye—' said the voice.

Jane puzzled for a moment; she could have sworn that the West Coast LA accent had slipped into the West Coast of Scotland variety.

'I mean…yeah.' The twang returned. 'And when she heard you were adapting Jane Lockhart's *Happy Ending*, she was excited.' The voice rose an octave. 'We were all excited.'

'I'm excited,' Willie beamed. 'But it's not just adaptations—I have original material, too.'

'That's terrific,' enthused the voice.

It was clear to Jane from the way he oversold it that the LA movie executive couldn't give two hoots about Willie's original material.

'You can share all that with our senior VP…uh… Bob…and our deputy head of acquisitions…Www… Wanda…? Vonda. Yeah, Vonda. They're flying over this Friday. You live in London, right?'

'Mainly,' lied Willie. 'I have a place upcountry too,' he dropped in casually.

'Well, apologies, it may involve dragging you out to the middle of nowhere. We're scouting Steven's next pic.'

Willie perked up and Jane had a premonition about what was about to come out of his mouth.

Don't say it, she willed him. Don't say it.

'Steven?' Willie shifted the phone to his other hand. 'Steven Segal?'

Jane winced.

'Uh, no.' The voice dripped with disapproval. 'Soderbergh. He'll probably drop by and say hi. If that's OK?'

So-der-bergh, mouthed Willie excitedly. 'Aye, that'd be OK,' he said, endeavouring to make it sound like he and Stevie were always bumping shopping trolleys in Whole Foods.

'I'm sending you the itinerary. See you Friday, Mr Scott. Looking forward to meeting you.'

'Likewise. Can't wait to meet you, *bubeleh*.'

There was a click and the call ended.

'*Bubeleh*?' asked Jane.

Willie shook his head. 'I have no idea.' He walked briskly round to her side of the desk and pulled her to him. His eyes shone with excitement. 'Jane, I think this might be it. The big one.'

'I thought *Happy Ending* was the big one,' she said with a note of chagrin.

'Well, yeah. Obviously it is *a* big one,' Willie back-pedalled, 'but, c'mon, *Soderbergh*. We're talking Hollywood royalty and indie cred up the wazoo.' He studied his phone, as if some residue of the call lingered; it was no longer a mere handset, it was a relic through which the deity had spoken to him. 'I've been waiting my whole career for that call.' He looked up. 'You should come.'

'I don't think so.'

'C'mon, we'll make a trip of it. I'll book us a nice hotel, we'll take in a show, all that tourist bollocks.'

She kissed him, saying it was a lovely offer, but this trip was about him; he needed to focus without any unnecessary distraction. She didn't say that the prospect of a few days alone in her flat was making her turn whooping cartwheels in her head. Laughing with him over lunch, now eager to see the back of him, she was aware that her feelings for Willie pinballed from one moment to the next. It was exhausting.

*

Willie spent the remainder of the week working on his treatments: the original film ideas he'd mentioned on the call with LA. He explained to Jane that it wasn't enough simply to walk into the room and talk to these guys—they were used to a show. He stalked about the flat practising his pitch. He put on voices, injected meaningful pauses, even threw in a few props. When he was satisfied that he had it down pat he turned his attention to the other part of the sell. Movie execs had notoriously short attention spans, he told Jane, so it was important to grab them with what he called a 'log-line'; a pithy phrase that encapsulated the movie in twenty-five words or less.

'OK, OK, here it is.'

Jane was staring out of the window wondering about dinner when he rushed breathlessly into the living room clutching a sheaf of pages. This would make it the sixth occasion that afternoon; on each he had presented her with a log-line more honed and polished than the last. They were all for the same movie idea, which, as far as she could tell from his excitable description, involved a World War Two tank division battling occult forces through France after D-Day.

Willie cleared his throat. He waved a hand, painting an imaginary cinema marquee: 'Demons.' He paused for dramatic effect. 'In tanks.' He beamed. 'What d'you think?'

'Well,' Jane began. 'It's definitely shorter than the last one.'

His face crumpled. 'You hate it.'

'I don't hate it. It's just, maybe I'm not the best person to judge a film about possessed tanks.'

'Fair point.' He shuffled the pages. 'OK, OK, try this one.' He flicked the new top sheet with the back of his hand. 'A tight-knit family makes a desperate bid to escape the clutches of a totalitarian regime during a talent competition.' Another meaningful pause. 'On Mars.'

'Right,' she said, mystified.

He elaborated. 'It's kind of *Alien* meets *The Sound of Music*.'

Jane couldn't help herself. 'So…in space no one can hear you yodel?'

'Oh, very bloody amusin'.' He scowled, then fell silent, clearly mulling what she'd said. He piped up. 'Can I use that?'

Friday rolled around. Willie was booked on the first shuttle to Heathrow. He stood by the window looking anxiously for his cab, about to call the dispatcher when it pulled up out of the pre-dawn murk.

'That's me, Janey. I'm off.' He snatched a single piece of carry-on luggage and hurried out of the room.

'Hey, what about my kiss?' she said sleepily. She was still in her pyjamas and planned to go back to bed as soon as he'd gone. Tonight was the pub quiz final and she needed to rest up. Until the phone call from LA, Willie had planned to be there to support her. Not that she minded, but he hadn't said anything about missing it. She suspected that in all the excitement about his trip it had simply slipped his mind.

He trotted back into the living room, dropped his case and took her in his arms. His lips brushed hers.

'Go,' she said when the kiss had ended.

He gazed at her fondly. 'In a second.' He stroked her hair. 'Jane, this is an important trip for me. These guys are working with Soderbergh. And they called me. That just never happens.'

'Yeah, you're right, it doesn't,' she agreed. Something about the phone call had been bothering her. Maybe that was it.

'And it's all because of you,' said Willie. 'Truth is, I'd never have got their attention if I wasn't adapting your novel.'

'Oh, rubbish. You're a great writer.'

Willie thought for a moment. 'Aye, you're right.' He gathered his case and started for the door.

Jane remembered something and crossed quickly to her desk. She picked up a large buff envelope and hurried after him.

'Willie. Here.' She held out the envelope.

'What's this?' he asked suspiciously.

'Relax, it's not a court summons,' she said, mildly aggrieved. 'It's my novel.' She waggled her head. 'Well, the first thirty chapters. You could read it on the plane, and if you have any thoughts, notes, y'know...'

'Aye. Terrific.' He took the envelope and stuffed it unceremoniously into his bag. The door clicked shut behind him and he was gone.

Jane stood for a while listening to the sound of the empty flat then turned on her heel and padded back to her bedroom.

'Charming,' said Darsie, who lay stretched out on the bed like some starlet, clad in a gauzy red silk dressing gown, hidden behind an eye-mask. She lifted one corner of the mask. 'He could at least have pretended to be interested.'

'He's excited about his meeting.'

Darsie propped herself up on one elbow. 'Why are you making excuses for him?'

It was a good question. 'Because...' she began, and then realised that she didn't have a good answer.

'Do you love him?'

The answer was yes. On paper, at least. Sure, he could be insufferably self-regarding, but when he wasn't puffing himself up he was kind and funny and vulnerable and handsome. A great guy, on paper. Her whole life was on paper. 'Just because I don't hear violins doesn't mean I don't, y'know…'

Darsie rolled over. 'I understand. He's no romantic hero.'

'No, thank god.'

Darsie sat up. 'You don't want a hero?'

'What the hell does that even mean? In my experience men are not heroes. Men leave. They do terrible things and then they walk out of your life. So no, I'm not waiting to be swept off my feet.'

'Well, I want a hero.'

Jane couldn't hide her disappointment. 'I wrote you to be more than that. You're not just some paper-thin heroine in a bodice ripper, you have *levels*.'

'Y'know what, you can keep your levels. If it's a choice between being deep or being happy, I'll take happy.'

Was that the choice—engaged sorrow or unthinking happiness?

'So that's why Tony Douglas is such a bastard.'

Why was she bringing up the hero of her novel? Strictly speaking he wasn't a hero, more an anti-hero, although she disliked using either term, reducing as they did complex characters to ciphers.

'He's horrible, mean-spirited, and yet I keep going

back to him,' mused Darsie. 'Is that the sort of man you want?'

'No. Of course not. And I'm not defined by a man.' She paused. 'He's not *that* horrible.'

'Oh, he's dreadful. The things he's done to me...' She shook her head slowly and then stopped. A curious expression slid across her face. 'Wait, you like him, don't you?'

'Of course not. I mean, not like *that*. I like him as a character. Between the sheets—*pages.*'

'Do you like him better than me?'

'It's not a popularity contest I'm writing, it's a novel.' She crossed to the window. 'Some characters can do the most dreadful things, but if they're compelling enough then once you're hooked you go with them. It's not just that you want to know what happens, but even if what they're up to is morally questionable you find yourself—against your better judgement—willing them to succeed. You'll forgive them anything.' She shrugged. 'It's one of the differences between fiction and real life.'

She turned to the bed. Darsie had gone.

CHAPTER 17

'I Made It Through the Rain', Barry Manilow, 1980, Arista

TOM HAD BEEN surprised at the ease with which he and Roddy had fooled Priscilla into believing they were Fox movie executives looking to connect with her client, but even more gratifying was how easily they had persuaded Willie into getting on a plane to London—at his own expense, no less—and then forging into the depths of the Home Counties for an imaginary meeting. Based on the dismal showing of their previous machinations, he had half expected Willie to see straight through the ruse and march into Tristesse to deliver another beating. He winced at the memory of the previous one; the bruises hadn't completely faded.

'I thought you said you could do an American accent,' Tom complained to Roddy soon after he'd hung up on the faked phone call.

'That *was* American.'

Tom grunted non-committally. 'Off and on.'

'Well, you didn't exactly help. Wanda…Vonda. If

you're going to mouth a phoney name you could at least make it obvious.'

However, both agreed that despite Roddy's vowels and Tom's consonants this latest plan had got off to a brilliant start. It was a propitious moment—they were rid of Willie. It was time for phase two.

'Now we work on *papa*.'

'I want it on record,' said Roddy grimly. 'This is going too far. She wouldn't talk to her dad for years—they're rebuilding their relationship.'

So far Tom had tried and failed to make Jane miserable by sabotaging her career and then her relationship with her boyfriend; all that remained was her dad. Tom liked Benny Lockhart, didn't want to hurt him, but there was no other option.

And it wasn't as if he was trying to cause a permanent rift between father and daughter; a temporary falling out should do it. Briefly he'd considered enlisting Benny in the plan. That way the older man would know it wasn't a real quarrel and avoid any potential heartache. But Benny was no actor and if the scheme were to work then Tom needed him to feel every raw emotion. When Roddy voiced his doubts Tom didn't admit that he had them too, and instead resorted to his usual refrain.

'I'm just trying to help her finish her book. She'll thank me in the end.'

*

Dark clouds rolled in over the Campsie hills that ranged along the northern edge of the city, bringing the threat of rain and a deluge of fair-skinned men in boldly patterned knitted sweaters. Tom drove carefully through the packed streets, threading his car amongst the throngs waving flags and singing heartily in their Nordic tongue.

It was the night of a crucial World Cup Qualifier, a clash between Scotland and the unfancied Faroe Islands. Despite his long residence in the country Tom took little interest in the qualification chances of the Scottish national side, but earlier that day Roddy had helpfully laid out their prospects.

'It's a disaster,' he'd said, 'we only need the one point to make it to the finals for the first time since 1998.'

That made no sense to Tom. 'Why is that a disaster? The Faroe Islands aren't exactly Brazil. You've never lost to them before, right? One point is all but a certainty.'

'Shhhh! Shhhh!' Roddy waved his hands frantically. 'For pity's sake, man, do you want the football gods to hear you talk like that?'

Tom had dismissed Roddy's paranoia; for him there was a far more important fixture that night. Through an accident of scheduling the final of the pub quiz was due to start soon after the big match kicked off. Tom was certain that even should Scotland falter at Hampden Park, France would triumph at the Walter Scott Pub.

He turned confidently onto Gallowgate and headed east. Just before he'd left him Roddy had tried to confer on tonight's plan yet another of his codenames.

'I don't want to hear it,' said Tom peremptorily.

'Aww, but it's a good one.'

'I don't care. Every time you give something a name, it dies on its arse.'

'That's not true,' Roddy objected. He folded his arms, miffed. Then a moment later offered a conciliatory nod. 'OK, so yes, it's true.' He looked shocked. 'Bloody hell. I'm jinxed.'

By the time Tom parked his car on the corner outside the pub, the rain had arrived. He pulled his jacket over his head and made a dash inside.

The place was packed, the regular crowd swollen with football supporters unable to get a ticket for tonight's game. The air was thick with the reek of sweat and wet woollen coats. Growling men gathered around the satellite TV, soaking up the pre-match build-up, nervously downing pints and talking down their chances of victory. A thin man with a sallow, pinched face who'd been in the crowd the last time Scotland had made it to the finals, rocked in the corner.

It was a little after seven o'clock; the game kicked off at half past, the quiz started at eight. Tom searched the crowded pub. Benny Lockhart leaned on the bar between his teammates. He seemed to be concluding a pep talk so Tom held back, allowing him to finish.

'How you feeling?' Benny asked the man with the bobbing Adam's apple.

'Good,' he replied.

'Sharp?'

'Sharp,' he agreed.

Benny turned to the other man. 'Rory?'

'Brand new,' said Rory. He looked over his shoulder at the quizmaster and then said slowly, 'Mind you, I'm a bit worried because I don't know what he's gonna ask us.'

Benny pinched his brow. 'Aye, well it's a quiz, Rory.'

'Oh, right.' Rory nodded. 'Aye.'

Tom chose that moment to announce his presence. 'Monsieur L…'

'Tommy!'

The two men shook hands warmly. Benny insisted on buying him a drink.

'Big night, huh?' remarked Tom.

'No kidding. Winning team gets a holiday to America. And two tickets to Disneyland.'

'That's wonderful. Good luck with that.'

Benny smiled up at him. Tom hated that he had to deceive him, but kept reminding himself that it was for the greater good. A cold pint of Tennent's duly arrived.

'I know you and Jane haven't always seen eye to eye,' said Benny, 'but I'm sure she'll be pleased you're here.'

'Where is she?' Tom looked innocently about the pub.

'Not here yet. But the quiz doesn't start till eight.' He inclined his head towards a clock behind the bar. There was still nearly three quarters of an hour to go.

'Ah, well,' said Tom, raising the lager to his lips, concealing a half-smile behind the glass. 'Plenty of time.'

*

She'd left plenty of time to get to the pub for the quiz, but the cheery blast on the horn signalled that the cab was already here; now she'd be even earlier than planned, which would be a relief to her dad. Although just five or six miles separated them, for Benny the genteel West End with its curling Georgian crescents and Arabica-tinged air was a mysterious uncharted place and she might as well have been coming by flying saucer from Venus.

Outside the flat the minicab idled at the kerb. Jane slid into the back seat. The radio was tuned to the match; a pre-game interview blared platitudes. A Christmas tree freshener swung from the driver's rear-view mirror and in it she caught his reflection. He wore a flat cap pulled down over his brow, a chunky woollen scarf wrapped round the lower half of his face and in the narrow strip between them his eyes were obscured behind a pair of black spectacles with thick lenses.

'That was quick,' she said. 'I wasn't expecting you for another ten minutes.'

'Aye, well, I was just roun' the corner, hen,' he said, his voice muffled in the scarf. 'Where to?'

'East End, please. The Walter Scott.'

The driver stirred the gearbox and with a crunch located first gear. The cab lurched into the road. There was a steady swish and squeak from the windscreen wipers as they made progress through the wet streets.

'You look familiar,' he said. 'You on the telly?'

'Oh no,' she said with a chuckle, then conceded, 'Well, I've done a few interviews…'

He snapped his fingers. 'You're that writer! Jane Somethin'…My wife read your book. What's it called again?'

'*Happy Ending*.' He *did* recognise her. How…odd.

'Aye, that was it. *Happy Ending*? She was greetin' her eyes out by the end, it was that sad. And you wrote it.' His flat cap swivelled as he turned his head in admiration. 'That's amazing.'

Jane demurred with a faint smile, quietly pleased at his reaction.

'She was in floods. Said it was the saddest thing she'd ever read. Really depressing.' He glanced back. 'God, you must be a right miserable cow.'

Stung, she sat back, pushing herself deep into the seat. Outside the window the city passed by in grey gloom. Red sandstone terraces that would glow in the evening sun were cold and mute, rain washing out their colour. The last of the daylight gurgled down storm drains.

She wondered how Willie was getting on at his meeting. He hadn't called her all day, which was probably a good sign since it meant he was too busy. She'd hoped his absence would free her up to beat her writer's block, but there had been no magical breakthrough. Instead she'd made brownies and vacuumed for three hours. On the radio the studio presenters wound up their interview and handed over to the match commentators for kick-off. In the background she could hear the giant football crowd churn with anticipation.

They passed a railway station. She was vaguely aware of the sign over the entrance as it slipped by, but fully five more minutes elapsed before the name on the board worked its way into her consciousness. Rutherglen. Not only was she not going to Rutherglen, it was the wrong side of the river from her intended destination. With a flutter of panic she leaned forward to address the driver.

'Where are we going?'

'The Rabbie Burns.'

'I said the Walter Scott.'

'You sure?

'Of course I'm sure!' she snapped.

'Hey, hey! No need for that. They're both iconic pillars of our national literature arguably responsible for the over-romanticisation of Scottish history that persists to this day.' He sniffed. 'Easy mistake to make.'

'OK, OK.' She glanced at the time on her phone. 'Just…please hurry.'

There was still time. But only just. She scrolled through her contacts and dialled her dad to let him know what had happened. It'd be fine. So long as the traffic wasn't too bad she'd get there before the quiz started.

The phone rang six times before connecting.

'Dad!'

'Hullo, aye…it's Benny Lockhart…I can't get to the phone right now so please leave me a message.'

With a twinge of concern she guessed that he couldn't hear it ring in the noisy pub. There was a dull tone. Jane decided not to leave a message; it would only make him worry. She'd see him soon enough. The cab hit a pothole and her stomach lurched. The bump dislodged the driver's scarf. It unwrapped itself, baring his mouth and chin. She squinted at him in the mirror.

'Do I know y—?'

He shoved it back across his face before she could take a good look.

'Out of fags,' he said quickly. 'Gi'e us a minute.'

'What? No. I have to get to the…'

He stamped on the brake, the sudden stop drawing hoots of protest from cars behind, then fumbled for the handle. The door flew open and he flung himself through it, stumbling over the sill in his hurry to escape. Picking himself up he lowered his head and pelted past Jane's window.

She scrambled out of the cab. 'Come back!' she shouted after his rapidly receding figure. 'I have to get to the…pub.' Her shoulders slumped. He'd gone, disappearing into the traffic and the night.

The driver's door flapped. She ducked her head back inside the car. The ignition was empty; he'd taken the keys. Slamming the door in frustration she began to walk briskly along the slick pavement, willing a black cab to materialise out of the rain. Then she remembered the number of a taxi company in her phone. She got through on the first ring. Nothing available for half an hour. The big match, y'understand.

In half an hour it would be too late. Desperate now she stepped into the road to flag down a car, waving her arms at the approaching traffic, trusting that amongst them one good Samaritan would stop. Cars and vans swerved past, sweeping her with watery light from their headlamps, blasting their horns in irritation. One driver rolled down his window and for a moment she was sure she was saved, but instead of offering her a ride he unleashed a foul-mouthed tirade and then with an upward thrust of his middle finger was gone.

She tried her dad again. He wasn't picking up. Fat drops of rain pattered against her phone. The weather was worsening and she hadn't bothered taking her umbrella tonight since she hadn't been planning a bloody walk. She cursed the minicab driver; why had he abandoned her? Was he so desperate for a cigarette that he'd legged it into the night? Had his wife been so upset by *Happy Ending* that he was taking some strange revenge? And what was all that chat about Walter Scott and Burns—was he an aspiring writer with an unpublished novel of his own? She was mystified.

Up ahead a cluster of figures took refuge at a bus shelter. She saw several arms extend to hail a bus and seconds later one rolled past her, coming to a stop with a squeal of brakes in front of the bedraggled line of people. She had no idea if it was the right bus, but it was pointing in the right direction. And it was dry.

She jumped aboard and made her way along the aisle as it bounced down the road, finding a seat next to an old woman in a white knitted hat that steamed gently as it dried out.

'*Dreich* night, hen,' remarked the old woman, gazing dismally out of the window. 'As black as the earl o' Hell's waistcoat.'

For one insane moment Jane contemplated calling Tom for help. She got as far as to highlight his name in her phone contacts list, before common sense prevailed. Firmly tucking away the phone she studied the route map above the window. The bus was making good progress in the general direction of her destination, but in about a mile it would turn off the main street taking her farther from the pub. There was nothing else for it—she'd have to walk.

*

'Unbelievable! How did Miller miss that?!' The match commentator's anguished howl was taken up by the denizens of the pub as Scotland's star striker contrived to poke the ball past the post of an open goal.

'Dismal,' groaned Benny Lockhart. 'Pathetic.' He

turned to Tom, shaking his head. 'See, it's at times like these I think it might be nice to be someone else. Someone who wasnae a Scottish football supporter.' He paused. 'Though I cannae see mysel' as a German.' He put his head to one side. 'Maybe a Brazilian?' He nodded, warming to the idea. 'I like goin' to the beach.' He patted his belly. 'Though it's a wee while since I fit into my Speedos.'

Tom watched as Benny reached into a battered holdall.

'Here, what d'you think?' He pulled out a collection of coloured skip-caps sporting Mickey Mouse ears, each embroidered with the name of a team-member, except for Jane's, which in addition to her name also displayed the word 'Captain'.

'Me and the boys have discussed it, we're going to make her captain.'

That still left one question. 'And the mouse ears?' asked Tom.

A soft smile spread across Benny's face. 'When she was little she always wanted to meet Mickey Mouse. Saved up all the pocket money her ma gave her for a trip to Disneyland. Every birthday it was the same—all that wee girl ever talked about was Mickey Mouse.' His tone darkened. 'Every birthday until her seventh.'

The memory clouded Benny's face. Tom wanted to tell him to stop. That he knew. But it was too late.

'Her ma had taken her to Woolworths for her present. They were late getting back. I was at home, mad that my dinner wasn't on the table.' The words caught in his throat. 'That was the night I walked out on them.'

Tom felt a shudder of unease. He knew the story—it was Jane's after all—but this was different, this was the other side. Until now he hadn't heard it from the villain's point of view.

'Son, I wish walking out was the worst thing I did that night.' Benny stared vacantly into the middle distance. 'But no. I thought I'd teach them a lesson. So that's when I did it.'

'Oh god…' Tom mouthed, knowing full well what was coming.

'I emptied Jane's piggybank of all her Disney money,' he said quietly. 'Went out and spent every penny on drink.'

Tom listened dry-mouthed as Benny relived the memory.

'You know why they were late home?'

'Ah…yes,' he confessed and saw comprehension dawn on the other man's face.

''Course you do—it's in the book, isn't it?' He dredged up the horror. 'Her ma had dropped dead in Woolworths. Her ma was dead in the Pick 'n' Mix aisle in Woolworths and I was out spending her Mickey Mouse money on booze.'

Benny played nervously with Jane's cap, turning it round and round in shaking hands. His eyes flicked to Tom's half-empty pint of lager and he licked his lips.

Tom felt sweat prickle his forehead. Could he really bring himself to continue with a plan that might break Benny—again?

'I know I can never make it up to that wee girl,' said Benny, trying to keep his voice steady, 'but if we win the prize tonight, I'm going to take her to Disneyland.' He paused. 'No' the shit one in Paris, obviously.' He raised an apologetic hand. 'Nae offence.'

Benny leaned on the bar.

'Years later I found out that the police brought Jane home two minutes after I left. Two minutes, son.' He glanced up at the wall clock. Ten to eight. 'She'll be here. I'm sure nothing's happened.' He swallowed. 'Not again.'

A cry of distress rocked the pub. 'Another near miss for the plucky Faroe Islanders!' bellowed the TV commentator, adding in a high-pitched squawk, 'Is history going to repeat itself tonight?

Tom looked at Benny. 'Will you excuse me for just one moment?'

'Sure, son.'

He moved along the bar, out of Benny's earshot, dug out his phone and dialled with shaking fingers.

The plan had seemed so simple. Aided by Roddy's illegal radio scanner—obtained cheaply off a former *News of the World* reporter—they would eavesdrop on the minicab channels until they heard a dispatcher send a cab to Jane's address. Roddy, disguised as a driver, would then arrive outside Jane's flat before the real cab she'd booked turned up. He'd take her far enough away from the pub that there'd be no way she could make it to the quiz in time. Her dad would be disappointed, she'd be upset—enough to get her writing again. So simple. God, he was such an idiot.

'Roddy!'

'Tom…'

'Call it off,' he barked into the phone. 'Bring her here, immediately!'

'Tom, she's gone.' His voice was frantic. 'I'm back at the car. She's not here. We've lost her.' There was a horrified pause. 'In Rutherglen.'

Tom lowered the phone without hanging up. Roddy rattled on, his voice distant. The hubbub of the football supporters seemed to fall away. Tom stood in the dreadful silence. A voice pierced the stillness.

'Captains,' said the quiz master, 'please bring your team-lists to the adjudicator's table.'

*

The tail lights of the bus faded behind a curtain of rain. Jane was the only passenger to disembark at the stop. She looked around. A set of traffic lights cycled from green to red in the deserted street. A short row of terraced houses lay in darkness, half their windows boarded up, obscene graffiti scrawled on their crumbling walls. Beyond them, across a patch of wasteland bordered by a razor-wire fence, a line of high flats pierced the black sky. Sickly yellow light shone from a handful of windows and even from this distance she could hear the wind groaning around the towers. The pub lay on the other side.

She edged past the end of the dilapidated terrace, searched the fence line for a way through, and found a ragged hole in the base that looked like it had been chewed out of the wire. She dropped to her knees and scrambled through the hole, catching her coat sleeve on a spur of metal. There was a loud tear as it ripped through to her skin. She got to her feet and struck off into the darkness,

*

'I'm one team short,' the quizmaster announced from the adjudicator's table.

Tom looked anxiously at Benny, who clutched Jane's Mickey Mouse hat in one hand, the team-list in the other.

'I must have the list right now,' the quizmaster intoned, 'or you forfeit your place.'

Benny's teammates urged him to go up.

'Come on, Benny, come on!'

Sweat poured off his forehead. 'Two more minutes, lads. Two more minutes.'

*

Jane scrambled across the wasteland beneath the looming tower blocks. The muddy ground was pockmarked with craters sloshing with dirty rainwater and littered with discarded supermarket trolleys and old tyres. A pack of yowling dogs appeared out of the darkness, red raw lips pulled back over gnashing teeth. She recoiled, then a moment later saw that they were on a leash. They strained towards her, forelegs clawing the air, their fat owner anchored in the mud, arms popping as he struggled to hold them back. She skirted past quickly.

Up ahead on a low rise the dim outline of a huddle of people. Guttural voices carried on the air, spitting vile oaths. The tinkle of breaking glass as a hurled bottle smashed nearby. Jane adjusted her course to go around them, stumbled on a hoard of bottles at the edge of one of the rain-filled hollows. With a yell she went down, slapping against the mud. Drenched through, exhausted and on the verge of tears, for a moment she considered giving up. Why bother putting herself through this? It must be too late by now.

She lifted her head. In the distance she could make out the glow of streetlamps beyond the last of the high flats. The pub was on that street. Rousing herself for one final push, Jane heaved herself up off the squelching ground. She teetered awkwardly on the edge of the hole. Checked her shoe. The heel had snapped off. Pulling her coat around her, she limped on.

*

'I'm sorry,' Tom said in a low voice. 'I'm so sorry.'

Benny's eyes were watery. 'Hey, son, it's no' your fault. Maybe the taxi got a puncture.' Then he added gloomily, 'Or maybe she just decided no' to come after all.' He shrugged. 'No more than I deserve.'

Tom wanted to confess. He could feel his heart thumping.

The quizmaster cupped the microphone, turned to the adjudicator and mouthed a question. He answered with a solemn nod.

'OK, that's enough,' the quizmaster removed his hand from the microphone. 'Right then, let's get on with—'

A howl rose up from the rest of the pub as the Faroe Islander's number ten dribbled the ball past three Scottish defenders before passing it through the keeper's open legs. The back of the net bowed outwards, almost apologetically.

'DISASTER FOR SCOTLAND!' the match commentator wailed.

On the TV Scottish players crouched wretchedly on the pitch, heads in hands. The commentator heaped on the misery. 'They'll be dancing in the streets of Torshavn tonight!'

Benny's team-list stirred in a sudden breeze. It took Tom a moment to realise through the waves of defeated moans that the door to the pub was wide open, and another to see that in the doorway stood Jane, hair whipped across her rain-streaked face and clumped with mud, one coat sleeve ripped. She wobbled on a single shoe.

She saw him and frowned, clearly puzzled by his presence.

'Jane?!' It was Benny, eyes widening with surprise and pleasure. He started towards her then checked himself, turned quickly on his heel and crossed to the adjudicator's table. Mouth tight he slammed down the team-list. Expressionless, the quizmaster checked his watch and then after what seemed a lifetime nodded curtly.

Benny's teammates punched the air and took their places for the start of the quiz.

'You OK, darlin'?' Benny asked.

She nodded wordlessly.

'Here. This is for you.' He gave her the skip-cap. She turned it round to see the word 'Captain'. Her eyes glistened.

Tom had seen enough. Jane had made it, albeit just in time and almost certainly at the expense of several years of his own life, shortened by the stress of what he now saw was a sorely misguided plan. He had no one else to blame but himself. For now, all was well in Benny Lockhart's world—and that's what mattered. Reluctant to hang around and be forced to answer the inevitably awkward questions, he slipped past the reunited pair and made for the door. The quizmaster's voice followed him out.

'Question one. Literature,' he began. 'Who was William Shakespeare's wife?'

*

Tom splashed across the street and got into his car. He sat for a moment gazing out at the rain, then stabbed the key into the ignition. The engine bleated like a drowning sheep. He banged a palm against the steering wheel, his frustration more to do with the events of the evening than the all too predictable failure of his car to start. After a dozen more tries he gave up and called Roddy to come and collect him.

An hour later they were parked in Roddy's car outside Mario's Fish and Chicken takeaway in Merchant City. Tom told him the whole sorry tale of what had transpired in the pub. Roddy listened quietly, wincing at the details as he ate hot chips out of a paper bag. The engine ticked over at idle and the cabin was filled with the smell of diesel and vinegar.

Roddy leaned across the handbrake and offered Tom the bag. He shook his head brusquely; he'd lost his appetite. Like a tongue probing a rotten tooth he continued to go back over the evening, torturing himself with what might have been. What if he'd succeeded? What if Jane hadn't shown up at the last second? The fan heater blasted hot air from the dashboard and yet he felt ice-cold.

'Your plan was rubbish. Again.'

'On the contrary,' said Roddy, 'my plan has been highly effective throughout. Only, we weren't looking at the right target.'

'What are you talking about?'

'Tom, it's made *you* utterly miserable. Look at you. If you were a writer you'd be ready to compose an epic poem.'

It was true. He hadn't felt this awful in years. Who

would have guessed that malicious plotting was bad for the soul?

'The fact is,' mused Roddy, 'we're not dog-killers.' He reached for another chip. 'I mean, what's the worst thing we actually achieved? Kidnapping a pot plant.' He popped the chip into his mouth and stared out as he chewed. 'There's our fatal flaw—at heart, we're nice guys.'

Tom was barely listening. He'd come to a decision. 'I'm going to tell her everything.'

'No,' said Roddy, alarmed. 'You don't want to do that.'

But for the first time that night he knew with utter certainty that this was the right path. There would be no more ridiculous plots designed to upset Jane. 'I'm going to come clean, apologise and then I'm going to stay the fuck out of her life.' He paused. 'Forever.'

CHAPTER 18

'Naked in the Rain', Red Hot Chili Peppers, 1991, Warner Bros

HER DAD HAD insisted she take home the trophy. They'd won the quiz on a tiebreak: which country originally made Panama hats? She'd only known the answer thanks to her shopping spree after the Austen awards. When she shouted out 'Ecuador!' and chalked up the winning point, her dad had leapt from his seat, arms aloft in triumph, knocking over the table and spilling their drinks.

She'd never seen anyone so happy. There was something so pure and uncensored about his delight. Hadn't she said she wanted to get to know him? Well, here he was, utterly unguarded; and she wondered if she'd ever reconcile the bullying father who'd abandoned her with this smiling man.

Then he told her haltingly that he wanted to take her to Disneyland and she'd lost it; burst into tears, full-on hiccupping sobs, snot running down her face, the works. She'd had to clean herself up in the ladies. Standing over the sink, staring at her dishevelled reflection in the mirror, she'd noticed the now faded words that Darsie (Jane?) had scrawled in lipstick weeks earlier. *Where's my happy ending?* Maybe it was out there, she considered, buying the first of many congratulatory rounds for his mates.

They'd celebrated until closing time and then she'd taken a cab home. A black cab, not a minicab. She set the new trophy down on the shelf next to her Austen award for Best New Writer. The golden statuette of the Regency lady stood primly alongside the squat pub quiz award, a small plastic version of Rodin's 'Thinker', bent head topped off with a tartan bunnet. She chuckled at the juxtaposition of literary and *gallus* that tied her two worlds together; the trophies looked like they'd get on famously. Which was more than could be said for her and Tom.

When she'd blown through the door of the pub he was the first person she'd clapped eyes on. What the hell was he doing there? Come to harass her again about the novel, she assumed. During Nicola Ball's book launch she'd told him she was in the quiz final; perhaps he thought she should be making better use of her time finishing his damn novel. *Her* novel, she corrected herself. She couldn't recall seeing him again during the evening and presumed that he'd slunk off. Good riddance. She shook herself. Why on earth was she thinking about Tom?

She tried Willie again. The call was batted straight to his answerphone, so she left another message asking him to ring her back, hoping her voice didn't betray her anxiety. He'd been out of touch all day and that wasn't like him; he'd call her from the corner shop when he went out for a newspaper.

Deciding she wouldn't sleep until they'd spoken, she busied herself in the kitchen making meringues. He still hadn't rung by the time they were in the oven. She picked up a book. She was reading Nicola Ball's latest novel in proof and had been enjoying it, especially for the fruity sex scenes—the girl had a facility for writing gaspingly good bonking that belied her demure exterior.

As she read an idea began to form. However, for this she'd need a certain amount of Dutch courage. She went into the kitchen and scoured the wine rack. There were two bottles. One of them turned out to be Balsamic vinegar—god, she'd become so middle class—the other was a bottle Tom had brought round just before they'd broken up.

She slid it from the rack. A 2003 Volnay Burgundy. She had no idea what that meant, but it sounded expensive and Tom had excellent taste in wine. He was a walking French cliché. She poured herself a glass; it was lighter than she'd expected, a foxtrot on her tongue, with a flavour that reminded her of parma violets. After downing the glass and another in quick succession she was ready.

Write naked, Willie had said. Initially she'd dismissed the suggestion as the hopeful wish of an old pervert, but the more she'd thought about it the more it made sense. Free your mind, cast off your inhibitions along with your knickers. Jane hunched over her laptop, wearing her Mickey Mouse skip-cap. And nothing else.

Darsie cleared her throat with a discreet cough. 'I won't do nudity unless it's essential to the plot.' She sat prissily in one of the living room chairs, eyeing Jane over the top of an open magazine.

Jane caught sight of herself in the darkened laptop screen. Oh god. How had she become so unutterably stuck that sitting in the buff seemed like a brilliant idea? She struck a key so that the screen bloomed, wiping away her reflection. She shifted awkwardly in the chair. The moulded plastic rubbed against her bare bum.

'So,' teased Darsie, 'feeling uninhibited yet?'

'It's coming along great, actually,' said Jane defensively, angling the screen so that Darsie couldn't see that the page below the Chapter 37 heading remained resolutely blank.

Darsie lowered the magazine with a frown. 'Why are you lying to *me*? If you really were working do you think I'd be sitting here reading *Stylist*? No, I'd be in your book, probably having my heart broken by that bastard Tony Douglas. Again. By the way, he'd better get his comeuppance at the end.'

'What if ultimately you're meant to be together?' pondered Jane.

Darsie gave a brittle laugh. 'Oh, I very much doubt that.' She looked panicked. 'You're not going to make me end up with him, are you?'

'Would that be such a terrible ending?'

Darsie raised the magazine, blocking Jane's view of her face. From behind it she began to cry softly.

Jane reached out a hand. 'Oh, don't do that. I'm sorry. I know Tony's been awful to you—'

'He ran over my dog,' wailed Darsie. 'The dog my dad gave me before he died, Tony Douglas killed it.'

'Well, no, actually he didn't,' confessed Jane.

'What?'

'You find out in the last chapter. Well, you will, when I write it.'

'Go on.'

'Tony wasn't driving the car. He tried to rescue Wentworth, rushed him to the vet, but he was too late. He tried to tell you—'

'At the club,' said Darsie as it dawned on her. 'He was late and I thought he'd decided not to show, as usual.'

Jane nodded.

'And then I said those things to him.' She clapped a hand to her mouth. 'Those terrible things. And he had a go at me. Oh god, the fight—it was awful.'

Jane smiled; she was particularly proud of that scene. Writing it had been incredibly liberating. By the end both characters were broken and hollowed out, and when she'd inserted the final stop she too had been a wreck, their relationship seemingly in an irretrievable place. It was good stuff, even though she said so herself. Tom would love it. He was always pushing her to go further.

'What are you grinning at?' snapped Darsie.

'Nothing.'

'We're talking about my life, Jane. My *life*.' Darsie fell into quiet reflection for a moment and then leaned forward. 'See, this is the problem with a dual narrative,' she complained. 'You just don't know what the other one's thinking. That leads to misunderstanding and the next thing you know you end up alone, miserable and dog-less.' She brightened. 'He could bring me a puppy! In the final chapter. Tony could show up at my door with a wee puppy. I'd forgive him and we'd live happily ever after. That's a great idea. Go on. Write that.'

'A puppy?'

'Yeah.'

'You don't think that's a bit…well…shit?'

'Hell, no. I get a puppy.'

'I'll bear it in mind,' said Jane.

A stack of pages lay on the desk. Earlier she had printed out everything she had of the new novel. Until that moment the book had been nothing more than a few hundred kilobytes in a folder on her desktop marked 'Untitled'. The mountain of paper made it something real. She gathered the manuscript in both hands, enjoying its heft, then riffled through the pages. The chapter numbers flew past, snatches of sentences, the novel accumulated in a rush—and then abruptly ran out. She had hoped that by reading it through on the page rather than on a screen it would trigger an epiphany about the final chapter. It hadn't.

The doorbell rang. She unpeeled herself from the chair and dashed down the hallway. It was Willie. Had to be. She was about to throw open the front door when she remembered she was naked. No doubt he would be pleased to see her in her undressed state, but just in case it was a neighbour looking for fun-run sponsorship rather than her boyfriend she pressed her eye to the peephole.

'You must be joking,' she muttered.

It was Tom.

'Jane?' He leaned towards the door, his head bulging unnaturally in the fish-eye lens.

'Just...go away.' He looked drawn, tense. And fully dressed.

'I've got to talk to you. Please open the door...'

She was about to tell him where to go when the phone rang. It was Willie. Had to be. She padded back into the living room. Darsie offered up the phone.

'Thanks.'

'No problem.'

The caller ID was blocked, but she was sure it was him. 'Willie?'

There was a brief silence then a click and a cheery automaton said, 'You need to hear about our great deal on home insurance.'

The last thing she needed to hear about was—

Bleep bleep bleep!

'Jane, your meringues!' Darsie pointed to the kitchen. Black smoke poured from the oven. Above it the alarm bleated.

'Oh shit!' She dropped the phone and hurried into the kitchen, bare feet slipping on the linoleum floor. She caught the edge of the counter-top and steadied herself, then stuck on a pair of oven gloves and flung open the oven. Smoke billowed into the room. She waved at it uselessly as she slid out the tray of singed meringues.

Above the insistent sound of the smoke alarm she could hear Tom calling out urgently.

'Jane? You OK? Jane!'

There was so much smoke he must be able to smell it. But at least he was on the other side of the door.

There was the rasp of a key sliding into a lock.

The spare key above the lintel.

Oh, no.

Clutching the tray of smoking meringues, she sprinted down the hallway, intent on reaching the door before he gained entry. But it was too late. Tom stepped inside and she skidded to a stop in front of him.

For a moment neither said a word, then he arched his eyebrows and gave a low whistle.

Aside from the meringues, she was stark naked. She was glad she'd whipped them into a stiff peak. His eyes roamed up and down her body.

'Stop looking!'

He covered his face with a hand and then instantly

spread his fingers and grinned. She made a face as if to say, how childish, then ducked into the bedroom, returning a few minutes later wrapped in a dressing gown. He was no longer in the hall. She found him in the kitchen, standing on the counter flapping at the smoke alarm with a tea towel until it stopped. He jumped down.

'What the hell are you doing here?' she demanded.

'I came to apolo…'

She saw his eyes drift past her to fall on the manuscript on the desk.

'Is that my novel?'

They stood for a moment, like a couple of sprinters on their starting-blocks. And then both lunged for the novel. Tom got there first.

'Give that back!'

She pursued him round the room.

'I paid good money for this—I'm going to read it.'

'You don't get to read anything until it's finished. That's the deal. Give it back!'

Tom slowed to a stop. He hung his head and, appearing to relent, passed the novel back to her.

'OK. Yes. You're right.'

'Thank you,' she said, feeling the familiar weight of the manuscript. She ran her thumb along the spine. 'Good to know you can behave like a grown-up once in a—' Something was wrong. It felt a tad light. 'Where's the rest of it?!'

She looked up and he was gone. There was the slam of

a door and then a click of a bolt being thrown. He was in the bathroom. The sonofabitch had locked himself in the bathroom with—she counted quickly—the first three chapters.

She hammered against the door with her fists. 'Come out of there, you thieving bastard! Give me back my novel!'

In reply came the flick of a page being turned.

'Don't you dare. Not one page. That's what we agreed.'

Flick.

'OK, now you're just taking the piss. No one reads that fast.'

Flick.

Oh, he was so maddening. She decided that he was enjoying her irritation, and that her furious pleading was serving only as a pleasant soundtrack to his reading, so she left him to it and went back to the living room to drink more wine. About half an hour later he reappeared. He stood silently in the doorway, the chapters rolled into a scroll held in one hand down at his side.

In her head she'd planned to shout a lot, berate him for his behaviour, say something withering about it not being a surprise given how he'd treated her previously and then eject him from the flat. The plan started well enough.

'How could you do that? I can't believe you. Even you!'

But then it encountered an obstacle; a lump in the custard—first draft neurosis. She took a sip of wine.

'So,' she said anxiously, 'what did you think?'

She knew that to answer correctly was akin to tempering chocolate; in order to avoid unpleasant crumbling the respondent had to heat and cool with perfect control. The answer should balance praise and criticism, ten parts to one; characters' names should be recalled with perfect clarity, one or two favourite passages recounted with close reference to the text, the writer left with a lingering taste of validation.

Tom shrugged. 'It's merely the first few chapters so who can say?'

Jane opened her mouth to object, but before she could say anything he continued. As he spoke he moved slowly and steadily towards her.

'However, putting to one side that you are a whining, overpaid author who clearly got lucky with her debut, I'd say this is a very good start.'

He held out the rolled up chapters like a baton. They were close enough now that all she had to do was reach for them where she stood.

'Well, coming from a never-even-has-been owner of a third-rate publishing company, I'd have to say…thank you.'

Their hands gripped either end of the scroll.

'Naturally, I have a few notes.'

She held his gaze.

'Naturally.'

For the next hour they discussed the opening chapters.

At first Jane was aware that they were dancing awkwardly around each other, holding back their true feelings about the text, but then almost without noticing she felt herself slip into the comfortable pattern they had established while editing *Happy Ending*.

She watched Tom's hands gesticulate through the air in wild circles then tight ones as he honed his point. He paced the room in his familiar long stride, palm held against one stubbly cheek as he figured out aloud what he was thinking. His insights were pointed, awkward, sometimes they stung. A novel was about choices; it was rarely a question of right or wrong, but of making the smart choice. Tom's were unavoidably, irritatingly smart. She had forgotten how good he was at this.

He pointed to her laptop. 'Would you mind if I...?'

She sat back. 'Be my guest.'

Dragging Willie's chair round to her side of the desk so they were next to one another he scrolled to the beginning of the novel, flexed his fingers and began to type.

She read over his shoulder as he worked, scratching out a word here, adding another there, losing an extraneous speech tag and ruthlessly hunting down adverbs. He paused, and she pulled the laptop towards her. His changes had sparked a fresh idea. The old version fell away and a new possibility branched off. What if Darsie and Tony meet earlier, before he discovers she's just a waitress?

She wrote it up quickly, amazed at how easily it came to her; she'd forgotten how good it was to be able to do this. She had never been an elegant typist; self-taught, she worked the keyboard like a hen-party drunk trying to prove she isn't, always about to lose her feet, steadying herself just in time to avoid crashing unconscious in a Sauchiehall Street doorway. She lurched from one key to another, giddy with pleasure. The feeling swelled. She was reconnecting to a part of her she feared had gone for good. She wanted to carry on writing, not stop—never stop.

Tom leaned over her, scanning the work as she wrote, nodding furiously. Yes. Yes. Yes, Jane.

She turned to him, her cheeks flushed with wine and bliss. The sweet taste of violets on her tongue.

'This wine is amazing.'

'I know. It's from my family estate.'

She laughed, gesturing with her glass to the wall. 'And that painting's from my dad's private collection.' She took another sip and ran a finger across the label on the wine bottle. 'I'm something of a wine expert, y'know.'

'You are?'

'Oh, yeah. Six years working in Tesco you pick up a few things.'

'Please.' He motioned to the bottle. 'Enlighten me.'

'OK. Right. Well, you won't know this, not having my extensive experience of aisle twelve, but if you want to tell if a wine's any good there is one thing you look for.'

'Nose? Colour? Length?'

She gave a dismissive pout. 'Pert bottom.' She picked

up the bottle and held it above their heads. 'That,' she said pointing to the dimpled base. 'The perter the bottom...*perter*?'

'More pert,' he offered.

'The more pert the bottom,' she resumed, 'the finer the wine.' She lowered the bottle to the table again.

'That,' he said slowly, 'is the biggest load of bollocks I've ever heard.'

'It is?'

He nodded. 'There is more than one way to ensure great wine.' He paused. 'For example, go to France.'

'They have wine in France then?'

'Have you ever been?'

'Does a day trip to Calais count?'

'Not really.' He refilled her glass. 'You should go. I know this château in the south with a wonderful vineyard. There you will find many pert bottoms.'

'Your family estate?'

'Yes.'

She watched him, unsure if he was teasing her. If he was, then she couldn't tell. He seemed unusually sincere.

'As an expert,' he said, 'you will also be aware that although the grapevine is most productive in sunnier climes it produces wine of the very highest quality where it is at the margin of its existence.'

She thought about that for a moment. 'So a Scottish wine might be really good?'

'You still need *some* sun.'

She looked at him. 'French sun. Scottish rain.'

'I believe that would produce a highly favourable wine.'

He leaned in. Their lips almost brushing. His breath warm and sweet.

Her phone chirped and the moment shattered like a dropped snowglobe.

She considered ignoring it, the number wasn't one she recognised. But there was a good chance it was Willie. She picked up the phone. 'Willie?'

'Hi, Janey.'

Ordinarily she would have winced at the nickname, but there was something in his tone that made her overlook it this time. She left Tom sitting at the desk and moved to the other side of the room.

'So, how's the trip going? Did you meet Soderbergh?'

He started to answer and then stopped himself. She heard a catch in his voice. He gathered himself. 'There was no meeting. I've been stuck in the arse end of nowhere. I couldn't get a cab. My phone died. I've been walking for nine hours. In the rain. I just found a call box.'

'Oh, Willie.'

'I'm cold and wet and just feeling so...' She heard him hunt for the right word. He sighed. 'Miserable.'

Behind her Jane was aware of Tom slipping out of the room. And suddenly she was unhappy too. She told herself it was because of Willie, not because Tom had gone, taking the sunshine with him.

'But y'know what,' said Willie, 'I'm kind of glad the trip turned out so badly because it's made me realise a few things. I miss you, Janey. You're the best thing in my life.'

She could hear it in his voice, knew with dreadful certainty what the next words out of his mouth would be, almost as if she was writing them herself. She held her breath. Don't go there. Please. Not now.

'I love you,' he said.

She heard him sigh with perfect bliss, gathering confidence from saying the words aloud. He wasn't finished. There was a gathering pause at the other end of the line and then he said, 'Let's get married.'

CHAPTER 19

'I Wish It Would Rain Down', Phil Collins, 1990, Virgin

'THAT WASN'T THE PLAN,' said Roddy.

They were standing near the head of the lunch queue outside Mother India's Café. The pungent aroma of cumin and saffron drifted out of the door onto the street.

'No kidding,' said Tom. It was the day after he had barged in on a naked Jane; the image of her standing in the hall was vividly etched in his mind. Regrettably, so was the moment when Willie had called. In that instant it was clear to Tom that he'd outstayed his welcome and not wishing to intrude on what was obviously an intimate conversation he had swiftly departed. He was in the hallway when he heard her repeat Willie's proposal. *Married?*

He and Roddy had contrived to send Willie on a wild-goose chase so that they could focus on driving a wedge between Jane and her dad. Instead, somehow they'd brought Willie and Jane together. Talk about a plan backfiring.

'Kind of Wordsworthian,' said Roddy. 'Willie's per-ambulatory journey along the rain-dappled English lanes, reflecting on his place in nature, feeling so wretched that he begins to ponder his very existence and concludes that he needs to make a change. A big married change.'

'Do I look like I give a flying fuck?'

'Fair enough.'

'And you can't have dappled rain. Sunshine is dappled. Dapple. Bloody stupid word anyway.'

The queue shuffled forward.

He'd gone to Jane in order to come clean and apologise, although he couldn't remember if he'd actually said sorry. He presumed not. Given what had subsequently happened his act of contrition would have been a sideshow. An apol-ogy—no matter how heartfelt—paled beside a marriage proposal. He certainly hadn't confessed to her about his stupid plan. And when he'd opened the familiar glossy black front door to leave her place it had flashed through his mind that it was for the last time. She was moving on. Moving to Klinsch & McLeish. Moving on with Willie.

'A lifetime with Willie Scott,' he muttered. 'If that doesn't make her miserable, nothing will.'

'Look,' said Roddy, a note of exasperation entering his voice, 'I know things haven't worked out for the two of you, but surely you don't really, actually, totally want her to be unhappy?'

It was the cornerstone of their plan. But she was hap-pier than ever—engaged to be married, for god's sake. He had failed. In every previous relationship he had always made them cry, even when he hadn't intended to. So why couldn't he do it to her? 'It's complicated.'

'Roddy!'

Tom looked up to see Nicola Ball making her way along the pavement. She waved and Roddy waved back.

'Is she actually skipping?' asked Tom.

'I would say she has a skip in her step, yes.'

'So…you two?'

'Yup.'

'Are you sure?'

'About what?'

'She's a writer. I'll grant you the sex can be imaginative—but when you look in her eye you'll always wonder if you're going to end up in her next book.' Tom shrugged. 'In the end you're just material.'

He could tell that Roddy wasn't listening to a word.

'She likes curry,' he said, smoothing his hair. 'How many girls do you know who like curry? And not just tikka masala, I'm talking biryani.' He shook his head in wonder. 'And afterwards we're going to the Art Gallery.' He nodded across the road at the exuberant red sandstone façade of Kelvingrove Museum directly opposite. 'To see the *Annunciation*.' He gave a beatific smile. 'Curry and Botticelli—that might be my perfect day.' Then added after a thoughtful pause, 'And sex. Obviously.'

Nicola bounded up and the two of them embraced. They nuzzled each other and Tom had to look away.

Her new book was selling slowly, but at least it was selling. However, the numbers were nowhere near the level to extricate him from the hole he'd dug Tristesse into. And barring Nicola suddenly gaining overnight celebrity by committing a series of grisly murders that propelled her onto the front pages, or, in an ironic twist, being knocked down and killed by one of the precious buses she wrote about, they were unlikely to amount to much. Still, he wanted to sign her up for another two books. She wrote beautifully and if he could gently steer her towards a subject more befitting her lapidary prose then he was sure she had a great novel in her. But she was a long-term prospect, and as things stood Tristesse Books was not. He had another meeting with Anna LeFèvre later today when he expected her to bring out the torture equipment reserved for serious defaulters.

Finally Nicola acknowledged his presence.

'Tom,' she said, her demeanour turning formal.

'Nicola.' He inclined his head in a mocking neck-bow.

'Lovely news about Jane.'

'What is?'

She tutted. 'Her and Willie.'

For a moment he'd forgotten. It came back to him like a punch in the gut.

'Roddy told me. So romantic. Proposing to her in the rain.'

'He was in a call box.' He saw disapproval in Nicola's face; the social compact dictated he go along with the invented story. 'I'm sure they'll be very happy together,' he heard himself say.

'Married writers,' she mused. 'Going for long walks to solve tricky plot points, discussing the day's work as they prepare dinner, pillow-talk editing.' She sighed.

'Are you kidding?' he cut across her. Such simpering fantasy could not be tolerated. He would set her straight. 'Married writers means two utterly self-absorbed people pretending to listen to each other, but only really inter-ested in their own work. Bitter when the other receives a good review, furious when one is invited to a festival but there isn't a place for the other, jealously comparing the size of their royalty cheques. As for pillow talk, try sepa-rate bedrooms and most of the sex is imaginary.'

He was out of breath. In the awkward silence that fol-lowed his rant the only sound was the snort of air through his flaring nostrils. Why was he so angry? He wasn't sure he even believed what he was saying, but the soft-focus picture Nicola painted had piqued him.

'Your table is ready,' said the host at the door.

Roddy linked arms with Nicola and turned to Tom with a rigid smile. 'See you later then.'

'I thought we were having lunch?'

'*We* are.' Roddy angled his head towards Nicola.

'So why have I spent the last half hour waiting in this queue?' He could feel the anger rising again. 'What am I—a bookmark?'

'OK, OK,' said Roddy. 'Chill. Come for lunch.'

'Yes, please join us,' said Nicola.

She looked petrified. Tom felt his stomach lurch; he hadn't meant to frighten anyone, it had just sort of happened. 'I'm sorry,' he mumbled. 'I'll see you later.' He headed off along the pavement.

'No, come on,' said Roddy. 'Come back.'

'Can't. Don't know what I was thinking—got a meeting. Nicola?'

'Yes, Tom?' she said hesitantly.

'You are most definitely one of the foremost writers under the age of thirty in Scotland.' He smiled broadly.

Her face lit up and she burrowed into Roddy with pleasure. He caught the departing Tom's eye and gave him a big thumbs up, mouthing 'curry, Botticelli and sex'.

CHAPTER 20

'Rain in My Heart,' Frank Sinatra, 1968, Reprise

THE BEDROOM GLOWED with late afternoon light the colour of Lucozade.

When Jane walked in Willie was exactly where she'd left him two hours before, sitting up in bed wrapped in a tartan dressing gown, working on his typewriter which was propped on a wooden tray in front of him. The tray acted as a resonator, exaggerating the clack of the key-strikes. He interrupted his typing to cough consumptively into a fist.

He'd arrived home last week from his disastrous trip down south looking deathly pale and with a streaming cold. Jane's first, uncharitable, thought had been that in such a state he'd be forced to take time off his writing. But she'd been wrong. On his bedside table towered a stack of perfectly squared-off pages, each side a sheer vertical cliff. An unclimbable alp of words. It seemed to her that following the trip, he had recommenced his work with even greater intensity than before. He couldn't have contracted a fever? Not that she wanted him to be sick. Just a little fever. Something minor to slow him down.

She hovered in the doorway. They hadn't talked about the marriage proposal since his return. He hadn't mentioned it and she hadn't brought it up. She wondered if he'd changed his mind. He'd popped the question at the end of a long and emotional day, but perhaps in the aftermath he was regretting his impulsiveness. If she were being pedantic—and if this wasn't a perfect opportunity, nothing was—then he hadn't popped any question. On the phone he'd said 'let's get married'—a passive form of words that hadn't demanded a response from her. Technically speaking, anyway. Some women would have evinced delight and rapture; she remembered her surprise—shock—and then the call was over. In a daze she'd turned round to find Tom had gone.

Willie's subsequent silence on the subject had provoked in her a mixture of relief and indignation. Proposing to someone wasn't like putting up a shelf, something you could just say you'll do and then forget about. Then a few days ago when folding away some laundry she'd stumbled upon a ring-box in his pants drawer. She'd debated for at least half a second whether or not to peek inside and when she flipped open the lid to discover a pair of cufflinks she felt only relief.

'Can I get you anything?' she asked. 'A cup of tea? Piece of cake?'

He ignored her, continuing to hammer the keys until he

had filled up the page, and then with a flourish he ripped it out and slapped it down on top of the stack. He turned to her with a broad smile.

'The phone.'

'The phone?'

He gestured to the handset on the table. He could have reached it himself, but she was closer. She passed it to him. With a wink, he dialled and turned on the speaker.

'Global Creative Management, how may I direct your call?'

'Priscilla Hess,' said Willie.

There was a click, then a new voice said distractedly, 'Yes?'

'Priscilla,' said Willie with a flashy smile at Jane, 'it's your favourite client.'

'Peter!'

'No,' he said, sounding wounded. 'Willie.' He linked his hands behind his head. 'Listen, sweetheart, get out the big pen. Time to bill the bastards for my first draft.' He swivelled his head towards the tower of pages. 'I just finished the script.'

Jane gawped. Finished? How could he have finished? She couldn't write a word and he had *finished*. This was so unfair. On the other hand, it did mean she'd be free of his incessant typing, at least until he began the next draft.

There was one other topic they hadn't broached since his trip. When he'd departed for London she'd thrust a portion of her new novel into his hands. What did he think? Had he even read it? She'd dropped numerous hints but he'd singularly failed to pick up on any of them, and in one memorable instance—they'd been waiting for an order at the local Chinese takeaway—he had mistakenly believed she was trying to initiate sex. Either he was oblivious, she reasoned, or he was making a Herculean effort to avoid having to tell her what he really thought.

Her gaze fell on his completed screenplay. Reluctance to read worked both ways. She wasn't sure if she dared read *Happy Ending* the movie, certainly not after he had hinted at the destructive changes he'd made in adapting her novel. The script sat there like some arcane tome bound in flayed human skin, waiting to unleash an evil spirit upon anyone who opened its pages. Not that she was overreacting or anything.

Willie finished the call with Priscilla and hung up. 'We should celebrate,' he said.

'We should,' she agreed blandly. What were they celebrating exactly? His massacring her novel?

He coughed again and then wrinkled his nose. 'Now how about that cup of tea?'

Darsie was waiting for her in the kitchen, sitting on the countertop wearing a white Empire line dress and a what-the-fuck expression; a character combination that in the course of writing six novels and assorted juvenilia Jane Austen had somehow contrived to omit.

'He's sick,' said Jane.

'Oh, come on, he's just taking the piss now.'

'He said he loves me. Wants to marry me. You heard him.'

'Actually I didn't. Maybe it was in your vivid imagination.'

'And I kind of love him too.' On paper, anyway. 'I think he makes me happ—'

Willie's cry cut across her declaration. 'Any chance of that cup of tea, doll?' His voice dissolved into a wracking cough.

Jane studiously avoided Darsie's look of I-told-you-so, filling the kettle and setting it to boil.

She motioned to Darsie's dress. 'Interesting. Like Eliza Bennet with a licence to kill. What's with the gear then?'

'I'm wearing it in honour of your impending nuptials.'

Jane held up her hands, palms out. 'Hey—there'll be no talk of nuptials. Nobody's talking about a wedding. We're not even engaged.'

'I fear I misunderstand your meaning,' said Darsie. 'Is not marriage the desired end? Does not every Austen novel reach its satisfactory conclusion only with the advent of a proposal?'

'Well, yes. True. Marriage is conventionally, as you say, the end. But not now. Eventually. Maybe.'

'I favour spring for the wedding. With the apple blossom in full flower and the dusky scent of bluebells—aw bollocks, forget it. I can't keep this accent up. Jane, you're mental. You're not marrying that *eejit*. You know it and I know it. And let's face it, I am you, so you know it twice over.'

Jane pondered her character's words.

Darsie jumped down off the counter. 'I see what you're doing. Stop it. Stop it right now. Don't start with your internal narrative. I want to hear whatever you're thinking. Out loud. Admit it, you don't love Willie. You can't. Oh, Jane! Do anything rather than marry without affection.'

'I...I...'

The kettle began to shake and steam plumed from the spout as the bubbling water inside reached boiling point.

Darsie wagged a finger. 'Don't you dare sublimate your anxiety into a metaphor. Especially not one as crap as a boiling kettle.'

The cut-out kicked in with a click.

CHAPTER 21

'When It Rains It Pours', 50 Cent, 2005,
G-Unit/Interscope

TOM KNEW THAT the meeting with Anna was going to be
uncomfortable as soon as he spotted the bottle of ketchup
on her desk.

'What's this?' he asked, tentatively picking it up.

'Your cash flow,' replied Anna. She gestured to a chair.
'Now sit on *yer erse* and listen.'

He took a seat and she proceeded to talk him through
several impenetrable spreadsheets. When he looked at her
blankly and shrugged, she gave an exasperated sigh and
said she would summarise the company's financial position in language he understood.

'If Tristesse Books is a vegetable then it's the last wrin-
kly French bean in the supermarket.'

'Come on, surely it's not so bad,' he protested.

'You can't buy any more books.'

He rubbed his cheek. 'That's OK. I'm not planning on
taking on any new authors.'

'Yeah, I don't mean that. When I say you can't buy books, I mean *paperbacks*. And if I were you I'd think twice about newspapers and toilet roll.'

Tom felt sick. He knew things were serious, but had no idea they'd sunk this low.

'How much money have you got in your wallet right now?' she asked.

He dug it out and withdrew a single ten-pound note. She stretched across the desk and plucked it from his fingers.

'Hey! What are you doing?'

She brandished the note. 'Tristesse Books owes my bank thousands of pounds. I'm taking what I can get.'

'You can't just snatch money out of people's hands.' He paused. 'Can you?'

Anna raised an eyebrow.

'But that's my dinner money,' he pleaded.

'You're a big lad—missing one meal won't hurt you.'

He folded his arms and shifted uneasily. 'What about an overdraft extension?'

'Based on what exactly?'

'You know what,' he mumbled. 'Or should I say…who.'

'Ah yes, the ever reliable Jane Lockhart.' Anna's name-badge had worked its way loose from her jacket and she began to reattach it. 'Have you told her how much you need her?'

Tom frowned.

Anna shook her head briskly, grasping the misunder-standing. 'I meant need her new novel.'

'Yes, because authors work so much better under extreme stress. Jane lives in her head, she inhabits a make-believe world—she's fragile. I couldn't…'

'Why are you protecting her?' Anna sounded exasperated.

He wasn't sure. Jane had given him nothing but aggravation. Her delay in submitting the manuscript threatened not only the business he'd sweated to build, but now even his ability to buy a roll and sausage.

'Her new novel is wonderful.'

Anna leaned in, interested. 'So, she's finished it? Why didn't you say?'

Tom gave a pained look. 'Not finished exactly. But *nearly*.'

She sighed. 'No novel, no overdraft.'

'Then we have nothing else to discuss here.' He stood up to leave.

'Yes we do.' She drummed her fingers on the desk. 'Pandemic Media.'

'I told you,' he snapped. 'I don't care if they've increased their offer again.'

'They haven't.'

'Oh?'

'Word's out that you're neck-deep in the shit. They've reduced the offer. They still want you but you're not worth as much as you used to be.'

'It's irrelevant,' he said with what he hoped came across as a dismissive sweep of his arm. 'I'm not for sale.' He stalked to the door.

'I like you, Tom. You might look like a Chanel model, but you're a smart guy.'

He hesitated in the doorway. He liked Anna too; her caustic tongue and plain speaking were refreshing, though rarely comforting.

'So, tell me,' she went on, 'what the hell are you doing here? Why give yourself all this hassle? The Pandemic money is still generous. Do the deal, find some pretty *jeune fille*, settle down somewhere sunny and enjoy your life.'

It sounded simple when she said it like that. Maybe it was simple. A change would be good, mix things up a little. The suggestion held some appeal. Perhaps he'd go back to France for a while. Stay long enough to start thinking in French again and allow the strange Glaswegian dialect he'd acquired to lapse. Perhaps he'd stay long enough to forget Glasgow altogether. When he thought about it, there wasn't much left for him here.

Anna sat behind her desk, awaiting his answer.

'I couldn't do that,' he said with a half-smile, 'I'd miss the rain.'

'Forty-eight hours,' she said brusquely. 'Either you do the deal with Pandemic Media, or, as they say where you come from, *tu es totally screwed*.'

He turned to go.

'Wait.' With an indulgent sigh, Anna drew out the ten-pound note and slapped it down on her desk, sliding it towards him. 'Don't buy fried food.'

*

The office roof had sprung a leak. He returned from his meeting to find rainwater puddling in the corridor. At first he was thankful that it hadn't spoiled any of the new books waiting to go out to stores, but then he made a quick calculation and with a horrible sinking feeling realised that the insurance claim would likely be worth more than the proceeds of any book sales. He went in search of a mop and bucket.

He'd often listened to established authors give wannabes the same advice: if there is anything else you could do, any other profession you could follow that would make you happy, then do that instead of write. Writing is hard, lonely and invariably unprofitable. As he positioned the bucket under the leak, he reflected that precisely the same guidance could be applied to independent publishing.

Through the window overlooking the courtyard he watched a courier dodge puddles as he approached Tristesse's front door clutching a package, which Tom felt sure must be from some or other creditor. He considered hiding behind a nearby book stack, but then the courier spotted him through the window and gave a cheery wave.

Reluctantly, he opened the door and signed for the delivery.

He sat down at his desk with the suspicious package. As he reached for his letter-knife his eye fell on Jane's plant. It seemed to him that even though his dim office was not the most conducive spot for life to prosper—plant or otherwise—it had indeed flourished since its abduction. He was no gardener but had tended it with great care. He took a leaf between his thumb and forefinger. Maybe it liked him. Once this was all over he'd return it, although he'd have to come up with a credible reason that explained why he was in possession of her treasured plant. That was a problem for another day.

Warily he slid the knife along the top of the package, working it open an inch at a time as if it might explode in his hands. Slowly, he drew out the contents. It wasn't from an angry supplier or the credit card company. It was from Willie.

In large letters across a cover page was typed: '*Happy Ending*—Screenplay by Willie Scott'. And beneath, in a much smaller font: 'Adapted from the novel by Jane Lockhart'.

Willie had included a business card, edged in gold, his name embossed along the top, and a handwritten message, 'Read it and weep. Best wishes, Willie.'

Tom didn't hesitate. He picked up the screenplay and hurled it across the room. Muttering furiously to himself in French, he marched out into the corridor, colliding with the now half-full bucket of rainwater. He swore as the cold water seeped through his right shoe, soaking his foot. Willie was such a tit. His arrogant message was the work of someone who believed that he had won. But he and Willie weren't in any competition. What did Willie have that he wanted? Nothing.

In fact, in other circumstances a film version of *Happy Ending* would be the greatest gift Willie could have given him. The bump in book sales when the film came out would be huge. Unfortunately, it didn't look like Tristesse would be around long enough to benefit.

Tom retraced his steps to the doorway of his office. The script lay splayed out over the back of the sofa. He decided categorically, finally, absolutely not to read it, right up until the moment he sat down on the sofa and opened to the first page.

A wicked thought snuck up on him. Willie was a writer and if there was one thing Tom knew it was writers. He knew how to cosset them, but moreover he knew how to destroy them. He would read the screenplay like any other submission, and then hit Willie with a set of notes. These would be no ordinary notes; they would be the Ten Plagues of notes—so damaging, so foul, that their legend would reverberate through the ages. Writers would talk of them in horrified whispers for generations. Willie would never recover.

'Fade in. Exterior. City street. Night,' he read.

The rain-slick sidewalk shines wetly beneath sodium streetlamps the color of rotten teeth. The drizzle-infused air is punctuated by the intermittent drone of combustion engines and the searching sweep of car headlights. Far below street level, an underground train rumbles through Victorian tunnels.

Above, in the looming tenement building, from behind a half-closed window edged with an incandescent line drawn by a 60-watt lamplight, drifts the faint mewling of Coldplay's 'Clocks'.

The quick clip of heels. A figure appears out of the darkness at the end of the street. Tucked beneath the perfect round form of a bright red umbrella, JANET shelters from the relentless downpour.

Tom read on, marvelling at the screenplay. Willie had taken everything that was rooted and heartfelt about Jane's novel and made it generic and sickly sentimental. Crucial moments were missing from scenes, stripping them of their meaning and texture. Characters were skinned alive and in a miracle of reverse alchemy, sparkling dialogue culled from the novel had become dull and lumpen. Everywhere it was possible to misrepresent or alter, he had done so; every page offered a fresh horror that proved how little he understood the novel. How little he understood Jane. It was compelling in its awfulness.

Ninety-seven pages later Tom had reached the final scene. Of all Willie's offences, none was more egregious than what he had done to the ending. Tom read with growing disbelief.

EXT. GLASGOW HOUSING SCHEME—DAWN

JANET and her DAD walk out through the rusting gates of the run-down estate. As they step into a new day, the RAIN finally STOPS.

A pale sun struggles over the grey tower-blocks, and as its rays touch the discarded bottles and syringes that litter the wasteland beyond the gates, it transforms them into something almost beautiful.

JANET reaches for her DAD's hand. He grips it hard. Won't let go. Not again. Never again.

DAD

I love you, Janet.

JANET

And I love you, Dad.

She shivers in the cool of the early morning. He removes his coat and places it round her shoulders.

Then he looks back one last time at the crumbling tower-block, once a memorial to their shared tragedy, now a soaring symbol of their triumph.

DAD

Well, Janet, who'd have believed three weeks ago that we'd both get our happy ending?

And as they walk off, hand-in-hand, we FADE TO BLACK.

THE END

Tom called Roddy as soon as he had finished. At the other end of the phone he could hear him addressing his class.

'Which is why Shakespeare never left New York again. OK. Chapter twenty-four. Read. Or be punished.' His voice grew louder as he turned to the phone. 'What is it? I'm right in the middle of teaching Generation Uhh.'

'He's changed the ending.'

'I don't follow.'

'Willie. He's only gone and changed the ending of Jane's novel.'

Roddy let out a long, low whistle. 'That's bad. All you changed was her title and she thinks you're a complete and total wanker—'

Tom could hear titters from the kids, and then Roddy's voice again, in teacher mode.

'That's Juan Kerr,' he said without missing a beat. 'He was a nineteenth-century South American revolutionary.'

Tom held the screenplay open at the last page. 'This will break her heart.'

'Uh, isn't that what we've been trying to accomplish all along?'

'I suppose.'

'You suppose? Come on, this is the moment. Seize the day. Once more unto the breach!'

'You're quoting *Henry V* to motivate a Frenchman?'

'Listen, *mon ami*, it's time to get over Agincourt,' said Roddy. 'If you want your novel, then man up. It couldn't be simpler, all you have to do is make sure she reads Willie's screenplay. She'll be distraught. Melancholy. Miserable. Mission Accomplished.'

'Yeah,' said Tom doubtfully. He looked down at the screenplay, took a deep breath and made a decision.

*

After searching for him in what felt like every possible hangout in the West End—there were even more poseurs' cafés than he remembered—Tom finally found Willie in Paramount, a wannabe American diner on Argyle Street. Tom had passed by it for years without venturing in, but he could see how the place might appeal to an ersatz Hollywood screenwriter.

Willie sat beneath a poster for Martin Scorsese's epic boxing movie, *Raging Bull.* The battered, haunted face of Robert De Niro stared over the top of Willie's head as he tucked messily into a bagel.

Tom looked him up and down. He was wearing running shoes that resembled human feet, loose-fitting shorts that gaped alarmingly about his thighs and a matching black T-shirt, lightly stained with sweat. It looked like he'd just been for a run. In between bites of his bagel he attempted to engage the attention of two young women at the next table. It was clear to Tom that Willie believed he was being more charming than they did.

'So, you fancy a leg-up in showbusiness…?'

There was a thud and Willie's coffee cup rattled against its saucer as Tom slapped the copy of his screenplay down in front of him.

'You've given it a happy ending,' said Tom.

Willie smiled at the two girls and then looked up slowly to meet his accuser's gaze. 'And your point?

'The point is Jane's novel doesn't end happily.'

Willie lowered his bagel and brushed crumbs from his sleeve. 'Who the hell wants to walk out of a movie feeling miserable?'

Had the man never heard of art-house cinema? Tom stopped himself from responding; this wasn't the moment for a debate. 'You have to change it back.'

'Uh, I don't think so.' There was chuckle of disbelief in his voice.

Part of Tom wanted to let Willie have it his way, let the smug screenwriter make the same mistake that he had. But this wasn't about him. 'She doesn't know yet, does she?'

Willie stirred his coffee.

'Do you have any idea what this'll do to her—to both of you? I made a mistake and I can't take it back. But, Willie, if you truly love her, change it.'

Willie leant back, laced his hands behind his head and regarded Tom with a quizzical air.

'What's going on here?'

The man was infuriatingly slow on the uptake. Did he have to spell it out? 'You just don't get her, do you?'

'Oh, I get her all right.' A sneer curled his lip. 'Every night I get her—any way up I fancy.'

Tom wasn't sure why the innuendo at Jane's expense bothered him so much. It wasn't as if he was some old-school gentleman confronting a cad in order to protect her honour, and yet as soon as Willie said the words he balled his hands into fists and raised them to his chest in what he hoped was an approximation of a boxing pose.

'Right! Come on.' He shuffled his feet and waved his fists. 'You and me. Here. Now!'

He knew as soon as he opened his mouth that it was a terrible miscalculation. But he didn't care. One punch, he prayed, just let me land one good punch. Willie rose up like a black wave, tipping back his chair, sending it clattering to the floor. The ventilated legs of his shorts flared, exposing the café to an unwelcome flash of hairy balls cupped snugly in white mesh. The other patrons looked on in horrified silence at the unfolding brawl.

The last time they'd come to blows, Tom had allowed Willie to throw the first punch. At least, that was how he remembered it. This time he wasn't taking any chances. He drew back his right arm and flailed at Willie. The blow glanced harmlessly off his chest.

'Hit a sick man, would you?' Willie growled. Elbows pressed tight to his body, he began to advance on Tom. 'I am a piece of bamboo,' he chanted. 'Firm but flexible. Rooted but yielding.'

There was a blur as his arm shot out in a deadly effective straight line. The last thing Tom saw was De Niro's tenderised raw meat face staring out balefully from the film poster.

CHAPTER 22

'Scottish Rain', The Silencers, 1988, RCA

'READ IT. GO ON, you know you want to.' Darsie held out a copy of Willie's screenplay.

They were outside, in the square of garden that filled the back court amidst the flats. The rain had given way to late afternoon sunlight that slanted down past the high tenements.

Jane swung a watering can over a flowering quilt of Busy Lizzies. Despite the earlier downpour the bed was bone-dry, as usual; the spot in the corner where she'd planted the flowers protected from all weathers beneath the overhanging buildings. The only permanently dry corner in Glasgow.

'I'm not reading it,' she said firmly. 'I told you. I don't need to.' After thinking it through she had decided to take the high ground. She had to trust Willie. He was an experienced writer—he knew his business. He knew what he was doing, even if the alterations she suspected he'd made to her novel might make her uncomfortable.

'But what if he's changed stuff?'

'I'm sure he has. A film is not a book. Changes are not only inevitable, but desirable. If you ask me, adaptation is sorely underestimated as an art form. I prefer to think of Willie's screenplay as a response to my novel, rather than a slavish copy.' She'd been practising this speech for days, repeating it like a mantra in the hope that it would still her anxiety. She was still waiting for the Zen calm to descend.

'Yeah, but what if he's put in a car chase, or something, y'know, really crap?' Darsie opened the screenplay to the middle and scanned the page hopefully.

'It doesn't matter what he's done,' said Jane evenly. 'The novel will still be there on my bookshelf, just the same as before. The film will have another life of its—'

'No way!' gasped Darsie.

'What?' she snapped, her serene acceptance ruffling in an instant. 'He's put in a bloody car chase, hasn't he?'

'Uh, not exactly.' Darsie looked up, deep in thought. 'Remind me, does the bridge explode in the novel?'

Jane snatched the screenplay out of her hands, sat down on the lawn and turned to the first page.

She came out here about this time to read on those infrequent days when the grass was still warm from the sun and the light had softened after the peak of its midday harshness. It was a comfortable, shady spot where she'd passed the time with some of her favourite novelists. Not today. She started to read.

Despite everything she feared, there was a part of her that still held out hope that Willie's script would be a love letter; that it would say more about his love for her than he'd so far been able to put into any other words. But as she read each terrible new scene, wincing at every clunking misstep, she felt her body tense and her throat constrict, until by the end she was struggling to breathe. She fell back on the grass, closed her eyes and let out a moan of despair.

'I'm not going to say I told you so,' said Darsie.

'Shut. Up.'

Jane trudged back up to her flat, every step on the worn stone an effort. *How could he?* She slammed the heavy front door behind her and stomped into the living room. *How dare he!*

She wrenched open the stiff bay window and perched on the ledge, looking out over the green canopy of trees, so thick with leaves that they hid the road beneath. At this time of year her flat was like a tree house in the woods, cut off from the rest of the world. Not cut off enough, she decided.

Darsie appeared at her side with two large glasses of red wine.

'Where's yours?' Jane asked, grabbing them both. What was it about the men she dated that they all felt the need to rewrite her? Tom had changed her title and Willie, well, he had changed everything else.

A breeze fanned the trees. The sound always had a

calming effect. If she gritted her teeth perhaps she could forgive a lot of what Willie had perpetrated on her novel—but not that ending. What was he thinking? She'd ask him, simple as that. He was due back from his run any time now. They'd sit down together and talk it through like grown-ups, and then he would do what she told him.

Or perhaps he had a truly excellent reason for rejecting her shattering final chapter, the ending that readers told her through their tearful letters that they loved, the high watermark of her writing career, thus far. It was the right ending, the *best* ending. She heard the front door open and close. He was back. She felt her heart race. It was the only ending. She would demand that he reinstate it and ditch his own insipid attempt. Either it went, or he did.

'Janey?'

Willie strolled into the living room, wrapping a length of bandage around the bloodied knuckles of his right hand. For a moment Jane forgot about the script. 'What happened to you?'

He flexed the hand and smiled. 'Ran into an old friend.' He flopped down on the sofa and stretched out. 'Bit early for that, isn't it?' He motioned to the two glasses of wine, adding with a puzzled expression, 'Who's the other one for?'

She put them down on her desk next to his screen-play and turned to close the window. After he'd proposed she'd made a list of writers married to other writers. Siri Hustvedt and Paul Auster, Maggie O'Farrell and William

Sutcliffe, Nicole Krauss and Jonathan Safran Foer. To her surprise it seemed that it could work. The discovery had made her cautiously hopeful. Two writers living and working together—she would pen novels and he would adapt them for film. A perfect, symbiotic relationship. But it had already gone wrong for the two of them.

'Meant to say, Janey, I read your new novel.'

She had been prepared to lambast him for crimes against adaptation, but this threw her like a sideswipe in one of his stupid car chases. 'You did?'

He nodded. 'Just the chapters you gave me.' The bandage on his knuckles had worked its way loose. 'It's terrific.'

She waited for him to elaborate, but when he didn't she asked, 'Is that all?'

He started to rewrap the bandage. '*Really* terrific?'

That's not what she wanted. She wasn't fishing for praise, she wanted—and she had to laugh at the irony—she wanted him to be…engaged. Tom had had more to say on the first sentence than Willie had on the first thirty chapters.

'So, now that I've read your thing, you should read mine,' he said.

Ah, so that's what this was about. I'll show you mine if you show me yours. She glanced at the script. 'I have read it.'

Willie perked up immediately, spreading his arms wide in invitation. 'And?'

'Willie…'

'Now, try not to be defensive. Remember, it's an adaptation. You can't have every scene from the novel in the film or it'd be twelve hours long. And to be honest, you had a lot of unnecessary stuff in there. There were whole chapters I could do with a single look. And a lot of your dialogue doesn't work so well when you say it out loud—yes, I know, but you need a screenwriter's ear to hear it. So I punched it up, gave it some—' he made a fist and moved it back and forth like a piston '—real emotion.' He got up from the sofa. 'All in all I'm pretty pleased.'

She bit her tongue. 'But it's a first draft. Things will change, right?'

'Sure, sure,' he said with a generous wave. Then stopped. 'Well, maybe a few tiny things. My first drafts are most writers' fourth or fifth.' He crossed to the desk and gathered up his screenplay in both hands, holding it out like a votive offering. 'It's all in here,' he breathed. 'With the right director, this is a go script.'

Then go, she wanted to say. Just take it and go! 'But Willie, what about the ending?'

He gave a shrug of incomprehension. 'What is it with you people and the ending?'

'What are you talking about? Which *people*?'

'Oh, I bumped into your publisher,' he said casually. A drop of blood fell to the floor. They both gazed at it, and then he brushed it away with his foot. 'Cup of tea?'

'No. No, thank you.' She watched him head into the kitchen. 'Why were you talking to Tom?'

'I sent him the screenplay. Wanted to rub his nose in it.' He held up his hands in a gesture of admission. 'I know, I know, not very mature, but you don't mind, do you? He's a prat.' He rubbed his bandaged hand. 'Well, the lanky French prat got what he deserved.'

'You hit him?!' She cringed. 'Again?'

'He hit me first,' he said indignantly.

'Oh, Willie, what were you thinking? Why did you go looking for him?'

'I didn't. He came looking for me. Had a beef about my ending. Like he knows anything about filmmaking. Every French film I've ever seen ends the same way,' he said, rising to his theme. 'A shot of some guy in a hat sitting alone in a room smoking a cigarette. In black and white.'

'What was his beef?'

'Hmm?'

'Why didn't Tom appreciate your ending?'

Willie gave a dismissive pout. 'Uh, it was about you. He said you wouldn't like it.'

She struggled to understand the implication of what he was saying. Tom had read Willie's screenplay and then confronted him about the ending, earning another beating for his audacity.

'But you do, right? You like my ending, don't you?'

'I…'

'I know it's not the same as yours, but it's what people

want. You've got to trust me on this. I've never said it before, but your book is bloody depressing. No one wants the hero to die in the final chapter.'

She thumped a palm against her chest. 'I want him to die. That's why I wrote it like that. And a hundred thousand satisfied readers agree.'

'Yeah, but did you ever think that maybe a hundred thousand could have been a million,' he was in her face now, 'if you'd just written one more chapter—*he's not really dead!* Whammo! They walk off into the sunset.'

Then he said it. And in his expression she saw that he truly believed he was playing his trump card.

'For god's sake, Janey, the book's even called *Happy Ending*.'

*

Willie moved out the following afternoon. There was no shouting, which in Jane's experience was always a sign that nothing was left worth fighting for. She was surprised at how little stuff he had to pack up since for most of the time he'd lived there it felt like he'd colonised her flat. He explained to her that he followed the philosophy of Al Pacino's character in the movie *Heat*, who boasted that he had so few ties he could walk away from his life in thirty seconds. Willie reckoned he had it down to about twelve minutes including tablewear, but it was a work in progress. What about his desk? she'd asked. Oh, shit. He'd forgotten about that. The desk was really going to mess up his exit. He told her he'd send someone to collect it in a few days.

'Where will you go?' she asked.

He shrugged. 'Back to my mum's.'

'Not Hollywood?'

'Oh, yeah, of course. LA, baby! But, y'know, not now. When the time is right.'

He stood in the doorway, a cardboard box full of clothes, books, photos and his two film posters rolled up under one arm, his typewriter tucked beneath the other.

'I don't understand how you can do this over a dumb ending.'

'No,' she said. 'You don't.'

He looked mystified and then shrugged. 'Well, if it's any consolation I don't think it would've worked out with us. To be honest, Janey, I just don't get all that worshipping your pain stuff.'

She closed the door and listened to his footsteps recede down the stairs until they faded into the background hum of the day.

She resented his parting accusation; she didn't worship her pain. Of course in her writing she drew on her painful upbringing, but she didn't venerate it, whatever Willie believed. What did she care? She didn't have to answer his charge any more.

It was a pain dating men with opinions about her work. Her next boyfriend would be functionally illiterate, she decided. One of those men who never cracked open a book unless it was a car manual. She'd read on Jezebel that the average woman used twenty thousand words a day and the average man just seven thousand. That was still too many. Next time she was aiming for a sub-thousand bloke—guttural, but with fastidious personal hygiene. During the day she'd labour in her study, alone, only to join him in the evening for dinner. He'd greet each new novel of hers with a bland 'that's nice, dear' and she'd be fascinated by his job in finance. She wouldn't dedicate a novel to him since he'd never bother to read the inscription. There was just one problem with this perfect picture.

It sounded lonely.

*

The following day Jane's dad helped her move Willie's desk out of the flat. By mid-afternoon the outline of four claw feet in the dust and a couple of brass drawing pins in the wall were the only reminders that he had ever been there. When they were done, Benny hugged her and said he could stay, if she wanted company. To her surprise she nodded and they sat and talked about nothing in particular until dinnertime. But it only postponed the inevitable moment when he did finally leave, and she was alone in the empty flat.

She wandered through the vacant rooms half-expecting to find Darsie lounging on the sofa drinking champagne to celebrate Willie's eviction, but her heroine was nowhere to be found, which was a shame as it would have been nice to hear her voice.

Willie had even cleared all of his bottles from the bathroom cabinet—and gone off with her Sensodyne, she noted. She was about to leave when she noticed something poking out from under the bath. It was a page from her manuscript. Briefly she puzzled how it had got there and then guessed what had happened. Tom must have dropped it the night he stole the first three chapters and locked himself in here.

She knelt down. The page was marked up with notes in his familiar red pen, first impressions scratched out hurriedly as he read. But amongst them was something else. He'd written her name. There it was scrawled in the margin in his distinctive hand—just her first name. She tried to tie it to the paragraph opposite, looking for some significance, something to explain what it was doing there, but it seemed that in the midst of his reading he had simply felt the need to write out her name. When she read it she couldn't help but hear it in his voice.

She screwed up the page and felt the cold tiles on her back as she slumped against the bathroom wall and studied the shape of the swaying bough through the frosted glass of the window. She wasn't sure how long she sat there, but the next thing she knew it was dark and she was at her desk, the Prophetic Sad playing on her turntable.

I tell myself I can't hold out forever.

She looked round the room: the withered umbrella

plant; the row of red and white Klinsch & McLeish spines along her bookcase; the pub quiz trophy. The page on which he had written her name.

But you can't see my tears in the rain.

The laptop lay open, the page frozen at Chapter 37. The cursor blinked.

Jane began to write.

CHAPTER 23

'I Can See Clearly Now (the Rain is Gone)', Johnny Nash, 1972, Epic

'THAT'S QUITE A SHINER.' Benny Lockhart scrutinised Tom's latest black eye, or, more accurately, the black eye he had sustained on top of his previous black eye. His vision had almost returned to normal after his latest run-in with Willie's fist, but the eye still throbbed and the skin around the socket was the colour of a ripe plum.

'Was it over a woman?' inquired Donald MacDonald.

'Over an ending,' explained Roddy.

Donald nodded with the appreciation of a man who had experience of such things. He sloshed a whisky chaser into his pint, adding, 'Of course, your compatriot, Alexandre Dumas, fought his fair share of duels.'

'Yeah, this was less pistols at dawn, more pissed-up in Partick.'

Tom surveyed the diverse group propping up the bar in the Walter Scott. A poet, an alcoholic, a teacher and a

Frenchman walk into a pub. It was the set-up to a joke, although the punchline escaped him for now.

He'd asked them all here tonight. In less than twenty-four hours Anna was expecting an answer regarding Pandemic Media's offer. Tristesse Books was on the ledge, a bloodthirsty crowd far below chanting 'jump'. Partly he wanted to canvass the other men's opinions, but mostly he wanted their company as he drank himself into oblivion, or as close to it as his limited resources would allow.

Donald peeled back the sleeve of his tweed jacket to expose a sandy-haired arm mottled with liver spots. He pointed to an old scar.

'FR Leavis, 1965. We came to blows over a review he gave me.' He took a step back from the bar and with surprising agility kicked his leg up onto it then rolled back his trouser-leg to reveal another ancient wound. 'Norman Mailer. Skye Book Festival, 1969.'

Not to be outdone Roddy turned his head to one side and tapped a finger over a tiny mark behind his left ear. 'Inter-schools badminton championships, under-15s, quarter-finals, 1998.'

'That, young man,' said Donald, squinting, 'is hardly a wound. Indeed it is no more than what my six-year-old granddaughter would refer to as a *boo-boo*.' He took a thoughtful pull on his pint. 'Health and Safety killed off the brawlers. These days you can't throw a punch without a risk assessment.'

Tom nursed his pint of lager and studied Benny. Jane's dad remained conspicuously silent as the others recounted the origins of their injuries. Tom had no intention of bringing him into this particular conversation, since his answers were likely to be far more troubling than bad reviews and badminton. However, Donald had no such inkling.

'What about you, sir?' inquired the poet. 'A man of the Glaswegian persuasion must surely have a notable mortification of the flesh, or two.'

Benny nodded slowly. 'I've handed out a few doin's over the years, aye, got my head kicked in a few times too. But never over a book.' He stared into his orange juice. 'Money and women.' He put his head on one side. 'Mostly women.' He turned to Tom. 'Why were you so worked up, son? It's just words.'

How could he explain it to Benny? Their experiences were so different. Perhaps unbridgeable. Tom's life revolved around words: shaping them, binding them, publishing them. In his world what Willie had done demanded confrontation. It was ignorant. It was criminal. But in his dudgeon an uncomfortable thought needled away: was it any worse than what he had done by changing Jane's title without telling her? With a pang he remembered that despite his best intentions, he had never quite got round to apologising for that—and it was too late now.

'Let me get this right, son.' Benny leant on the bar. It was clear to Tom that his explanation hadn't satisfied

Mr Lockhart. 'You read Willie's play, got mad about the ending and told him to change it—a man who'd already decked you in a garage in Bridgeton under totally humiliating circumstances in front of a hundred folk?'

'A hundred and fifty,' added Roddy helpfully.

'And I wouldn't say *totally* humiliating,' said Tom quietly.

'Over an ending?' Benny shook his head incredulously.

Donald chuckled into his pint. 'I believe Mr Lockhart's exposition contains a subtext.'

'I don't know about that,' said Benny. 'I just think there's more to this than meets the eye.' He rolled his shoulders and gave an awkward cough. 'Now I'm no' very good at "expressin' my feelings" but you young guys, you're into all that shite, aye?'

'I know men who have degrees in that shite,' said Roddy.

'Aye, well.' Benny swallowed. 'See, the only feelings I give a damn about are my Jane's, right? I fucked up her life for long enough, now I want to make it better.' He looked at Tom. 'And I think you do too.' In a reflex action, seeking Dutch courage for what he had to say next, Benny gulped down the rest of his orange juice and banged the glass down on the bar. 'You didn't get your head caved in for an ending, son.' He squirmed. 'You love her.'

Tom didn't reply at once. After all his talk of words he couldn't find a single one. Donald laughed out loud—a deep, joyful sound—and began to declaim in a booming voice. Poetry curdled the thick air.

As he recited his paean to true love, the rest of the pub fell uncomfortably silent at the dubious development in their midst. When he finished the only sound was the TV commentary rounding up the racing results and then the burble of regular conversation closed over the hush like returning seawater as the drinkers turned back gratefully to their pints.

Roddy gawped. 'That was beautiful. One of yours?'

'Edwin Morgan,' said Donald tersely. 'Bastard.' He turned to the barman. 'Mein host, another round for my friends.' He thumbed at Tom. 'And a double for the young man having the amorous revelation.' He laughed again. 'Oh, and before you ask me for my advice on women, don't. Three divorces, all my fault, apparently. According to my beloveds I made the same mistake each time.'

'And what was that?' asked Roddy.

'No idea.'

Tom's tongue had ceased working, awaiting instructions from his brain, which was replaying Benny's words in a loop. You *love* her. *You* love her. You love *her*. It was a lie, what they said about realisation. The writers had it wrong; realisation didn't 'dawn', nothing so disconnected as sitting on a rock with your arms around each other watching the sun come up. Realisation was a plummeting elevator. The precipitous snap of steel, followed by a churning freefall. But at least you knew where you were going. Finally.

He'd come to Scotland to escape the endless sunshine that bleached ideas and enervated imagination. She'd come to him out of the rain-dark streets. But he'd made the same mistake everyone else had. Confused the writer with the writing. She wasn't some miserable novelist in thrall to her pain. The sun came out.

He loved her.

'Tom? Tom?!' Roddy's voice sounded far away. 'I think he's having a stroke.'

'Nonsense,' said Donald MacDonald, in a field by the sound of it, the wind blowing away his words. 'What we are witnessing here is a *coup de foudre*, a thunderbolt of love. And in the original French too.' He clapped his hands. 'Marvellous!'

Tom felt a hard hand grip his shoulder, calluses rubbing through his shirt, and he was back. Benny's eyes locked on his.

'I'll be honest wi' you,' said the older man, 'If you don't get over there right this minute an' tell her how you feel, then you and me are gonnae have words.' His hand dug into the fleshy part of Tom's shoulder. 'And I'm no talking about your kind of words, I'm talking *real* words, from my side of town. Y'understand?'

'I understand,' said Tom. 'But…'

'But what?' said Benny sharply.

He'd tried to do the honourable thing by her. She'd chosen the other man. He hadn't respected her title, but felt he had to respect that. 'She's with Willie now.'

Donald MacDonald elbowed his way between Tom and Benny, his bushy eyebrows clashing in the centre of his forehead like two small storm clouds. 'I beg your pardon, *monsieur*, but you should be ashamed of yourself. A Frenchman unwilling to declare his *amour* for fear of upsetting marital convention?' He shook his head in disgust. 'A sad day for the *République*. The Tricolour will hang at half-mast.'

'She isn't,' said Benny.

'What?'

'With him,' he explained. 'Willie moved out.'

Roddy, who until that moment had been listening to the unfolding revelations in open-mouthed silence, let out a girlish squeak of excitement at this sudden reversal.

'Behold,' boomed Donald, 'the *peripeteia* around which our story turns!'

'He's gone?' Tom had to confirm he'd heard right.

'I bloody hope so,' said Benny, clutching his lower back, 'I'm no' carting that desk back up those stairs.'

'Well, what are you waiting for, man? The Muses have conspired to give you a third act.' Donald gestured magisterially to the pub door. '*Allez-y!*'

CHAPTER 24

'Looks Like Rain', The Grateful Dead, 1990, Arista

THE END CAME swiftly. After weeks of pent-up frustration the last chapter burst onto the page as fast as she could type it. Occasionally an idea would overtake her fingers to leave a pile-up of misspelled words and random letters, which she would have to go back over and decipher. But she knew where she was going. She pushed on towards the novel's climax. In the end it was so obvious she wondered what had kept her from seeing it all this time. Darsie and Tony Douglas were clearly not meant to be together. More than that, she'd realised that they weren't meant for anyone else either.

Neither would make it out alive; both had to die in the final chapter.

She wiped away a tear for their imminent demise. Even now she had the power to make things turn out all right. One word could change the outcome. In her head she heard Darsie's desperate pleas, but hardened her heart against them and bent to her task. The world didn't need another happy ending.

First she killed off Tony. A serial betrayer whose love for Darsie was a sham, he deserved to die. But even as she dispatched him she took no delight in his end. A flurry of keystrokes sent him to his shocking fate at the hands of the razor gang.

Then it was Darsie's turn to shuffle off the mortal coil. It would be an epilogue of sorts, set some twenty years after Tony's murder, Darsie's passing altogether slower and more painful than his swift, brutal exit. She needed to suffer all that time, broken with the knowledge that he never loved her. *Where's my happy ending?* Don't look for it here, sweetheart. Over six agonising pages she dies trembling and forgotten in an empty corridor of the hospice calling out his name.

And then it was over. She rested her fingers against the warm keys and looked up from the page, half expecting to see Darsie lounging on the sofa and in the next moment knowing that she would never see her again. The gauzy, vivacious Darsie snuffed out, her dirty laugh silenced forever. The loss palpable. That feeling of closing a book and saying goodbye to beloved characters, but amplified by the knowledge that she did this. In cold ink.

There was no point hanging around. The sooner she delivered the novel the sooner she could get on with the rest of her life. She brought up Tom's email address and attached the manuscript, but as she was about to press

'Send' she hesitated. One click and it would finally be over between them.

She discarded the half-composed email, telling herself she couldn't bear him thinking she was avoiding the awkwardness of a confrontation. Far from it, she relished the opportunity. She loaded her printer with a fresh ream of paper, hit print and settled down to wait for the finished manuscript. She would look him in the eye, hand him the novel and tell him precisely what she thought of him. One last time.

*

He wasn't in. The office was closed and the flat above it in darkness. She clutched the newly minted manuscript, still warm from the laser printer. So much for the dramatic showdown. It was one of real life's letdowns that people rarely showed up on cue.

She cupped a hand to the large plate-glass window that overlooked the courtyard and peered inside for any signs of life. As she scanned the silent and empty office a face smiled back at her from the shadowy space between two tall book stacks. She jumped back. It was her own face, smile set in cardboard. The life-sized promotional cutout was an old friend, having accompanied her on every leg of her debut book tour before being retired to the store cupboard. Tom must have fished out the doppelganger in preparation for the launch of the new book.

She remembered the day the picture was taken, turn-

ing up at the office, excited at the prospect of a professional photoshoot only to discover that Tom was to be her
David Bailey. On seeing her disappointment he had pro-
fessed a deep interest in portrait photography and affected
an indignant air when she teased that maybe he was just
trying to save a few quid on a proper photographer. Then
he'd led her upstairs to find that he'd set up a tripod and
camera. In his bedroom.

When she'd given him a dubious look he explained
that the light in here was perfect. His bedroom? Yes.
He'd pointed to an airy window explaining that its
north-facing aspect offered the classic portrait light. Think
of Vermeer's *Girl with a Pearl Earring*, he'd said, and
then instructed her to get her kit off.

When she'd roundly objected he gestured to an outfit laid out on the bed: a pair of houndstooth trousers, an orange shirt and a silk waistcoat. She loved it
all. It was exactly the sort of thing she'd choose herself. And in the right sizes. You bought this? He'd been
offended by her surprised tone, given her one of those
Gallic shrugs. It was the first time she'd undressed for
him.

'Jane.'

Aware that she was smiling at the memory she swiftly
wiped it from her face. But it wasn't him.

'What're you doing *here*?' asked Roddy.

He seemed confused to see her. In fact she would say
he was disappointed to find her outside the office.

'Did Tom get hold of you?'

So he was looking for her, presumably to continue plaguing her for the stupid novel. Well, today he was in luck. 'No, I haven't seen him. But I know what he wants.'

'You do?'

She noted the surprise in his voice. Why so taken aback? It wasn't as if her delayed novel was news.

'And do you feel the same way?' he asked tentatively.

'About what?'

'About him?'

Infuriating, deceitful, egotistical? She was sure he had a similar list of her bad points. She shrugged. 'I expect so.'

Roddy reacted to her answer with a gasp of pleasure. 'That's wonderful! Seriously, great stuff.' He punched the air. 'Result! I'm dead chuffed.'

Unsure why her continuing disdain for his best friend should elicit such a giddy response she offered up a thin smile and let him ramble on.

'It's in the air. You can feel it all around. Donald MacDonald said it. Well, Edwin Morgan wrote it, but Donald said it. Your dad was right.'

'My dad? What's he got to do with…whatever the hell you're on about?'

'We were in the pub. I had to leave them there because I have a date. With Nicola. Just came back to get changed. I bought a new shirt. It's *verde*. Nicola likes me in *verde*. Says it brings out the colour of my eyes.'

'You were in the pub with my dad?'

'Yeah. Me, Donald, your dad—and Tom, of course.'

Tom and her dad had met up behind her back. Her dad had always liked Tom, but couldn't he see that this wasn't the time to be firming up their friendship? While she was endeavouring to detach herself from the clutches of her former publisher her dad was making him his new drinking buddy. It wasn't right.

Roddy opened up the office and went inside. He held the door for her. 'I'm sure Tom'll be back soon. Why don't you wait?'

'I don't think so. I just came to give him this.' She held out the manuscript. 'It's my novel. I finished it.'

Briefly Roddy lifted his eyes to the cloudy heavens. 'It's all just coming together today, isn't it? Well done. Seriously, I know it's not been easy.' He lowered his voice. 'Out of interest, would you say you've been feeling any more melancholy of late?'

'Melan—?'

'Never mind.' He studied the manuscript and blew out. 'I can't tell you what a relief it is to see that. Between you and me, your book is the only thing keeping this place,' he clapped a hand against the doorpost, 'from going tits up.'

'What are you talking about?' It was the first she'd heard that the company was struggling. Although now when she thought back to her meeting in Edinburgh with Klinsch & McLeish, Dr Klinsch had made a puzzling reference to Tom's troubles. At the time Jane had assumed that the good doctor was referring to her—she was Tom's biggest trouble, unable to finish her promised novel. It turned out she had been more correct than she knew.

'Tristesse Books is in deep *shtuk*.' He put his head on one side. '*Was* in *shtuk*. Not now. Your novel has saved the day, if you'll forgive the cliché. Ever notice that things like this rarely happen in real life? I mean, in the nick of time, one second left on the clock.' With time on his mind he glanced at his watch. 'Dammit. Nicola hates being kept waiting.' He grinned. 'I think it's writing about all those bus timetables.' With that he launched himself upstairs taking them three at a time. Jane leaned through the doorway and called after him.

'Roddy…'

She could hear him through the thin ceiling, clattering about on the floor above as he dressed for his date.

'Where shall I leave it?' she asked more to herself than him. He couldn't hear her above the sound of his own singing, an enthusiastic if tuneless rendition of 'Singin' in the Rain'. She debated leaving the manuscript at the door, but was pricked by the idea that Tom would find it there and jump to the wrong-headed conclusion that she was scared to step over the threshold. She refused to give him the opportunity.

Closing the front door behind her she made her way cautiously along the corridor. It was the first time she'd been back here since that day. The day she discovered he'd changed her title. It was hard for other people to understand why it was such a betrayal. In the interven-

ing months even she had occasionally wondered if she'd
overreacted. After all, the book, with its new title, had
exceeded all her expectations. But no. That wasn't the
point. It was as if they'd had a child together, agreed on
his name, but on the way to register it Tom had changed
his mind. So instead of a 'Luke', they'd ended up with a
'Pubert'.

Why was she thinking about their children?

A plastic bucket squatted beneath a leak in the ceiling.
The tick of falling rainwater followed her down the corridor into Reception. Nothing had changed. From the heady
tang of freshly unboxed books and the thick layer of dust
on the shelves, to the complete absence of anything living—unless you counted mould. What was it with men
and their spaces that left to their own devices they would
be sure to instal a gumball machine and vintage jukebox,
but never any greenery? Before they'd broken up she'd
suggested to Tom he might sprinkle a few standard-issue
office ferns around the place. Nothing thrived here, he'd
said. No kidding.

The Reception desk lay hidden beneath a mass of
unopened mail, proof copies of books and three wobbling
stacks of manuscripts. If she left hers amongst this lot
there was a good chance it wouldn't be found for years,
perhaps then only by some future archaeologist excav-
ating for evidence of an ancient civilisation rumoured to
have subsisted exclusively on a diet of fried egg and sausage rolls.

She decided to leave the manuscript in Tom's office.

She stared at his door, hoping to find in its cheap oak-veneered panels the courage she needed to turn the handle and enter. She knew that he wasn't on the other side, sitting behind his desk sporting that languid grin, pushing his hand through his stupid wavy hair. That wasn't why she hesitated. Once she entered she would be in the place where their story had begun, and as soon as she put her manuscript on his desk and walked away it would be over. End where you begin. It was a common novelistic device. The familiar sense of place transported the reader in a flashback to the beginning when everything was simple and hopeful, and it was this delicious agony of nostalgia that suffused the final moments of the story. Nothing had changed, and yet everything had changed.

She couldn't remember opening the door, but then she was on the other side. Perhaps she'd walked through it like the ghost of herself. She stood in the semi-darkness of his office, listening to the sound of her own breathing. Crossing the floor she passed the same battered sofa they'd shared, the same low chair he'd made her occupy while they edited *Happy Ending*. Several rows of one bookcase were lined with copies of her novel. She ran a hand along their spines.

She stood before his desk. The bust of Napoleon, the Glasgow snowglobe, the metal holder crammed with his ubiquitous red pencils. Amongst the familiar objects she noticed something unexpected. A business card. One of

Willie's. She picked it up and recalled their last conversation when he'd told her about Tom's objection to the screenplay. An image sprang to mind of Tom on his white horse defending, if not her honour, then her novel. Was it possible that she had been too hard on him? If so, then this act was an acknowledgement of that; perhaps even the first small step on the road to a rapprochement.

She made space on the cluttered surface and set down her manuscript. That was when she saw it, tucked behind a pile of books at the edge of the desk. She could so easily have missed it, and that would have changed everything.

Her umbrella plant.

There was no question in her mind that it was hers: the same plant her dad had given her, the same plant she'd nurtured for years. She would have recognised it anywhere. But if it was here then what was the withered plant she'd returned to in her flat all those weeks ago? A substitute? But to what purpose? A cruel prank perpetrated by a disgruntled ex-boyfriend? That didn't seem like Tom's style. He was far more Machiavellian than that. A creeping sensation at the nape of her neck began a cold-fingered crawl across her scalp. It wasn't a plant, it was the tip of an iceberg.

She heard thudding on the stairs. Seizing the plant she marched out of the office to find Roddy—hair combed, shoes shining, shirt green—about to leave for his date. He reached for the door handle.

'You!' she snapped.

He froze at the sound of her voice, his high-spirited singin' trailing off.

'I want a word with you.'

She saw him look round slowly, then an expression of fear cloud his face as he registered the plant gripped in her hand like a punch. He offered up a weak-sauce smile.

'Jane…'

'Roddy?'

'I can explain.'

'Was this your idea?'

'No, no,' he protested, desperately flapping his hands. 'It was Keats.'

CHAPTER 25

'Rain King', Sonic Youth, 1988, Enigma

SHE WASN'T IN. Stirred up by Benny, Donald and Roddy in the pub, he'd flown across the city in a passionate frenzy to Jane's flat, ready to profess his love. It felt reckless. It felt good. He had run. He'd actually done the romantic running thing. Not all the way here, that would have been unfeasible. But unable to find a parking space right outside her building he'd abandoned his car in a spot three streets away. And then he'd run. Thinking of her with each pace. Thinking of the first time he'd seen her, at Tristesse, scrabbling about adorably on her hands and knees. Thinking about their first kiss, in the cottage in front of the open fire. Thinking about her naked. Mostly thinking about her naked.

On the way over in the car he'd detoured to buy flowers, petrol station blooms. So when she didn't answer the door he suddenly became a sweaty guy standing outside his angry ex-girlfriend's flat clutching a bunch of dyed chrysanthemums in an unlikely shade of blue never seen in nature. He decided to wait downstairs for her to return.

He leant against a low garden wall, hunched into his coat, arms folded around the garish flowers. Impulsive romantic declarations were all well and good, but at the very least the object of your affection ought to be in the same vicinity when the mood struck. Waiting around in the cold kind of put a dampener on the whole thing.

The waiting also brought time to think and with that a prick of doubt. What if she didn't feel the same way? He supposed that was less a doubt and more a certainty. She hated him. That brought an odd smile to his lips. He realised he was relishing the challenge to set her straight. And when she finally came strolling round that corner, hair streaming in the wind, arms swinging at her sides, he would stand before her and there would be no fumbling, halting romantic declaration. That was a peculiarity of the English lover and he was of the line of Cyrano, Abelard, Lancelot. OK, they all died at the end, but the point was that they were eloquent in the throes of love. It was in his blood. Years spent in this rain-sodden country had not dulled instincts he was born with. At least he hoped not. That would be a total *scunner*.

He paced up and down in front of her building to keep warm, conscious of suspicious glances emanating from behind the twitching curtains of neighbouring property. He sneezed. Definitely coming down with something. Come on, Jane. Where was she? He nipped to the corner shop for a bag of smoky bacon crisps and a Twix, then returned to his beat. After about an hour a traffic warden ambled past cheerily scrutinising windshields for expired parking tickets. He was about to dash back to his car to feed the meter when two things happened. The rain that had been threatening all day at last arrived and Jane turned into the street.

He didn't hesitate, striding towards her, chrysanthemums held before him like a sword. She was holding something too, but he was just too far away to make out what. She hadn't seen him yet, her head down, face half-hidden in her hair. The taps opened, the shower turned into a deluge. The flowers bent back under the onslaught. Wind blew rain into his face and he wiped the drops from his eyes, closing the distance between them in a dozen long strides. He started to say her name, but then saw what was in her hands.

Oh.

Shit.

'What the hell are you doing here?' She regarded the flowers with wary disgust.

'Uh…um…I…'

'You know what, I don't care. Get out of my way.'

She pushed past him, the leaves of her umbrella plant brushing against his arm, close enough for him to see that she'd been crying. Instinctively he reached out.

'Get off me!' She recoiled, her wet hair whipping. 'Get away from me.'

'Jane…'

'I don't want to hear it. I don't want to hear any more of your bullshit.' A stifled sob of disbelief. 'You made me think my plant was dead. You tried to sabotage my deal with my new publisher. You had a go at my relationship with Willie. All of that I could forgive. But the pub quiz. My dad.' She shook her head slowly.

She knew it all; every witless part of his plan. *She'll thank me in the end.* You moron. You complete and utter tool. He could see her hurt turn swiftly to anger.

'You tried to wreck my life, Tom.'

She stuck out her chin and marched for the entrance to the flats.

'It wasn't like that…' Even to his own ears his objection sounded weak and pathetic.

She stopped, whirled about and with a furious grunt hurled the plant at him. It landed short, the pot cracking as it hit the ground, contents spilling across the pavement, leaving a straggle of leaves and clumps of damp compost. The rain was falling so hard now that it was already washing the remnants of the plant towards the gutter. He dropped to his knees, scrambling to rescue what he could. Precious leaves and roots slipped through his wet grasp and circled down the drain.

When he looked up, the tenement door was already swinging shut behind her disappearing figure.

*

'I'm gonnae kill you.' The threat as cold as lager. Benny Lockhart's face was flushed, his breath coming in rapid wheezes. 'I should snap that fucking pretty neck of yours.' He clenched his fists at his sides, turned his back on Tom and walked away, evidently trying to curb his anger. 'Christ on a bike! What the hell were you thinking, son?'

Tom had come to the Walter Scott to confess. He'd missed his chance to come clean to Jane, but at least he could tell her dad what he'd done. He was fully prepared to take another beating. Wanted Benny to have a go at him. Not that he expected absolution. *What was he thinking?* The answer was simple: at the point when he'd attempted to wreck Jane's fragile relationship with her dad he had not been thinking. He hadn't simply crossed the line; he'd struck a red pen through it.

Benny walked stiffly back to the bar. The two men sat side by side on a pair of stools, not looking at one another, their eyes fixed straight ahead.

'I thought you loved her.' Benny's voice shook with anger and confusion.

'I do.'

He gave a harsh laugh. 'Some way of showing it, son.'

'I screwed up.'

'That what you call it?'

'I'm sorry. Truly sorry.'

'It's no' me you have to apologise to, son.'

Following his encounter with Jane in the street he'd headed home to lick his wounds. He'd found her manuscript on his desk. She'd finished it. The cover page declared the novel 'Untitled'. Did that mean she had a title but wouldn't share it, or that it was open for discussion? It almost felt like a private joke between them. Almost. Eagerly he devoured the final chapter, reading it three times before putting the manuscript to one side. He reflected on the significance of the moment and then went in search of booze.

A couple of hours later Roddy had returned with Nicola to find Tom asleep at his desk next to an empty six-pack of Babycham. It was all he could find in the flat and he was too broke to contemplate buying anything else.

'The happiest drink in the world,' proclaimed the label. Someone had given it to him as a joke.

Roddy prodded him awake, filled him in on what had happened when Jane dropped off the manuscript. He swore he had resisted for as long as possible telling her about their plan, but Jane had forced it out of him.

Tom told him not to sweat it—this was his mess and he would clean it up. To himself he admitted that might well be impossible.

The next day he'd returned to her flat in the hope of talking to her. There was no reply when he rung the bell, but on his way out he met a neighbour on the stairs who'd seen her get into a cab with a backpack. He'd tried her phone, but it was off. That's when he'd decided to go see her dad.

'She's gone.' said Tom.

'Uh-huh.' Benny gave a non-committal shrug and Tom could tell immediately that he knew where she was. He had a good idea himself.

'She's at the cottage, isn't she?'

'She doesn't want to see you.'

'I don't care. I'm going. I'm going right now.'

'Fine. Go.'

'I will.' He didn't move from the barstool.

Benny turned to him. 'Well?'

Tom gave a sheepish look. 'You couldn't lend me twenty quid for petrol?'

*

He looked over at the empty passenger seat. The last time he'd driven this road she'd been sitting next to him. She'd asked him to her cottage in the Highlands so that they could continue editing her novel. A beautiful young woman asks a man she barely knows to a remote spot for a weekend *à deux*? He didn't want to fall prey to some cross-cultural misunderstanding, so before they left he'd consulted Roddy on the potential underlying meaning of such an invitation. Roddy insisted that it sounded like the beginning of a film. Porn or horror. Could go either way.

His parting words: 'Just don't insult any in-bred locals carrying chainsaws.'

As they'd joined the M80 he reminded himself of his golden rule never to sleep with an author. They talked—well, she talked and he joined in when she paused for breath—and whenever he felt the conversation stray into personal territory he would gently steer it back to business. No flirting. He self-censored, striking an imaginary red pen through any innuendo that occurred to him in the course of their chat. He studied her face, trying to discern disappointment or relief at the anodyne conversation.

Even strapped into the seat she was constantly in motion, stretching her long legs, tapping her feet in time to the music playing on the radio, twisting her hair round a finger, flailing her arms to emphasise a point. She was loose-limbed, carefree. She leaned over to change the station on the radio. Her skin smelled of a delicate floral fragrance; not perfume, he decided, it must be body lotion. Between Stirling and Auchterarder he exerted significant amounts of self-control to stop himself picturing her applying it.

By the time they passed Perth he wanted her.

Two and a half hours later they arrived at their final destination, the car bottoming out as it bumped along towards a large pile of stones at the end of a rutted track. The stone pile turned out to be their accommodation. The sight of the dilapidated cottage helped dampen his desire, the rain and the plumbing did the rest.

But his respite didn't last long. The weekend was a constant battle with the urge to hold her, kiss her, undress her. Instead he forced himself to talk about the novel. Only the novel. At times he felt he hid his longing so well he must have seemed aloof and surly. He knew that he couldn't make the first move. If she didn't reciprocate then he'd just be some creepy guy hitting on a lone woman in the middle of nowhere.

And then had come Chapter 17. Oh, marvellous, glorious Chapter 17. Subtext was a beautiful thing.

His phone chirped at the arrival of a voice message. Typical, just when he was getting to the good part. He pulled off the motorway and checked the display to find half a dozen missed calls and the same number of text messages, all from Anna. *Call me back, idiot.* The car shuddered at the thunder of a passing lorry. Listening to the blackboard squeal of windscreen wipers he watched the lorry's tail lights disappear in the grey murk, and then couldn't put it off any longer. He dialled Anna. She picked up on the first ring.

'Well?'

Far from it, he thought. There was nothing to discuss, no need for small talk. He gave her his decision about Pandemic Media. She asked him if he was certain. Then asked him again.

'Yes,' he confirmed, and rang off.

He glanced at the empty passenger seat, convinced he could still smell her scent.

He drove for another three hours, watching the signal strength bars on his phone dwindle until he was beyond the range of the network. It was dusk by the time he reached the cottage in the glen. Surrounding peaks were silhouetted against the grey sky. Fluttering shapes darted across his headlamps. The car bellied along the track, its under chassis grinding like a knife on a whetstone. Faced with a pothole the size of a moon crater he braked to a stop and the car expired with a seizing cough. He drew out the ignition key. Not so much killing the engine as putting it out of its misery, he thought.

Rain beaded on the windscreen. He looked out at the cottage in the gathering dusk. The windows were dark, the place seemed devoid of life. He experienced a moment of doubt. Was she even here? He couldn't blame Benny for sending him on a wild-goose chase. He deserved it. He left the car and made a dash for the front door, rapping on it three times. No reply. He huddled into his jacket, wishing he'd brought something warmer—and waterproof.

'Jane, I know you're in there. And I know it sounds crazy, but I was trying to help.'

Rainwater guttered onto the ground; the only sound in the world. The silence of the countryside unnerved him. He stamped his feet and clapped his arms against his body to keep warm. He could feel a cold coming on. Ten minutes in this wilderness and he was sick.

He was about to turn away when he heard muffled footsteps on the other side and the door opened a crack.

Red hair fell into the gap and he saw her face, furious and beautiful. She was angry with him and yet the mere sight of her made him want to smile. He stopped himself, figuring a grin would only inflame her.

'All you care about is how my book can help your damn company,' she snapped. 'Well, you got what you wanted.'

Before he could speak she slammed the door in his face. It wasn't the reaction he'd been hoping for, but it was what he expected. Unbowed, he trotted back to the car and popped open the boot. Inside, wrapped securely in plastic and held upright in a cardboard box, was his secret weapon. His last shot.

He knocked on the door again.

'Please open the door. I'm not good at this countryside stuff.' The wind moaned down the glen, shapes loomed on the darkening hillside. 'I think I saw a bear.' He shivered in the cold. 'Jane. I'm sorry.'

I'm sorry.

The door inched opened. Jane peered suspiciously through the widening gap. He held out what he had carried from the car.

CHAPTER 26

'And It Rained All Night', Thom Yorke, 2006, XL

AFTER MEETING TOM on the street, Jane had left him clutching his stupid chrysanthemums and hurried upstairs to her flat, her mood swinging from hurt to anger and back again with each step. She made a cup of tea, the ritual soothing and familiar, not noticing until she stirred in the milk that she'd inadvertently used three teabags. He was always amused by the regularity of her tea drinking, noting that it punctuated their editing sessions like a well-placed comma.

Oh, for god's sake! Now she couldn't even make a cuppa without seeing his annoying face. She wanted to be alone. No, she wanted to be anywhere that he wasn't. It seemed that not even her flat offered the isolation she craved. She dug out her backpack from the hall cupboard, hastily threw in a few things and called a cab to take her to the bus stop. When it arrived she crawled on hands and knees into the bay window and raised her head just high enough over the sill to confirm that he wasn't still hanging around outside.

The cab dropped her off at Buchanan Street. Buses rolled in and out of the station, filling the air with the oily tang of diesel. Her bus departed in half an hour. She sat in the waiting-room, sharing it with a couple of skinny backpackers, young and in love, noisily sucking at each other's face. She mumbled a small prayer that they weren't booked on her bus.

It was hard to believe that just a few hours ago she'd been standing in Tom's office, her anger towards him softening. She'd even experienced a flutter of self-doubt, wondering if she'd been too hard on *him*. And when she'd placed the finished manuscript on his desk she'd imagined how happy he'd be, and that had made her smile.

Discovering the umbrella plant had changed everything. The mystery of its abduction turned out to be easily solved. Eager to exonerate himself Roddy had spilled his guts, no enhanced interrogation necessary. There was no question in her mind that what Tom had done was unforgiveable. Far worse than changing her title.

She boarded the bus, found a seat and settled in for the journey. The miles rolled past and soon, lulled by the fug of the cabin and the grumble of the engine, she fell asleep. She woke with a start ten minutes from her destination.

With a hiss the hydraulic doors sprang open and she stepped out onto the side of the road, the sole passenger to disembark. There was still an hour before sunset, enough time to make it to the cottage before dark. The bus pulled away, quickly disappearing from sight around the next bend of the meandering road. She heaved the backpack onto her shoulders and set off along the verge. The road wound through moorland hemmed in by hills, their summits shrouded in mist. If the road was lonely then the track she took after about a mile that led to the cottage was utterly forlorn.

By the time she arrived she was cold and hungry. Worse than the physical privation was the realisation that coming here was a terrible mistake. She wanted to forget him and yet this is where it had started. Wherever she looked she saw traces of him. Here was where he fed her the sweets from Glickman's, there the lamp-cord he tripped over as she chased him round the room in pursuit of her manuscript. And here the hearth where they had explored Chapter 17, in intimate detail.

She poked the wood-basket next to the fireplace. It contained a single seasoned log, a few scraps of kindling and a box of matches. She shook the box hopefully, but there was no telltale rattle. It held one match. She laid a fire, such as it was, knelt on the hearth and carefully struck her only match. It rasped against the box, its head snapped off and fell into a narrow crack between two flagstones. Desperately she dug her fingers into the gap, but despite her frantic attempts she couldn't retrieve it. She swore loudly, the sound of her voice startling her in the silence.

He always complained that the countryside was too damn quiet.

Swaddled in the hearthrug for warmth she cracked out her provisions, laying them out on the rough-hewn kitchen table. One sandwich, possibly chicken, it was hard to tell. Two fairy cakes, flattened at the bottom of her backpack. One bar of chocolate, family size. Not exactly a feast but she had been in a hurry when she'd left Glasgow. Anyway, she wasn't hungry.

'Are you going to eat that?'

Darsie sat at the table, eyeing the chocolate bar.

'Because if not, I could probably manage a square or two.' She looked up at Jane. 'Who am I kidding? I want to take that whole bar and shove it in my gob. I've had a hell of a day. Coming back from the dead takes it out of a girl.'

Jane backed away from her heroine, bumping against the edge of the sink. 'You shouldn't be here.'

'You mean because you killed me off in the last chapter?' A trickle of peaty water stuttered out of the tap. Darsie angled her head thoughtfully. 'You know those stories where they finally kill the monster but then it turns out it's not quite dead?'

'This isn't one of those stories.'

'Well, *duh*, obviously. I'm not suggesting a last-second genre switch. Can you imagine the confusion that would cause your poor publisher? And the booksellers? I mean, where would you shelve something like that? Gritty urban romance turns into girl versus unstoppable evil in a cabin in the Highlands, with a downer ending. Actually, come to think of it, I can see that selling a truckload.' She slammed her hand down on the bar of chocolate, clawing it towards her. 'You really think you can kill me? Tell me, Jane, when you read it back did it ring true?'

'Yes.'

'Liar.'

'I finished the novel. You shouldn't be here.'

'So, why *am* I here, Jane?'

'Enjoy the chocolate.' She walked out of the kitchen. It had been a long day and despite her snooze on the bus she was bone tired. Retreating to the bedroom she lowered herself onto the narrow bed and fell into a fitful sleep. She woke once during the night to find Darsie standing silently at the foot of the bed.

'Go away! Leave me alone.' She pulled the blanket over her head. 'All I want is to be alone.'

*

She heard his car before she saw it, the familiar cough and splutter as it groaned to a halt outside the cottage. He'd found her, which meant that he'd looked for her. She didn't care, deciding in that instant not to let him inside.

He banged on the door. At first she ignored him—he'd made a wasted journey—but when it became clear that he wasn't going to leave without encouragement she confronted him on the doorstep. At first she thought he'd taken her words to heart. He returned to his car, but instead of getting into it he opened the boot. The lid screened him—and whatever he was up to—from view, but a few seconds later he was walking back towards the cottage.

Only the thickness of the door separated them.

'Please open the door. I'm not good at this countryside stuff. I think I saw a bear.'

A bear? Uh, don't think so. Tom was many things, but King of the Wild Frontier was not one of them.

'Jane. I'm sorry.'

Was that an apology? The wind had picked up and she wasn't sure she'd heard right. She had to make sure. She would see it in his face, know if his contrition was genuine. She opened the door.

He was holding an umbrella plant. A seedling, its solitary shoot sporting five perfect green leaves. It was a romantic gesture, a request for forgiveness, an attempt to reconnect. He shivered pathetically in the cold.

'Thanks a lot.'

She grabbed the plant and slammed the door again. Pressing her ear to it she listened intently for his reaction.

'OK. You're right. I deserve that.' A sneeze. 'I'll just go shall I? I'll…go.'

She heard his footsteps retreating and hurried to the window to confirm that he was leaving. He climbed into his car. Moments later the starter motor sent out a whine of distress. He continued in his attempt to start the engine, but it would not catch and its increasingly desperate *chug-a-chug-a-chug-a* echoed pitifully along the glen. Finally, he gave up and she watched him through the rain-streaked driver's window mouthing oaths and slamming the steering wheel in frustration.

He shouldered open his door and hauled himself out. Lifting his mobile phone to the slate-grey sky like some megalithic druid trying to summon the sun, he waved it about in an attempt to catch a signal. When that failed he drew back his arm and angrily hurled the handset far into the neighbouring field.

Cursing, he ducked down briefly out of her sight and when he reappeared was clutching two large handfuls of turf. He flung them at the car, stooped to collect more ammunition, and maintained the assault until its roof resembled a freshly sown lawn. Moving round to the front he continued his tirade at the inert vehicle, and then as Jane watched with mounting concern for his mental health he began to head-butt the bonnet, the dull thud of his forehead repeatedly impacting the sheet metal audible inside the cottage.

It was raining hard now. He leaned against the car, his back to the cottage, hugging himself to keep warm. His hair, always so effortlessly windswept, clung to his scalp like a wet Pomeranian. As she watched, his whole body convulsed in a series of wracking coughs. Still, she resolved, there was absolutely no chance she would let him inside.

*

'It's eight miles to the nearest village. I don't expect to see you when I wake up. Goodnight.'

She tossed him a blanket and left him to dry out in front of the fire. She'd finally managed to light it using the cigarette lighter from his car. She had no intention of sharing the hearth with him. Not tonight. Not ever again.

She stalked from the sitting room and then returned a moment later, deliberately avoiding eye contact. Sheepishly she collected the plant he'd brought with him and, hoping he hadn't noticed, slipped out of the room again. Not that the plant meant anything to her. The bedroom in the cottage could benefit from some greenery, that was all. It was just a plant.

She sat up in bed, eating chocolate and watering it from a chipped cup filled from the kitchen tap. As if this tiny little scrap of green could make a difference to what he'd done. It was laughable. What the hell was he thinking? That was a good question. Realising that tonight might be her last chance to obtain an answer she flung off the blanket and returned to the sitting room, clutching the plant in one hand and the chocolate bar in the other.

He had pulled the armchair close to the fire and sat there muttering into the flames.

'What were you thinking?' she asked to the back of the chair.

He stuck his head round and saw what she was holding. 'About the plant?'

'Yes. No.' She'd had it all straight in her head, but he did this to her. Every time. Made it all come out jumpy. Incoherent. She let her fury guide her. 'About me, idiot!'

She circled round to stand in front of him. He looked white as a corpse, as if all the colour in his face had been washed out by the rain. She saw in his sudden expression of deep concentration that he hadn't been expecting a chance to justify himself to her and was taking great care in choosing his words.

'No misery. No poetry,' he said at last.

She screwed up her face. 'Is that translated from the original bollocks? Because it sounds like it. It sounds like utter French bollocks to me.'

'Actually it's...never mind.' He covered his mouth with a fist and gave a hacking cough. 'OK. Here's the thing. You go to some dark places when you write. You bring out stuff most people prefer to keep locked up. So I thought that if I made you miserable—'

'—I'd be able to finish my novel.' She gave a mocking round of applause. 'Genius! Bravo!'

His head dipped. 'Yeah. Well, I was wrong.'

'Of course you were wrong. You don't have to be miserable to write. See, this is a problem created by male poets standing on cliffs staring into the middle distance and perpetuated by novelists whose emotional intelligence is as pared down as their prose. You don't have to wrestle your inner demons in order to produce great work, you can just as easily be sitting next to a warm fire with a nice cup of tea.' She'd never thought about where her impulse to write came from. Writing was a reflex. Like vomiting.

'You write because you have to, because it gnaws away at your insides if you try to ignore it, because if you don't write you might as well be dead. Because nothing else can make you so mad, so frustrated, so happy, and yes, so miserable. *Usually all at the same time.*'

Hang on. Something in what he'd said lingered.

'What did you mean, "I was wrong"? You got the novel, didn't you? In Tom and Roddy-world, the plan was a roaring success.'

He cleared his throat and shifted awkwardly in the chair. 'Not exactly. The last chapter…it doesn't work.'

She could feel her lips moving, her tongue forming shapes, but all that came out was a strangled choke.

'It needs a rewrite,' he said.

'How much of it?'

'All of it.'

She sank onto the hearthrug. Something had been nagging her about the last chapter ever since she'd finished it. The something in question was currently making her way across the room to take up a space on the floor beside her.

'Told you,' said Darsie, plucking the bar of chocolate out of her hand and breaking off several squares. 'Actually I think he's being kind. It's a terrible chapter. Jumps all over the place, doesn't tie anything up satisfactorily, oh and did I mention—' She shoved her face in Jane's and glowered. 'I. Die.'

'Go away.'

Tom frowned. 'Hmm?'

'Not you.'

He looked round to check who else was in the room. 'Jane, are you all right?'

'No, I'm bloody not all right. I want more chocolate.'

Reluctantly, Darsie proffered the remainder of the bar.

Tom reached over one arm of the chair and hoisted his trusty messenger bag from the floor. He unbuckled it and slid out her manuscript.

'Maybe it'd help if we talked it through…'

'You brought my manuscript?' The nerve of the man. The only reason she'd let him through the front door was so that he could apologise to her endlessly and unsuccessfully. Instead she found herself in the middle of an editing session. Trust Tom to turn a fiasco into an opportunity.

'Yes, I thought that once I'd prostrated myself sufficiently and begged you for forgiveness we could get onto the important stuff.' The hint of a smile crossed his lips and then it was gone like a ghost.

'Oh, he's so single-minded,' said Darsie, impressed.

Jane felt her jaw go rigid. Tom laid one hand on the cover of the manuscript. It covered most of the page.

'And what big hands you have, grandmama.' Darsie nudged Jane.

He took a long breath and considered the novel. 'I think the problem might be that you don't get to choose your ending. It has to follow naturally from what comes before, or it doesn't feel true.'

Darsie caught Jane's eye. 'And so insightful,' said her heroine with a twinkle.

'I want to start with Darsie,' he went on.

'Goody.'

'I don't understand her.'

'No kidding,' said Jane under her breath.

'I mean, why's she in love with Tony Douglas, a man who betrays her so utterly? He's emotionally crippled, obsessed with his umbrella factory, has an uncomfortable tendency for mean-spiritedness...'

She felt bad that he hadn't yet twigged. 'He has nice hair,' she offered, and saw him reach understanding the way a parachutist with no chute reaches the ground.

He shot out of the chair and dropped the manuscript as if it had bit him. It landed with a thud on the flagstones.

'OK, OK, so yes,' she confessed, 'maybe there is an *element* of autobiography.'

He snorted. 'An element?' He began to pace the small room, the top of his head brushing the low ceiling.

'Which means you're the reason I can't write.'

'Me?'

'At some point during the last few weeks it dawned on me that when I finished this novel we were finished too, and some insane part of me—'

'Hey, why you looking at me?' said Darsie indignantly.

'—doesn't want that to happen.' She hadn't intended to say it, conscious that to do so was to lay herself open to him. Typical, she'd been blocked for a month but when she actually wanted to keep a lid on it the words had rushed out. She paused. 'You're my block, Tom.'

He affected the same look of deep concentration as before. 'But I want you to finish it.'

She'd bared herself and in return he had disappointed her. Again. She got to her feet to harangue him. 'Of course you do. And for what? So you can turn a profit. All you care about is your company.'

'I've sold it,' he said quietly.

'What?' said Darsie.

'What?' said Jane.

'I've sold the company. Your new novel will be published by Tristesse Books, an imprint of Pandemic Media.'

Her mind whirled. 'You can't have sold it! That stupid company is you. Get it back. You can't do this to me. I'm on the moral high ground here. I'm not getting off now.' She let it sink in. He might as well have said that he'd sold a lung. No, he had two lungs, but only one Tristesse. 'You *sold* it?'

He nodded. 'And you can take all the time you need with the last chapter. I made it part of the deal.'

What had that cost him? Not financially. She knew he didn't care about that, but in every other way. She weighed the balance. He had hurt her with his high-handed attitude to her title and then the foolish scheme to beat her writer's block, but he had cared about her novel when no one else had. And still cared. He could have taken the new manuscript with the terrible final chapter she'd given him, published it and saved his company. Instead he had sacrificed the thing most dear to him to prove that there was something else more dear. Someone.

So, what happened next?

It was up to her. Real life so rarely presented moments like these. Life buffeted you from one conclusion to the next, open-ended until it ended. Life was a series of accidents, happy and unhappy. But at that moment she had become the protagonist of her own story, this ending in her hands. All she had to do was find the right words.

'Tom. I didn't sign. With Klinsch and McLeish. I couldn't do it.'

She studied his face, trying to read his reaction—was he pleased to hear this news? He gave nothing away. Then after a pause that lasted forever he said:

'You could stay.' He took a step towards her. 'With me.'

She could feel his breath on her face. 'I could.'

He started to speak and she held up a finger to cut him

off. 'If I hear the words "sad", "beautiful" or "music", you're a dead man.'

She wanted to hear him say something else. Had been waiting since the night in the cottage when they'd got all Chapter 17 on each other. She relished the sequel—ached for it—but before they made love she wanted to hear him say it. Those three little words.

He gazed at her steadily. 'I…block you.'

She held his stare. 'And I block you too.'

He slipped an arm around her waist and pulled her to him. In the split second before their lips met she felt herself resist. She would never end one of her novels like this. It was unrealistic and smacked of wish-fulfilment. In her stories the universe turned a cold eye on the lives and loves of her characters. She felt his fingers gently stroking the nape of her neck. What was she saying again? Something about the harsh uncaring universe…

They kissed but then in the midst of the embrace she broke off. She stared past him, out of the corner of her eye aware of him regarding her with the dismal expression of a Frenchman thwarted mid-snog.

Darsie stood in front of the fireplace, smiling sadly. The fire was dying, the solitary log reduced to a thin layer of hot ash, its glow fading.

'What?' he complained. 'What now? What could possibly be so important?'

She hadn't noticed until that moment but her head was filled with an endless, wearying hum. Only knew it now because for the first time since she'd become stuck on the final chapter the hum had stopped.

'I know how it ends,' she mouthed and turned for the door. She hadn't dragged her laptop to the cottage, but there was a notebook and pen in the kitchen. 'And I just want to make a few notes…'

She felt Tom's fingers close around her arm, gentle but firm. 'I don't care,' he said.

She glanced towards the kitchen. Doors. Tricky things to get through. When she turned back Darsie had vanished. And this time she knew it was for good.

He kissed her again. A smirk slid across his face. She recognised that look. Had missed its promise. That was a Chapter 17 look. His hands were on her, unbuttoning, unzipping. She pulled his shirt over his head and as she did so brushed his forehead. It felt hot. Feverish.

'You're on fire,' she said, suddenly concerned.

'You're pretty hot your—'

He pitched into her like a felled oak tree. Somehow she held onto him and manoeuvred his dead weight into the armchair, all the time calmly repeating his name. It would be OK. Everything would be OK. He slumped in the chair, unresponsive. They were eight miles from the nearest village. No working phone. She shook him, shouting his name now. Felt his neck for a pulse, her fingers desperately seeking the reassuring beat that would tell her everything was going to turn out all right in the end.

EPILOGUE

'Singin' in the Rain', John Martyn, 1971, Island

ON A HILL above the city they gather in the breezy cemetery. Rain is forecast, but with callous disregard for the appropriate mood, for now the sun shines out of a blue sky. Solemn-faced men and women line the graveside, six deep. A decent turnout.

Roddy stands hand in hand with Nicola. Behind them his English class, smartly turned out in their school uniforms, most unsure how to behave at such a gathering. Benny Lockhart offers Anna LeFèvre a handkerchief. Donald MacDonald looks old. The only sound is the wind in the yew trees. Jane watches their branches sway, remembers reading somewhere that the funerary trees are traditionally planted in twos. The bitter irony doesn't escape her here, where couples inseparable in life are finally parted.

Her eyes fall on the dark wooden casket that rests in front of an empty podium. She can barely look at it; the sight offends her. She wants to blame him. In her head she has berated him often: how could he do this to her? But she didn't say it when she had the chance and now it's too late.

She walks slowly up to the podium as she has rehearsed, bends her head and begins to read. She hears the words issue from her mouth, hardly listening to them. She steals glances at the audience. Nicola comforts an inconsolable Roddy, openly weeping into a red handkerchief, the spot of colour popping against the wall of black. Her dad fights welling emotions but she can see his lip trembling with the effort to resist. Hard men don't cry. And then she's at the foot of the page and the final paragraph. She experiences an inrush of feeling, like air rapidly filling a vacuum. The world shrinks and the words telescope.

'Why is it that the saddest endings seem the truest? In the stories I told myself I was always the heroine, always reaching for my happy ending. It didn't turn out that way. I won't get to spend the rest of my life with him. But I was loved, and that's enough.'

Her voice fades and all that remains is the breeze in the trees and the sound of quiet weeping.

And then another voice mutters behind her, the accent unmistakable: a wisp of French mixed with a few stray Scottish vowels. 'I knew this would happen,' says Tom.

She turns to see him staring regretfully up at the clear sky. 'I was going to hire a rain machine, but you have no idea how expensive those things are. I think they must charge by the drop.'

He sidles up to join her at the podium, clears his throat and addresses the gathering in a loud, confident voice.

'Ladies and gentlemen, *fellow mourners*, Jane Lockhart will now be signing copies of her new novel, *You'll Catch Your Death*.'

At his signal two men dressed as undertakers flip open the coffin lid. The white silk interior is lined with copies of Jane's latest book. On the cover the title and her name frame a stylised photograph of a beautiful but melancholy young woman sheltering beneath a red umbrella.

Months ago, as they'd edited the manuscript, working speedily towards publication, he'd presented options for the cover. Annoyingly, this was the first design he had shown her. She loved it immediately, knew in her gut that it was the one. The figure was exactly how she'd pictured Darsie and the title worked beautifully with the image. So, naturally she had rejected it out of hand, making a giant fuss in the process, forcing him to mock up a dozen more designs before suggesting they revisit the first one. All in all she considered that he'd taken her shenanigans with surprising good grace.

The title had come to her in a flash, that night in the cottage when he'd suffered his little fainting fit. That's how she referred to it these days, just to wind him up, but for about thirty seconds she was sure he was dead. And during those moments of abject terror the title had popped into her head. *You'll Catch Your Death*. She was ashamed to say it, but even as she tried to rouse his inert body she experienced a momentary spike of pleasure. It was a *great* title. And hot on its heels another thought—she blushed that it should ever have crossed her mind—if he *did* die then he couldn't possibly change it.

She'd shared the title with him on the drive home sitting in the cab of the AA rescue truck. Your near-death experience inspired my new title—isn't that funny? *Darkly amusing?* Oh come on you grumpy Frenchman, that's *funny*.

The AA guy said he really liked it.

Jane closes her own copy of the book which is resting on the dais. She taps the cover image fondly and whispers to her heroine, 'I'm sorry about your ending, but it was the right one.'

Tony Douglas had to die, as much as Tom Duval had to live. Darsie didn't get her happy ending after all, but Jane Lockhart did.

'Are you actually talking to your book?'

Tom is at her shoulder. She surveys the funeral-themed launch party that he's proudly organised. She'd objected to it when he proposed the idea, but not strenuously enough. And since he'd graciously let her choose the cover and hadn't offered even a pipsqueak of objection to the title, she felt she had to give him something. On the other hand…books in a coffin.

'I wish you hadn't done that,' she says, gesturing to

the casket from which Waterstones booksellers dispense copies of her new novel. 'It's really offensive.'

A string quartet plays Beethoven's 'Funeral March' from the 3rd Symphony, Tom having rejected Chopin's effort as too mainstream.

'You don't think it's all a bit tacky?' she says.

'Tacky?' He sounds indignant. 'We have canapés.' A waiter dressed as a pallbearer wafts past carrying a tray laden with vols-au-vent baked in the shape of headstones. 'Now get signing.'

Sophie Hamilton Findlay leads her to a signing table. The queue already stretches back past six rows of graves and a mausoleum. As she settles into the familiar rhythm of greeting eager readers and sending out Best Wishes she watches Tom at the edge of the crowd in deep conversation with Anna, his bank manager. She holds her breath, hoping it's not more bad news. He'd sold Tristesse to some faceless corporation. For her. And then she sees the two of them clink champagne-filled glasses and a grin split his handsome face. 'Oh, thank fuck for that,' she says aloud—and inadvertently to a mother and her young daughter waiting for their books to be signed. The mother's smile slips. Horrified, she apologises profusely.

She watches Roddy swing by, Nicola at his side, his class trooping behind them like ducklings. Ducklings with smartphones.

He motions towards the buffet table. '"The funeral

baked meats did coldly furnish forth the marriage table"?
Anyone? Anyone? Come on 6b, it's a classic.'

'Is it *Avatar*, sir?'

'Yes, Gordon, it's *Avatar*.'

He exchanges a weary look with Nicola. Whispers
something to her.

'No,' she says coyly. 'I can't.'

'Oh go on,' he urges. 'It's fun.'

He squeezes her hand and she relents with an indulgent
sigh. Roddy swiftly gathers the class around him, directs
them to the signing table. Jane feels thirty pairs of eyes
study her minutely.

He claps his hands sharply. 'Pay attention, class.'

Nicola clears her throat and addresses the children.
'Jane Lockhart, of course, follows Charlotte Brontë as
only the second writer in English to design and build her
own hovercraft.'

'Ho-ver-craft,' repeats Roddy. 'Write that down.'

A few of them assiduously copy the misinformation
into their notebooks, but Jane is pleased to see that most
ignore him in preference to filching a vol-au-vent from the
table. Roddy nods approvingly at Nicola.

When Jane looks up, her dad is at the head of the
queue.

'We've got to stop meeting like this,' she says lightly,
then leans in to add confidentially, 'You don't need to buy
a book, y'know. I get a load of freebies.'

And then she sees that he's clutching a copy of her

Happy Ending, or as it will always be known between them, *The Endless Anguish of My Father*. He kneads the book between callused fingers, his face twisted in concern, the vein in his temple bulging. 'You read it then,' she says, preparing herself for the inevitable outburst.

He nods slowly. 'Her dad. He was a real shit to her, a right nasty piece of work.'

'He's not y—'

He cuts across her objection. 'But in the end, she forgives him.'

And she sees that he gets it. Finally.

'Monsieur L!'

Tom sweeps in, buoyed up by whatever news Anna LeFèvre has just imparted, and points at the copy of *Happy Ending* in Benny's hands, grinning as he says, 'If you think that was bad, wait till you see what she's done with you in the new one.'

Jane sees her dad blench, starts to explain that Tom is joking. Aren't you, Tom? But Benny's OK with it—whatever she's written. After all, it's just a story.

'Mr Lockhart, Benny—excuse us, would you?'

Tom steers her past the queuing readers, apologising that there will be a slight delay in proceedings, but that Jane will be back signing momentarily. Feel free to have another canapé.

'I thought the Pandemic Media people were coming today,' she says as he hustles her across the cemetery.

'Uh-huh. They're here.'

She scans the gathering, looking for someone who might be a malevolent financier, though she's not sure what's *de rigueur* for the soulless investor these days.

'It's Anna.'

'Your bank manager?'

'Not any longer. Pandemic hired her to look after Tristesse. Apparently, they want someone in the company who won't let me get away with my usual extravagance. I feel that's a harsh characterisation.'

'This from the man who insisted on six different vols-au-vent and a string quartet.'

They stand facing one another at the edge of the cemetery on the hill, the roofs and spires of the East End spread out below them. The sandstone city glows in the afternoon sunshine, but for the first time that day she notices a stray cloud wander across the sky.

She studies Tom. The Scottish weather had almost done for him, but the sallowness in his skin has long gone, revitalised by the recent spell of sunshine. Riviera-blue eyes, well, they sparkle. What else could they do? As much as he tries to turn his back on it, he is a child of the sun. In a moment of abandon he'd promised to take her to meet his parents. Not to *meet* them, not like that. Apparently they run a *bijou* literary festival from their house in the south of France. Roddy had Googled it. More of a château, he informed her. Y'know, towers, parkland, visible from space. Seems the Duvals are descended from nobility, which means she's dating a prince. So much for her indie cred. The writer of gritty urban miserablism has turned into fucking Cinderella.

'What are you thinking?'

'Something dark and depressing. I'm definitely not having pink and sparkly thoughts. *Right*?' she insists.

'OK, OK.' He holds up his hands in surrender. 'You're inconsolably wretched and gloomy. Happy?'

More clouds straggle after the first. The wind picks up, blowing her hair and she smooths it back into place.

'So, you've fulfilled your contract,' he announces, sounding all business. 'We're done.'

'Yes. I suppose we are.' Not sure where this is going. She contemplates this set of affairs, sees him struggle with some great inner difficulty.

'Unless…' he begins.

'Yes?'

'It's been a long, hard journey, and you are, frankly, about the most infuriating person I've ever met, which considering I work in Scottish publishing is saying something.'

'Thank you.'

'But we couldn't have got here without each other. So…Jane, what I'm saying is…will you…'

The first drops of rain start to fall. The guests at the book launch scamper for cover. The 'Funeral March' ceases as the string quartet put up their instruments and follow suit. The undertakers quickly shut the casket lid.

Tom dips a hand into his jacket and pulls out a rolled up document.

She eyes it suspiciously. 'Is that...a contract?'

'Two more books and an option for a third.'

'Exclusive?'

'Naturally, we'd have to work very closely.'

'With lots of notes?'

'An *excessive* amount of notes.'

'OK. I do,' she says quickly. Too quickly. 'I mean—*I will*. Oh just give it here...'

And she is uncapping her pen and he is unfolding the contract at the signature page, and suddenly, almost by accident, they are kissing in the rain.

* * * * *

ACKNOWLEDGEMENTS

They say that a writer ploughs a lonely furrow. So, with that in mind, I'd like to thank my enormous support team.

My editor Donna Hillyer and the team at Harlequin. From the first drop of Sancerre it was meant to be.

Copy editor Robin Seavill for straightening out my Brontës and my Beethoven.

Lit agent Stan who has unwittingly unleashed another member of the Solomons family on to the reading public. A mere pawn in our plans for global domination. *Bwahahaha*.

Film agents Elinor Burns and Anthony Mestriner for their friendship and advice and for sticking by this one (and all the rest) through thick, thin and *meh*.

Producers Claire Mundell and Wendy Griffin, and director John McKay. This might be the first novel to have been produced and directed before it was written.

Karen Gillan and Stanley Weber for saving me from the inevitable question about who I'd like to play Jane and Tom in a film of the book.

My son, Luke. For not only giving me the opportunity to name him after a *Star Wars* character but also reminding me that everything's OK even when it feels like it isn't. Luke, I am your father. Never gets old.

And my wife, Natasha, a brilliant writer, all round Renaissance woman (though her specialty is the eighteenth century) and the love of my life.

WHAT DID YOU MISS OUT ON BECAUSE YOU FELL IN LOVE?

Kate Winters might just be 'that' girl. You know the one. The girl who, for no particular reason, doesn't get the guy, doesn't have children, doesn't get the romantic happy-ever-after. So she needs a plan.

What didn't she get to do because she fell in love?

What would she be happy spending the rest of her life doing if love never showed up again?

This is one girl's journey to take back what love stole.

www.mirabooks.co.uk

M327_LIAT

It is every mother's nightmare...only worse

Janine wants her child to live a normal life, so she lets her precious daughter go on her first overnight camping trip. But when Janine arrives to pick up Sophie after the trip, her daughter is not with the others.

Janine will not rest until she finds her little girl, because Sophie isn't like every other girl... she suffers from a rare disease.

Who could have taken her child and what will happen if they don't get her back?

HARLEQUIN MIRA
www.mirabooks.co.uk

What if the end were only just the beginning?

Harold and Lucille Hargrave's lives have been both joyful and sorrowful in the decades since their only son, Jacob, died tragically on his eighth birthday in 1966… Until one day Jacob mysteriously appears on their doorstep—flesh and blood, their sweet, precocious child, still eight years old.

All over the world people's loved ones are returning from beyond. As chaos erupts, the newly reunited Hargrave family finds itself at the centre of a community on the brink of collapse, forced to navigate a conflict that threatens to unravel the very meaning of what it is to be human.